MOLLY THYNNE
THE MURDER ON THE ENRIQUETA

MARY 'MOLLY' THYNNE was born in 1881, a member of the aristocracy, and related, on her mother's side, to the painter James McNeil Whistler. She grew up in Kensington and at a young age met literary figures like Rudyard Kipling and Henry James.

Her first novel, *An Uncertain Glory*, was published in 1914, but she did not turn to crime fiction until *The Draycott Murder Mystery*, the first of six golden age mysteries she wrote and published in as many years, between 1928 and 1933. The last three of these featured Dr. Constantine, chess master and amateur sleuth *par excellence*.

Molly Thynne never married. She enjoyed travelling abroad, but spent most of her life in the village of Bovey Tracey, Devon, where she was finally laid to rest in 1950.

BY MOLLY THYNNE

The Draycott Murder Mystery

The Murder on the Enriqueta

The Case of Sir Adam Braid

The Crime at the 'Noah's Ark': A Christmas Mystery

Death in the Dentist's Chair

He Dies and Makes no Sign

MOLLY THYNNE

THE MURDER ON THE ENRIQUETA

With an introduction by
Curtis Evans

DEAN STREET PRESS

INTRODUCTION

Although British Golden Age detective novels are known for their depictions of between-the-wars aristocratic life, few British mystery writers of the era could have claimed (had they been so inclined) aristocratic lineage. There is no doubt, however, about the gilded ancestry of Mary "Molly" Harriet Thynne (1881-1950), author of a half-dozen detective novels published between 1928 and 1933. Through her father Molly Thynne was descended from a panoply of titled ancestors, including Thomas Thynne, 2nd Marquess of Bath; William Bagot, 1st Baron Bagot; George Villiers, 4th Earl of Jersey; and William Bentinck, 2nd Duke of Portland. In 1923, five years before Molly Thynne published her first detective novel, the future crime writer's lovely second cousin (once removed), Lady Mary Thynne, a daughter of the fifth Marquess of Bath and habitué of society pages in both the United Kingdom and the United States, served as one of the bridesmaids at the wedding of the Duke of York and his bride (the future King George VI and Queen Elizabeth). Longleat, the grand ancestral estate of the marquesses of Bath, remains under the ownership of the Thynne family today, although the estate has long been open to the public, complete with its famed safari park, which likely was the inspiration for the setting of *A Pride of Heroes* (1969) (in the US, *The Old English Peep-Show*), an acclaimed, whimsical detective novel by the late British author Peter Dickinson.

Molly Thynne's matrilineal descent is of note as well, for through her mother, Anne "Annie" Harriet Haden, she possessed blood ties to the English etcher Sir Francis Seymour Haden (1818-1910), her maternal grandfather, and the American artist James McNeill Whistler (1834-1903), a great-uncle, who is still renowned today for his enduringly evocative *Arrangement in Grey and Black no. 1* (aka "Whistler's Mother"). As a child Annie Haden, fourteen years younger than her brilliant Uncle James, was the subject of some of the artist's earliest etchings. Whistler's relationship with the Hadens later ruptured when his brother-in-law Seymour Haden became critical of what he deemed the younger artist's dissolute lifestyle. (Among other things Whistler had taken an artists' model as his mistress.) The conflict between the two men culminated in Whistler knocking Haden through a plate glass window during an altercation in Paris, after which the two men never spoke to one another again.

Molly Thynne grew up in privileged circumstances in Kensington, London, where her father, Charles Edward Thynne, a grandson of the second Marquess of Bath, held the position of Assistant Solicitor to His Majesty's Customs. According to the 1901 English census the needs of the Thynne family of four--consisting of Molly, her parents and her younger brother, Roger--were attended to by a staff of five domestics: a cook, parlourmaid, housemaid, under-housemaid and lady's maid. As an adolescent Molly spent much of her time visiting her Grandfather Haden's workroom, where she met a menagerie of artistic and literary lions, including authors Rudyard Kipling and Henry James.

Molly Thynne--the current Marquess has dropped the "e" from the surname to emphasize that it is pronounced "thin"--exhibited literary leanings of her own, publishing journal articles in her twenties and a novel, *The Uncertain Glory* (1914), when she was 33. *Glory*, described in one notice as concerning the "vicissitudes and love affairs of a young artist" in London and Munich, clearly must have drawn on Molly's family background, though one reviewer reassured potentially censorious middle-class readers that the author had "not over-accentuated Bohemian atmosphere" and in fact had "very cleverly diverted" sympathy away from "the brilliant-hued coquette who holds the stage at the commencement" of the novel toward "the plain-featured girl of noble character."

Despite good reviews for *The Uncertain Glory*, Molly Thynne appears not to have published another novel until she commenced her brief crime fiction career fourteen years later in 1928. Then for a short time she followed in the footsteps of such earlier heralded British women crime writers as Agatha Christie, Dorothy L. Sayers, Margaret Cole, Annie Haynes (also reprinted by Dean Street Press), Anthony Gilbert and A. Fielding. Between 1928 and 1933 there appeared from Thynne's hand six detective novels: *The Red Dwarf* (1928: in the US, *The Draycott Murder Mystery*), *The Murder on the "Enriqueta"* (1929: in the US, *The Strangler*), *The Case of Sir Adam Braid* (1930), *The Crime at the "Noah's Ark"* (1931), *Murder in the Dentist's Chair* (1932: in the US, *Murder in the Dentist Chair*) and *He Dies and Makes No Sign* (1933).

Three of Thynne's half-dozen mystery novels were published in the United States as well as in the United Kingdom, but none of them were reprinted in paperback in either country and the books rapidly fell out of public memory after Thynne ceased writing detective fiction in 1933, despite the fact that a 1930 notice speculated that "[Molly Thynne] is perhaps the best woman-writer of detective stories we know." The highly discerning author and crime fiction reviewer Charles Williams, a friend of C.S. Lewis and J.R.R. Tolkien and editor of Oxford University Press, also held Thynne in high regard, opining that Dr. Constantine, the "chess-playing amateur detective" in the author's *Murder in the Dentist's Chair,* "deserves to be known with the Frenches and the Fortunes" (this a reference to the series detectives of two of the then most highly-esteemed British mystery writers, Freeman Wills Crofts and H.C. Bailey). For its part the magazine *Punch* drolly cast its praise for Thynne's *The Murder on the "Enriqueta"* in poetic form.

> *The Murder on the "Enriqueta"* is a recent thriller by
>   Miss Molly Thynne,
> A book I don't advise you, if you're busy, to begin.
> It opens very nicely with a strangling on a liner
> Of a shady sort of passenger, an out-bound
>   Argentiner.
> And, unless I'm much mistaken, you will find
>   yourself unwilling
> To lay aside a yarn so crammed with situations
>   thrilling.
> (To say nothing of a villain with a gruesome taste
>   in killing.)

There are seven more lines, but readers will get the amusing gist of the piece from the quoted excerpt. More prosaic yet no less praiseful was a review of *Enriqueta* in *The Outlook*, an American journal, which promised "excitement for the reader in this very well written detective story ... with an unusual twist to the plot which adds to the thrills."

Despite such praise, the independently wealthy Molly Thynne in 1933 published her last known detective novel (the third of three consecutive novels concerning the cases of Dr. Constantine) and appears thereupon to have retired from authorship. Having proudly dubbed herself a "spinster" in print as early as 1905, when she was but 24, Thynne never married. When not traveling in Europe (she seems to have particularly enjoyed Rome, where her brother for two decades after the First World War served as Secretary of His Majesty's Legation to the Holy See), Thynne resided at Crewys House, located in the small Devon town of Bovey Tracey, the so-called "Gateway to the Moor." She passed away in 1950 at the age of 68 and was laid to rest after services at Bovey Tracey's Catholic Church of the Holy Spirit. Now, over sixty-five years later, Molly Thynne's literary legacy happily can be enjoyed by a new generation of vintage mystery fans.

Curtis Evans

CHAPTER I

THE *ENRIQUETA* WAS a new boat with her reputation still in the making and, so far, luck had been on her side. She had accomplished her maiden voyage from Liverpool to Buenos Aires in record time, partly owing to her speed, but more largely to phenomenally good weather, and now, on her return journey and already thirteen days out from Brazil, it looked as though she were going to repeat the performance.

She was carrying her full complement of passengers and the crowd in the smoking room was of the size and quality that only goes with calm weather and an oily sea. Even the most saffron-hued among the Latin-Americans were enjoying their cigars wholeheartedly and the smoke clouds hung motionless on the heavy air of the stuffy, over-decorated saloon. To one fresh from the coolness of the deck the atmosphere, a rich compound of mingled tobacco, alcohol and humanity, came almost as a physical rebuff and, by eleven o'clock, it had driven all but the most hardened of the card players to their cabins. At a few of the tables, however, the play still went on steadily, accompanied by an almost equally steady consumption of liquid refreshment.

It was close on midnight before the first of the card-parties broke up. The interruption came from a plump little man whose luck had been out for the last three nights and who had earned for himself the reputation of being one of the heaviest drinkers on board.

"I'm through," he announced, rising unsteadily to his feet. "God, what a night!"

"Keep your tail up. The voyage isn't over yet, you know."

The speaker, a spare, long-limbed cattle rancher, swung his chair round and stretched his legs. The half tolerant, half contemptuous note in his voice would have roused the anger of either of the other players, but it was a long time since the man he addressed had been in a position to resent the attitude of anyone undiscriminating enough to put up with his company.

He stood, swaying slightly on his feet, the sweat glistening on his white face, his dull eyes fixed vacantly on the glass he had just emptied.

"When I say I'm through, I mean it," he said heavily. "And, what's more ..."

He broke off, evidently thinking better of what he had been about to say. For a moment he stood staring at the men who had been his boon companions for the greater part of the voyage. He seemed to have some difficulty in finding his voice, but when he did speak it was to the point.

"Curse you!" he said gently, his face devoid of all expression. But there was no doubt as to his sincerity. Then, without another word, he turned and left them.

As he threaded his way clumsily in and out of the tables to the door, the laughter of the three men followed him and he cursed them again, softly, but venomously.

He climbed to the upper deck and leaned over the rail, gazing out into the soft, starlit darkness. At first the cool air made him dizzy and it was some time before his brain began to clear and he was able to take stock of his position. As usual, the more he looked at it, the less he liked it. He had been pretty flush when he came on board and had won a very nice little sum during the first week. Then his luck had changed and he had been fool enough to go on playing. And there wasn't a soul on board he could touch for a penny.

His mind went back to the country he had left and tears of maudlin self-pity filled his eyes. He had been happy there, he told himself, until his wife had died and left him alone in the world. He had buried her, it is true, without a tear and had grudged her even the expense of the cheap funeral. It was only after her death that he began to miss her, or rather her pitiful earnings that had kept him in drinks during the greater part of their married life. For one short year he had supported her, working as correspondence clerk in a South American store, then he had thrown up his job, or the job had thrown up him, she had never been able to arrive at the true facts of the case, and it had dawned on her that she must go back to the stage if they were to live at all. For fifteen years the plan had worked admirably, from his point of view, and then she had died and left him stranded on a cold world. As he brooded over his loss, sagging against the rail of the *Enriqueta*, her desertion struck him as infinitely pathetic. After her death he had drifted along somehow, taking some curious bypaths on his way, until by chance he had fallen in with a member of his wife's old company and had managed to touch him for a loan. With characteristic optimism he had invested the proceeds in a lottery ticket and had won enough to pay for his passage home and leave him a considerable sum in hand.

Then, casting about for a further means of support, he had remembered his one remaining relative, a widowed sister. He had cabled to her, announcing his advent, in the role of heartbroken widower, and had shaken the dust of Buenos Aires off his feet, in the haste of his departure conveniently overlooking the repayment of the money he had borrowed from his wife's old friend. And now he found himself stranded once more, this time on the high seas and with no prospect of replenishing his empty pockets.

He pitied himself profoundly as he gazed across the dark waters, but even self-commiseration palls after a time and his mind began to dwell sentimentally on the sister he had not seen for nearly twenty years. He had last heard from her on the occasion of his father's death three years before. Incidentally, the old man's will had been infernally unjust, but he had never blamed her for that and certainly her letter had been, on the whole, friendly. It was apparent to him now that he had always been far fonder of her than she had realized. After all, blood *was* thicker than water, he reflected complacently, blissfully unaware that his cable was still undelivered, his sister having been in her grave for nearly two years. His name not being mentioned in her will, her lawyers had not thought it necessary to inform him of her death.

Somewhat sobered, but still a prey to a gentle melancholy induced by the contemplation of his sad plight, he roused himself and made his way to his cabin.

To reach it he had to pass a row of staterooms on the upper deck. Though his brain had cleared considerably since he had left the smoking room, his legs were still inclined to play him false and, halfway down the alley, he lurched suddenly and cannoned with his full weight against one of the stateroom doors.

The catch must have been insecurely fastened, for it gave under the impact and he would have fallen headlong into the cabin if he had not clutched at the sill to steady himself.

Sober enough to realize that he had committed an unwarrantable intrusion, he began to stammer a clumsy explanation.

Then his eyes fell on the man whose privacy he had invaded and the apology died on his lips.

"Good Lord," he cried. "You! Well, of all the luck! My dear chap, where on earth have you been hiding yourself?"

His voice was warm with the delighted surprise of a confirmed cadger who scents an unexpected victim.

"Doing yourself proud, I must say," he went on, oblivious of the ominous silence with which his effusive greeting had been received.

Uninvited, he pushed his way into the cabin, closing the door behind him, and cast an approving eye round the luxurious stateroom.

"Pretty snug, what?" he commented.

Then, as his fuddled brain slowly took in certain aspects of the scene before him, his pale eyes narrowed and his expression changed to one of crafty appreciation.

"I say, old chap," he whispered. There was a wealth of meaning in his voice now. "Let me in on this. Where's it all come from ..."

The sentence died away in a gasp, ending in a choking gurgle. Without a word, the man he addressed, who had neither opened his lips nor moved from his position opposite the door since the intruder's unceremonious entry into his cabin, launched himself at the other's throat. The attack was so swift and unexpected that it caught the other man unprepared. In any case he was in no condition to defend himself.

There was a thud as his head struck the panelling of the door behind him, then the elbow of his assailant hit the electric light switch and plunged the cabin into darkness.

For a space only the scraping of the two men's feet upon the floor indicated the silent struggle that was in progress. It ceased abruptly with the dull sound of a heavy fall.

Then silence.

CHAPTER II

NEWS TRAVELS QUICKLY and mysteriously on board ship. By the time lunch was over it was generally known that the plump, pasty-faced little man who had spent the greater part of his time hanging about the bar had died suddenly and it was not long before the rumour began to spread that his death had not been due to natural causes. As is usual in such cases it was difficult to get hold of any definite information. The officers of the ship, beyond confirming the fact that the man had been found lying dead at the foot of one of the companion-ways, proved resolutely non-committal and, for once, the prospect of a tip, however heavy, failed to loosen the tongues of any of the stewards.

The three passengers with whom the unfortunate man had spent the evening found themselves engulfed in a surprising and quite unprecedented wave of popularity, but they could do little to allay the curiosity of those who were now so ready to offer them liquid refreshment. Smith, the dead man, had left them shortly before midnight and that was the last they had seen of him. It was said that one of the passengers, on his way to bed in the early hours of the morning, had surprised a couple of deck hands scouring a dark patch that might have been blood on the boards at the foot of the companion, but nobody, so far, had been able to trace the rumour to its source or to discover the identity of the passenger.

The ship's doctor, a gloomy and saturnine person at the best of times, would vouchsafe nothing but that the man was dead and that there was not going to be a funeral at sea for the benefit of any kodak fiends on board.

By the following day even the most curious had been obliged to confess themselves baffled and the excitement over the affair had begun to die a natural death, only to be resuscitated abruptly in the afternoon by the news that the captain was interviewing in his cabin certain of the first-class passengers whose staterooms were on the upper deck. Unfortunately those who travel in staterooms are not very accessible to the general public, but one or two of them were waylaid and cross-examined. The results proved disappointing. The captain's questions had been few and to the point and, if he learned nothing from them, the passengers had gleaned even less from him. They had been asked whether they had been disturbed by any unusual sounds during the night and they had been obliged to confess that they had not. Beyond that they had nothing of interest to report.

"Anyhow, it looks as if there were something to be said for the murder theory," remarked a shrewd-looking, elderly man who had listened in silence to the reports from the captain's cabin. "'Something unusual' sounds a bit suspicious. Well, they're keeping it pretty close, whatever it is. I'm willing to bet that this is the last we hear of it till we land at Liverpool. Something's bound to come out then."

"If there's anything to come out. The fellow may have had a fit and injured himself in falling."

The speaker was a tall, square-shouldered Englishman, whose close-clipped moustache and erect bearing suggested that at one time he might have worn a uniform. He spoke listlessly, as if this incessant speculation on the man's death had begun to pall on him.

"If that's the case, why don't they say so and have done with it? As it is, they've got the whole boat buzzing like a hornet's nest. This hush-hush business is a mistake, in my opinion."

The other nodded.

"I've no doubt you're right," he remarked easily as he turned away.

He strolled past the long line of deck chairs and disappeared from view. A few minutes later he was at the door of the captain's cabin.

"My name's Shand," he said, by way of introduction.

As he spoke he laid a card on the table and, at the sight of it, the captain's expression of veiled annoyance changed to one of interest.

"New Scotland Yard," he read slowly.

Then: "You've got your credentials, I suppose, Chief Inspector?"

Shand handed them over in silence.

The captain glanced through them and returned them to their owner.

"Anything I can do for you?" he asked urbanely.

The inspector's eyes twinkled.

"I rather fancy it's the other way round. I was going to ask if there was anything I could do for you."

The captain looked up sharply.

"This Smith affair, eh?" Then, as a sudden thought struck him. "You're not on board on his account, are you?"

Shand shook his head.

"No. I've been over to Buenos Aires on an extradition job and missed my man by a day. I'm interested, though."

"In what way?"

"Well, my man slipped me. Doubled back to Europe, the day before I landed, but this man, Smith, was one of his associates in Buenos Aires and I was looking forward to getting certain information out of him that might have proved useful. Unfortunately I waited too long."

The captain looked at him thoughtfully.

"Do you think this could have had any connection with your affair?" he asked. "You know how Smith died?"

"I know nothing. Your people haven't been giving much away. There seems to be a general impression that he met with foul play."

"He was strangled," said the captain shortly.

Shand gave a low whistle.

"Strangled! That's fairly unusual."

"If you ask me, I think it's confoundedly unpleasant. As you may imagine, we're not broadcasting the news."

He sat for a moment turning Shand's card meditatively in his fingers. Then he looked up at him frankly.

"If you can see your way to giving us a hand in this I shall be grateful," he said. "It's out of my beat altogether. In any case, there's bound to be an inquest so that it will probably come within your province in the end. The thing's a mystery, so far."

"There's nothing among his papers, I suppose, to connect him with anyone on board? I don't mind confessing that I came to you in the hope of giving them the look-over."

The other shook his head.

"We've only made a very cursory examination, but there seems to be nothing. One thing we have pretty well established: robbery was not the motive. The man was almost broke. He had money when he came on board, but he has been playing heavily and, from what the men say who were playing with him that night, he could have had very little on him when he was killed. He laid his pocketbook open on the table when he was settling up, and according to them, it was. Practically empty."

"Where was he found?" asked Shand.

The captain opened an advertisement folder containing a plan of the *Enriqueta*. He made a cross with his pencil at the foot of one of the companionways and pushed the paper over to Shand.

"That's the place," he said. "He was found by one of the stewards just after one a.m. The man's got rather a curious story to tell, by the way. Like to see him?"

"I'd better hear what he's got to say. Is he an Englishman?"

"London born, I should think, by his accent. We're an English company, you know. He's been with the company fifteen years and he's got an excellent record."

While the man was being sent for Shand studied the plan before him.

"Assuming that Smith was on his way to his cabin from the smoke room, would this be on his route?" he asked, placing his finger on the cross.

"There would be nothing to prevent his going that way provided he had gone onto the upper deck for a breath of air, which is what he seems to have done. He was seen, leaning over the rail, sometime between twelve and half-past by two of the passengers who stood near him, smoking, for about fifteen minutes. They left him there when they turned in." The steward proved to be an intelligent looking cockney. Shand, having started the ball rolling with a leading question or two, left him to tell his story in his own way.

It appeared that he had been on his way to the galley with a tray of bottles and soiled glasses which he had fetched from one of the first-class cabins. As he turned the corner by the last of the row of staterooms he saw a man lying on his back at the foot of the companionway. Bending over him was another man. He could see them both distinctly in the glare of an electric light just overhead. Realizing that something was wrong, he put down the tray he was carrying and ran forward. To get rid of the tray he had to stoop and, in doing so, took his eyes off the men for a moment. When he straightened himself the second man was nowhere to be seen. After a short delay, during which he ascertained that Smith, whom he knew by sight, was, as he thought at the time, unconscious, he went in search of the second man, but could find no trace of him. He then gave the alarm and it was discovered that Smith was dead.

"You say that you saw them both distinctly in the light of the lamp?" asked Shand. "Would you recognize the man you saw bending over Smith?"

The steward shook his head.

"I couldn't swear to him, sir," he answered. "I could see 'im clear enough under the light, but there was a white bandage or it may 'ave been a muffler, round the lower part of 'is face. Uncommon queer, 'e looked, what with that and 'is green pyjamas."

"Pyjamas?"

"That's right, sir. Mr. Smith was dressed all right, but this other chap looked as if 'e'd got straight out of bed like. Bright green pyjamas, 'e'd got on, and this muffler thing round 'is face."

"Can you describe him at all?"

"Medium weight and on the thin side, I should say. 'E straightened up while I was lookin' at 'im. And 'is 'air was fair, or it might 'ave been white. It was difficult to tell just under the lamp."

"Ever seen him before, do you think?"

"Not to my knowledge, but then there was that muffler thing. I'd give something to know where 'e got to. 'E must 'ave been pretty nippy, too. I wasn't not more than a minute bendin' over that there tray and when I looked up 'e was gone. Must 'ave either slipped round the corner and past the staterooms or shinned up the companion."

"How much time did you waste over Smith before you went after him, do you think?"

"Not more than a couple of minutes. I see 'e was unconscious at once, then I lifted 'is 'ead and I see the blood. I never thought of 'im being dead. Just thought 'e'd 'ad a drop too much and slipped up and 'it 'imself, so I let 'im lie and went after the other chap meanin' to ask 'im if 'e'd seen 'ow it 'appened. But 'e was clean gone."

"Do you know of anybody on board with pyjamas that colour?"

"No, sir, and what's more I've asked others and they say they 'aven't seen none, neither. And the laundry 'aven't 'ad nothin' of that sort through their 'ands. I'll lay them pyjamas 'ave gone overboard all right, by now," he added shrewdly.

Shand laughed.

"Shouldn't wonder if you're right," he agreed.

Then, as the man was just going, he stopped him.

"You've no idea what the man was doing when you first saw him, I suppose?"

"I couldn't see. It was all too quick. 'E was bendin' over Mr. Smith when I first see 'im, but 'e straightened up almost at once. Then I stooped to put the tray down and when I looked up 'e was gone."

"He might have slipped into one of the staterooms," suggested Shand.

"'E might. But I never 'eard no door shut, that I'll swear and they was all closed, right enough, when I went along to look for 'im."

"Did you go up the companion?"

"Yes, and 'ad a good look round, but there wasn't no sign of 'im."

Shand thanked the man and let him go.

"Funny," he said, "about this white muffler. The steward seems pretty positive about it."

The captain smiled.

"I think we've traced the significance of that," he answered. "The ship's doctor spotted it. He found flecks of lather on the dead man's coat."

Shand stared at him.

"Lather? Soap do you mean?"

The captain nodded.

"Yes. The doctor's theory is that the man was shaving and the lather was still on his face when he attacked Smith. That's to say, if he did attack him. We've no proof that it was he who committed the murder."

"He might have been disturbed by the noise of a struggle and have come out of his cabin and found Smith," admitted Shand. "Funny thing that he hasn't come forward, though. And, if he didn't do it, why did he clear off like that when he saw the steward?"

"My theory is that he did kill the man. Smith must have disturbed him while he was shaving, probably went into his cabin. There seems no doubt that Smith had been drinking heavily, as usual, and he appears to have been in an ugly mood when he left the smoking room. He may have picked a quarrel with the man and been followed by him to the foot of the companion. The body was still warm when the doctor reached it and he is of the opinion that the man must have been killed just before the steward found him."

"If there was a quarrel someone must have heard it."

"No one has come forward to say so. I've interviewed most of the passengers from that deck, but they all declare that they were not disturbed in any way. Two of them were awake, one undressing and the other reading, but they heard nothing. Would you like to see what you can get out of them?"

But Shand shook his head.

"Better let me remain in the background," he said decisively. "If I lie low there's a chance I may pick something useful out of all the gossip that's going round. People won't talk freely before me, once they know who I am. But I'd like to have a look at Smith's papers."

The captain unlocked the drawer of his table and opened it. "I've got most of them here," he said. "His passport and cheque book and some private letters. I locked them up with the contents of his pockets for safety."

He laid a miscellaneous collection of objects on the table. Shand looked through them quickly.

"Nothing to help me here," he said at last. "The passport's made out in the name of Smith all right and I fancy that was his real name. The man I was after had been turning out some very pretty five and ten pound notes and I've reason to believe that Smith had planted some of them, but I've no real evidence against him. Can I see his money?"

The captain handed it over, a solitary five pound note, some English silver and some small change in South American currency.

"He'd come pretty well down to bed-rock," remarked Shand, as he examined the note. "This isn't 'slush' though. It's genuine enough. I'd like to get hold of some of the stuff he's been paying his gambling debts with."

"I can manage that for you, if you don't want to appear in the matter. He hadn't many friends on board and nearly always played with the same crowd. They're a rough lot, but ready enough to give any information they can about him. I've only to suggest that there was a doubt as to the genuineness of his money and they'll come forward quickly enough with any they got from him, if only to make sure that they haven't been done. Anything else I can do for you?"

Shand rose.

"Nothing except to let me run an eye over that money as soon as you get it. I'll go and have a look at the place where he was found. There's no doubt that he was strangled, I suppose?"

"None whatever. The doctor says he was choked to death and there are the bruises on his throat."

After dinner that night Shand spent a profitable hour in the captain's cabin over a mixed pile of English and American notes.

He looked up as the captain entered and pushed three five pound notes which he had laid aside over to him.

"I was right about our friend, Smith," he said. "Somebody's been stung. The rest are genuine, but those three are the work of the gentleman I just missed in Buenos Aires. Smith was passing the stuff all right. I wish now I could have had a word with him."

"Was he one of a gang, do you suppose?"

Shand shook his head.

"We've every reason to believe that our man works alone. He's a good man, an artist in his way and he can always find a market for his stuff. We've got nothing against Smith at the Yard and it was only by accident that I got onto his track in Buenos Aires. It's unlikely that he's a habitual criminal. He's probably one of those people who hang onto the outskirts of the real criminal world and are simply made use of by the clever ones. Unless they're unlucky or particularly clumsy they don't usually get into trouble. When Smith was in funds he probably ran straight enough."

"Then you don't think your man had anything to do with this?"

"It's unlikely, unless Smith could have told us more than I supposed. That he had been mixed up in the phoney money business, there seems no doubt, but the man we want is well on his way to Europe by now and, even supposing Smith to be in possession of dangerous information, I can see no reason why the gang, if there is one, which I doubt, should have waited all this time before putting him out of action. Smith could have split on them any day during the last week if I'd taken the trouble to approach him. I've a strong suspicion that this is a different business altogether and I'd give a good deal to know who the party is on this boat who is prepared to risk murder for the sake of getting a man like Smith out of the way. He must have had good reason to be afraid of him."

The captain, who had been examining the forged notes, threw them back onto the table.

"Good stuff," he said appreciatively. "I shouldn't have spotted them if you hadn't told me. It hasn't occurred to you, I suppose," he went on thoughtfully, "that Smith and the fellow who did him in may have met for the first time last night? Met on the boat, I mean. From all accounts, Smith wasn't intimate with any one on board and seems to have made very few friends, apart from the rather rough lot he played cards with. I fancy they're straight enough. Cattle ranchers and that sort of thing. If this chap had been keeping close in one of the staterooms, for instance, he may have run into Smith by accident. You're quite sure the man you are after isn't on board?"

Shand rose to his feet.

"Certain," he said decisively. "My man sailed on the *Argentina* all right. And, as I say, I doubt if he had a confederate on board this boat. No, my money's on the chap with the shaving tackle and the green pyjamas and I'm willing to bet that those pyjamas have gone overboard by this time. But I agree with you that they probably came from one of those staterooms on the upper deck."

CHAPTER III

SHAND WAS JUST finishing lunch next day when the captain passed his table. The Scotland Yard man was not so absorbed in the peeling of his orange that he did not catch the invitation in the other's eye or the quick jerk of his head in the direction of the door.

Five minutes later he was drinking his coffee in the captain's cabin.

"Well?" he asked. "Anything doing?"

"Nothing much, I'm afraid, but I thought you might as well have it. I had a message from Lady Dalberry this morning."

For a moment Shand was at a loss, then he remembered. "Of course, I'd clean forgotten we had her on board. The English papers were humming with that little romance when I left London. A bit of a mystery, isn't she?"

"Seemed straightforward enough to me," the captain said. "She's supposed to be a Swede, isn't she, according to the papers, and she looks it. Fair, good features, fresh colouring, and all that sort of thing. Foreign accent. Speaks quite good English, though. What they call a fine woman, I suppose, but a bit too much made up for my taste. I fancy she's older than she looks. In deep mourning, of course, but I've an idea that she won't take long to console herself."

"She's taking the body back to England, isn't she?"

The captain nodded.

"We tried to keep the thing quiet. It's extraordinary what a feeling there is against traveling with a corpse on board. But the Press was hot on the whole story, and, of course, it got out that she was sailing on this boat. As a matter of fact, curiosity proved stronger than superstition in this instance, and our passenger list was as large as ever. Not that they've got much satisfaction out of sailing with her. She hasn't shown up at all so far."

"Is she traveling alone?"

"Yes. Hasn't even got a maid. I fancy she's a bit at sea still as to what her jointure will be, and she's going slow with the money till she knows. It's a curious position altogether."

"I shouldn't imagine that she need worry about the money part of it. The first Lord Dalberry was one of the biggest coal-owners in the country, and even now they must be rolling in money. She'd have been a very rich woman indeed if it hadn't been for that accident."

"She was lucky to escape with her life," commented the captain. "Anyway, I had word from her this morning saying that she had heard from the steward that I had been questioning the other passengers on her deck as to whether they had noticed anything the other night, and that she would like to see me. As a matter of fact I'd decided not to bother her. Considering her position, it seemed a bit heartless, and it was most unlikely that she'd have anything of interest to report. As it happened, I was wrong."

"She had seen something?"

"Not seen, but heard, apparently. According to what she told me, she's been sleeping badly since the accident: the result of shock, and all that sort of thing. In consequence, she goes to bed late—about twelve, as a rule—and takes a sleeping draught before turning in. The night before last she sat up a bit later than usual, and it was close on one before she took the sleeping stuff. Apparently it takes a quarter of an hour or so to act, and she was lying in her berth waiting for it to take effect when she heard a noise outside her stateroom."

"Where is her stateroom, by the way?" interrupted Shand.

"On the upper deck. Number eight, just about half-way down the row. She says the noise was so curious that she sat up and listened. What first attracted her attention was the sound of shuffling foot-steps along the deck outside her door. They sounded so uneven that she came to the conclusion that the person, whoever it was, must be either drunk or ill. Then she noticed another noise—a scraping sound—as if something were being dragged along the deck. She listened as it passed her door, and then decided that it must be one of the deck hands with a sack or some other object too heavy to carry. Almost immediately afterwards she fell asleep, no doubt owing to the stuff she had taken, so that she never heard the man return, if he did come back. It's a piece of sheer bad luck for us that she didn't lie awake a few minutes longer, as she'd probably have been able to tell us which of the cabins he made for when he saw the steward. She'd have been bound to hear the door shut."

"She's no idea where the footsteps came from, I suppose?"

"None. I asked her that very question, but she says she heard nothing until her interest was roused by the sounds just outside her cabin. She thought no more about it until she heard of the affair from the steward."

"Did she strike you as a nervous, imaginative sort of woman? It's extraordinary what some people will manage to remember after an event of this sort."

"No. I should say her account's dependable enough. She didn't even seem particularly thrilled by the thing. Just thought it her duty to let me know. In fact, she's the only one of the passengers that hasn't attempted to pump me as to what we've discovered."

Shand found his thoughts dwelling a good deal on Lady Dalberry that afternoon. Though he had been quite genuine in his statement to the captain that he had forgotten the presence of Lord Dalberry's widow on board the boat, he had looked out for her with considerable interest during the first few days of the voyage, and had been disappointed to find that she evidently intended to keep to her cabin. He had caught sight of her once or twice, a spare, upright figure in deep mourning, pacing the deck in the early morning before the other passengers were about; and once, when there was a concert in the saloon, he had seen her sitting within earshot of the music, in a secluded corner of the deck, but he had been unable to get a closer view of her, and had never spoken to her.

In spite of her tragic history and the curiosity it had aroused, it is doubtful whether he would have given her a thought had it not been for his association with Jasper Mellish. When Chief Detective-Inspector Shand was just starting his career in the uniformed Force, Mellish had already achieved the reputation of being one of the fattest, laziest, and most capable of the Home Office officials. When Shand entered the C.I.D. chance brought him and Mellish together, and they had taken an immediate liking for each other—a liking which had soon crystallised into a friendship which had lasted through the latter part of Mellish's career, and which had persisted after his retirement five years ago.

In spite of his indolence Mellish was a person of many unsuspected interests. He possessed a fine singing voice, and used it with the skill of a born musician; his collection of etchings, though small, for he was not a rich man, had made his name familiar to collectors all over the world; he was chairman of various charitable committees and played an important part in the management of at least two of the great hospitals. It had been no surprise to Shand to learn that, among other things, he was sole trustee to the vast Dalberry estates, and it was from Mellish's lips that the detective had learned the details of the succession of tragic events that had brought the name of Dalberry so vividly before the eyes of the British public. Hence Shand's interest in Lady Dalberry, which, if short-lived, had been keen enough when he first heard that she was on board.

He was too occupied with the Smith affair, however, to waste much thought on her now. All through what remained of the voyage he moved unobtrusively among the passengers, quietly supplementing his meagre store of information. But as he stood on deck, waiting to land, on the day the ship docked at Liverpool, he admitted frankly to himself that his inquiries had brought him nowhere.

He was inclined to the theory that Smith, if he had an enemy, had been unaware of his presence on board the *Enriqueta* until the actual night of the murder. None of the information Shand had been able to gather pointed towards any nervousness or anxiety on Smith's part, and the few people who had seen much of him were unanimous in declaring that he had stated on various occasions that he had no acquaintances on board. They reported him to be a natural boaster and inclined to grow garrulous in his cups—the last person likely to conceal the fact that he had friends among the first-class passengers. And that the murder had been committed either inside or in the close vicinity of one of the first-class staterooms, Shand had no doubt. From Lady Dalberry's account, the body had probably been dragged past her cabin, and the abrupt disappearance of the man the steward had seen pointed towards his having taken cover in one of the staterooms on that deck. Shand had kept a close eye on the occupants of that particular row of cabins, but his investigations had led him nowhere. A certain number of them—an elderly clergyman and his wife returning to England after a protracted pleasure cruise; a prominent London banker, so crippled with rheumatism as to be incapable of violence; one of the secretaries of the British Legation at Buenos Aires, on his way home on leave; and an American writer, well known in journalistic circles in New York—Shand dismissed as above suspicion. Of the remaining few, any one of them might have been an associate of Smith's in the past and be possessed of sufficient motive for his removal. They were a heterogeneous lot, with little but their money to recommend them, but the detective was unable to find the smallest shadow of an excuse for connecting them with the crime.

He stood watching his own particular little batch of suspects as they filtered slowly up from their cabins and grouped themselves on deck. There was a glint of humour in his speculative grey eyes. A dull lot, he reflected, and it was difficult to picture any one of them buying, much less wearing, the suit of green pyjamas that had figured so vividly in the steward's story. And in all his long experience of criminals of all sorts he could remember no single case of a man who deliberately went to the trouble of purchasing a peculiarly gaudy addition to his wardrobe in which to break the law. Neither, for the matter of that, were murderers in the habit of lathering their faces heavily with shaving soap before embarking on a crime.

If, as he felt convinced, some member of that inoffensive looking little group of first-class passengers was, at least, closely connected with the death of Smith, the murder was obviously unpremeditated, and, it would seem, the work of a man with an unusually exotic taste in undergarments.

The boat had docked, and he was observing the passengers as they filed slowly across the gangway, when he was roused by a touch on his arm. Jasper Mellish, massive and imperturbable as usual, stood at his elbow.

"You look abominably fit," he drawled gently. "Have you got Lady Dalberry on board?"

"To the best of my knowledge you'll find her below," answered Shand, making no secret of his pleasure in the encounter. "She hasn't shown up yet. Glad to see you looking so well, sir."

The fat man gave a chuckle that shook his whole body.

"Why not say 'fat' and have done with it," he said. "I must go and find her. They tell me they've got poor Adrian's body on board."

"The funeral will be at Berrydown, I suppose?"

Mellish nodded, and crooked a finger at a young man who had been standing just behind him.

Shand had already spotted a little group of people who had evidently followed Mellish on board the boat: a slim, graceful girl, who, even at a cursory glance, he could place as one of those fortunate people who combine personal charm with unusual beauty both of feature and colouring, and an elderly man in black, whose face bore the mournful but detached expression of one who is about to assist at a painful ceremony in a purely professional capacity. He had family lawyer written all over him, and Shand mechanically transferred his attention to the young man who had come forward in answer to Mellish's signal. He took an immediate fancy to him. Indeed, he was one of those pleasant but unassuming individuals, with apparently little but youth and a certain air of general cleanliness and physical fitness to recommend them, to whom most people take a liking at first sight.

"This is Chief Inspector Shand of New Scotland Yard, Gillie," said Mellish, with a shrewd twinkle in his eye. "You may find it useful to have a friend at court one of these days. Lord Dalberry has come on board to meet his aunt," he added, by way of explanation.

Lord Dalberry laughed.

"If I get roped in by one of your men on boat-race night, I'll ask for you, inspector," he said cheerfully, as the party moved on in the direction of the staterooms.

Shand made his way slowly on shore. He had no pressing desire to reach London and make his report at the Yard. He was feeling anything but elated. In the first place, through no fault of his own, he had succeeded in just missing his man at Buenos Aires; in the second, his attempts to clear up the mystery of Smith's death had proved singularly futile. Fortunately, murder on the high seas was unlikely to come within the sphere of New Scotland Yard, and there was nothing to keep Shand hanging about in Liverpool.

He secured a corner seat in the boat train, and was standing smoking on the platform when the Dalberry party came in sight. It had to pass him on its way to the special mourning coach which had been attached to the rear of the train, and Shand, in common with most of the other passengers from the *Enriqueta*, found himself watching Lady Dalberry with considerable interest as she came slowly down the platform on the arm of her husband's nephew.

She had thrown back her heavy black veil, and, for the first time, he had a clear view of her profile. She was, as the captain had said, a typical Swede, and, in spite of the thick film of powder on her cheeks and the heavy make-up on her large, well-shaped mouth, carried with her that suggestion of life in the open air and general fitness which has become the hallmark of her race. Her erect carriage and clear-cut profile reminded Shand of a picture he had seen of one of the Norse goddesses. A fine woman, who looked as if she had always dealt adequately with life and had become a little hardened in the process.

Shand reflected that if she and Mellish came to blows, as they very easily might in the course of time, he would dearly love to witness the encounter. The path of a trustee is not a smooth one, and

Mellish, for all his kindliness, was a difficult man to lead and an impossible one to drive.

On his way to London Shand gave himself up to the enjoyment of one of the captain's excellent cigars, his mind running lazily over the annals of the Dalberry family as retailed by Jasper Mellish one blustering November evening in his cosy rooms in the Albany.

It was a tragic enough tale in its way. The peerage, a recent one, dated from the days when coal mines really did spell riches, and had been founded by the grandfather of the present holder of the title. On his death he had left three sons and one daughter. The eldest of the sons, Maurice, was a widower with two small boys when, at the early age of thirty, he succeeded to the title. His brother, Adrian Culver, a rich man as second sons go, and endowed with a goodly share of his father's energy, had visited the Argentine soon after his brother's succession, and, falling in love with the life, had decided to settle out there for good. His younger brother, Oliver, after a brief career in the Guards, had been killed in the third year of the war, leaving one son, the present Lord Dalberry. Marian Culver, only sister to Adrian and Oliver, had married Conway Summers, a wealthy American widower with one child. She had gone with him to New York, where she had remained till her death. She left no children of her own, and Summers, already immersed in those huge undertakings which were later to make him one of the richest men in America, was only too glad to take advantage of Lord Dalberry's offer and leave his motherless girl in his brother-in-law's charge, with the result that Carol Summers had spent the greater portion of her life at Berrydown, the largest of the Dalberry properties, and had grown to look upon it as her home. On Lord Dalberry's advice, Conway Summers had appointed Jasper Mellish trustee of the vast fortune his daughter would inherit on his death. Shortly after making the appointment he had succumbed to an attack of influenza, leaving to Mellish the task of safeguarding the property of the girl who, at her coming of age, would be one of the richest women of the day.

Shand guessed that it was Miss Summers he had seen with Mellish on board the *Enriqueta*, and he wondered idly what provision the fat man had made for his rather difficult charge, who was still under age and whose life at Berrydown had been brought to an abrupt end by the tragic death of her uncle and his two sons. All three had been killed instantaneously when the French air-mail crashed, half-way between the coast and Croydon. Indeed, it was only by a fortunate accident that Carol had escaped sharing their fate. She was to have joined them in Paris on the day before the accident, and would undoubtedly have been with them if she had not been persuaded to stay a couple of nights longer with the friends she had been visiting in Touraine.

Thus it was that Adrian Culver, who had put every penny he possessed into a ranch in the Argentine, and who had fully intended to pass the rest of his days there, woke one morning to find himself one of the richest land-owners in England. Three years before his succession to the Dalberry peerage he had married a Miss Larssen, a Swedish-American he had met on one of his infrequent visits to New York. Realizing that, owing to the responsibilities of his new position, he could hardly continue to live in America, he had set to work to wind up his affairs there, preparatory to sailing for England. The sale of the ranch had taken longer than he had expected, and it was not till over six months after his brother's death that he was free to leave America with his wife.

It was then that the second tragedy occurred which was destined to bring the name of Dalberry once more before a voracious public. Sending the bulk of their luggage on in advance, Lord and Lady Dalberry started by road for the coast, intending to take the journey easily, stopping at various places on their way to Buenos Aires, where they proposed to take ship for England. But they never reached their destination.

How, precisely, the accident happened would never be known, the car being too damaged to make any sort of investigation possible; but from the account of Lady Dalberry, the sole survivor, it would seem that the steering gear must have failed suddenly. Lord Dalberry, who was driving, evidently lost all control over the machine, which left the road, dashed head-on over the edge of a steep embankment, and crashed into a mass of undergrowth thirty feet below. Lord Dalberry and his wife's maid, the only other occupant of the car, were killed instantaneously. Lady Dalberry, by a miracle, was thrown clear, and, though badly bruised and suffering from shock, was so little hurt that she was able eventually to make her way up the embankment on to the road where she was found lying, almost unconscious, by the overseer of a neighbouring ranch.

In her first frenzy of grief it was difficult to convince her that her husband was really dead. She had, it appeared, struck her head in falling, and had been stunned for a time. On recovering, she had crawled to where her husband and the maid lay, the former half under the overturned car. Even in her partly dazed state she had realized that the maid, whose head had been badly crushed by the car, was dead, but she had tried in vain to liberate her husband and restore him to consciousness. Failing in her efforts, she had made her way to the road in the hope of getting help.

At first she had refused to leave the scene of the accident, and her rescuer had been obliged to take her back to the wreck of the car before he could convince her that nothing could be done for her husband. Then her courage had failed her and she had collapsed in earnest, and had only recovered consciousness as the car arrived which had been sent for to take her to the nearest town. Once there, she had shown amazing pluck, had refused to go to the hospital, and taking a room in the only hotel the little town boasted, had attended the inquest, and had herself made all the arrangements for the funeral of the maid and the transference of her husband's body to England. She had cabled the news of the accident to Lord Dalberry's lawyers, and announced her intention of sailing at the earliest opportunity. The American Press had done the rest, and the whole story, with all its gruesome details, was soon public property.

Just one month from the day of the accident she sailed in the *Enriqueta*, taking her husband's body with her, a heartbroken woman, on her way to a strange land, where, so far as she knew, there was not one soul whom she could call a friend. Her husband's nephew, the son of his brother Oliver, had succeeded to the title, and she did not even know what jointure he would be likely to allow her, and whether she could count herself a comparatively wealthy woman or not. Her husband had sunk most of his money in the ranch, and though this had sold easily enough, it had been of necessity a forced sale, and, for all she knew, the sum it had fetched might very well represent almost the whole of her capital.

Remembering the lack of ostentation with which she had travelled, the prompt manner in which she had come forward when she thought her evidence might be of value, coupled with the quiet dignity of her erect and vigorous carriage as she passed him on the Liverpool platform, Shand paid tribute to her pluck and common-sense, and at the same time wondered at his own lack of sympathy for the woman who had gone through so much, and was, apparently, facing life so bravely.

Somehow, since he had seen the clear, cold profile framed in the dense black of the widow's veil, he found it difficult to look upon her as a pathetic figure, and once more he caught himself wondering how long it would be before there was a clash of wills between her and Jasper Mellish.

CHAPTER IV

THE ONLY MEMBER of the Dalberry party who might be said to feel thoroughly at ease during the tedious journey from Liverpool to London was the melancholy looking solicitor who had come on board the boat with Mellish. As junior partner, these somewhat depressing excursions into the private lives of the firm's clients usually fell to his lot, and long practice had enabled him to go through the most painful and embarrassing experiences with a perfection of manner which was all the easier to maintain because it was purely mechanical.

Jasper Mellish, always a godsend on occasions such as these, kept up a gentle and mellifluous flow of conversation, which tactfully included Lady Dalberry, should she feel inclined to talk.

The two younger members of the party spent their time in trying to conceal their embarrassment, and wishing with all their hearts that the journey was over.

Carol Summers, as the only other woman present, was painfully conscious that the task of supporting and ministering to the bereaved widow lay with her, but her youth and inexperience, combined with the icy composure with which Lady Dalberry seemed to be facing a most trying situation, left her totally at a loss. Even the very real sympathy she had felt for her uncle's widow ever since the news of the accident had reached her did not serve to allay her embarrassment, and, to her shame, she realized that this sympathy was rapidly degenerating into acute curiosity. Over and over again she caught herself covertly observing the other woman, who sat, for the most part, gazing out of the window, her head thrown back against the cushions of the carriage as though the weight of the luxuriant fair hair that just showed beneath the rim of her close-fitting hat were almost more than she could bear. She had removed her heavy widow's veil, and in the cold winter sunlight that filtered in through the carriage window her face showed lines beneath its skilled but obvious make-up that proclaimed her as older than she had appeared at first sight. In profile, Carol decided, with the whole-hearted admiration of youth, her features were perfect, but when she turned, in answer to a remark of Lord Dalberry's and exhibited her full face, the girl was conscious of a sharp pang of disappointment. The whole upper part of the face was too wide, the cheek-bones too high, and the thick, fair brows above fine eyes too heavy.

Then those cold eyes swept in her direction, and, with a start, Carol realized that she was being addressed.

"We must see each other often when I am settled, and you must please help me in the choosing of the things for my house. I do not know your English shops, and I think I am a little frightened of London. It must be so big, from what I have heard."

Her voice was beautiful—a warm, deep, rich contralto, with a curious husky note in it. She spoke English carefully and with a marked accent, but she seemed to have no difficulty in finding words for what she wanted to say, and occasionally would use American idioms with an aptness that was startling. Later, in a moment of confidence, she told Carol that though she had been brought up in New York, she had not been born there. Her parents had migrated from Sweden when she was four years of age, and, though she was educated in American schools, she had never spoken anything but Swedish in her father's house. In spite of all that was to happen before Carol finally made up her mind about her uncle's will, she never quite succeeded in freeing herself from the spell of Lady Dalberry's voice, and it never failed to soften her towards its owner. It held all the warmth and sympathy that was so signally lacking in her face and manner.

"Lady Dalberry is anxious to get away from hotel life as soon as possible," put in Mellish, "and I have been telling her how heartily I agree with her. We must try to find her a suitable house between us."

"Meanwhile I hope you will make use of Berrydown, if you would rather be there until your own house is ready for you," suggested Lord Dalberry courteously.

Carol looked up quickly. She had known Gillie Culver, as he had been until his uncle's death, too long to be taken in by a purely formal exhibition of politeness. She had never before heard him speak with such complete lack of feeling. But to a stranger his offer sounded spontaneous enough, and Lady Dalberry evidently accepted it at its face value.

"It is more than kind of you," she answered, her beautiful voice warm with appreciation. "I shall see this Berrydown—to-morrow, I think?"

She stumbled a little over the end of the sentence and turned abruptly to the window. A feeling of constraint fell over the other members of the little party as they realized that she would see her husband's old home for the first time on the occasion of his funeral. No wonder the thought of the tragic ordeal before her had shaken her composure.

For the first time Carol was conscious of a spontaneous feeling of pity for the other woman, and only a natural shyness prevented her from crossing the carriage and sitting by her side. She glanced at Gillie, but beyond the quiet friendliness of his smile as his eyes met hers, he made no sign, and it was impossible for her to judge of the extent to which he had been impressed by the incident.

"I'm sorry we don't boast a town house at present," he went on. His tone was perfectly friendly, but Carol could still detect the curiously aloof note which had puzzled her a few minutes before. "Uncle Maurice turned it into a hospital during the war, and it was so knocked about that he sold it soon after the armistice, meaning to buy another. But my aunt was dead and he had no daughter, so that entertaining was not much in his line, and he got into the habit of taking a furnished house when he wanted to spend any length of time in town. I'm in rooms myself, so I can't offer you hospitality. I'm sorry. It would have been more comfortable for you than a hotel."

Lady Dalberry turned to him quickly.

"Of course I understand," she exclaimed. "As soon as I can I shall find a house. It will be better for me to be alone for a little, I think," she added gently.

"If there's anything I can do I shall be delighted," he assured her stiffly.

Carol gazed at him in astonishment: it was so unlike him to withhold his sympathy from anyone. This time even Lady Dalberry seemed aware of the curious reserve in his voice.

"This child will help me, I think," she said, and reaching across the intervening space she laid a hand on Carol's knee. "It is woman's work, house-furnishing. And she shall arrange one room for herself in the way she likes best, and come often to stay in it."

She flashed a glance at Dalberry, and it seemed to Carol that there was something very like a challenge in her cold eyes.

"Carol knows that Berrydown is still her home whenever she cares to go there," he answered easily. "The old housekeeper's pining for her, and the place is simply standing empty most of the time nowadays. The worst of Carol is that she is so much in demand elsewhere."

Lady Dalberry looked puzzled.

"You are living, where?" she asked, turning to the girl.

Carol laughed.

"I'm rather a stray dog at present. Poor Jasper's worrying himself to death trying to find a way to get rid of me," she explained, with an affectionate glance at Mellish. She had addressed him firmly by his Christian name at the early age of six, oblivious of the admonitions of a horrified nurse. "For the last six months or so I've been inflicting myself on a series of long-suffering friends, but I shall have to settle down some time. I ought to be house-hunting myself, I suppose. Jasper's got all sorts of antiquated ideas about a companion or chaperon or something equally depressing. We argue about it on an average of three times a week."

"As soon as you're of age you can do as you like," put in Mellish lazily. "Till then you've got to behave yourself, my child, though I don't mind telling you that I shall make myself uncommonly disagreeable any time within the next ten years if you insist on setting up house on your own. Not that you will take the slightest notice," he finished ruefully.

"He's getting a little fractious," explained Carol to Lady Dalberry. "You see, till now he's had me in the hollow of his hand, and he can't bear to think that his day is nearly over. On the twenty-eighth of March, exactly two months and nine days from now, I shall be twenty-one, and Jasper will give me his blessing and wash his hands of me for ever. There are times when it drives him almost frantic to feel that he won't be able to bully me any more."

"She's been counting the days," murmured Mellish plaintively. "The ingratitude of the minx!"

He and Carol were playing into each other's hands. The strain under which they had all been suffering since the beginning of the journey had at last begun to relax, and in their relief they had descended almost to flippancy. Lady Dalberry, face to face for the first time in her life with that essentially British characteristic which is, of all others, the most difficult for the intelligent foreigner to understand—the Englishman's overmastering impulse to make fun of those things about which he feels most strongly—was frankly puzzled; so much so that, though in the course of time she became really intimate with Carol, she never succeeded in realizing to the full the bond of genuine affection and respect that bound her and Jasper Mellish. Carol might jibe at the touch of his restraining hand, but she knew that he was never unreasonable, and she would have given up a great deal rather than hurt him. And, incidentally, she trusted him completely, and invariably turned to him for help and advice when in any difficulty.

"What are your plans for the next two months?" asked Dalberry with interest. "You can't stay on with the Randalls for ever."

"They want me to go to the south of France with them, but I'm tired of being abroad. It seems only yesterday that I got back from St. Moritz. I'd rather take a small flat in London. I think the life of a bachelor girl would suit me," she reflected.

"It might, but you won't have a chance to find out so long as I remain your long-suffering trustee. So you can put that idea out of your head," drawled Mellish.

"I believe you'll never be really happy till you've lost all my money for me," retorted Carol, with mock exasperation. "Then you can poke me away into a nice, strict home for destitute orphans, and visit me once a year just to find out whether I've been amenable to discipline."

"I did not realize that this child, like myself, was homeless," said Lady Dalberry, with a note of real sympathy in her deep voice.

"I had forgotten that she would, of course, have to leave Berry-down."

Dalberry's face flushed with annoyance.

"She knows the place is open to her whenever she cares to go there," he exclaimed, with what seemed to Carol quite unnecessary heat.

Mellish turned to him blandly.

"Lady Dalberry's quite right, my boy," he said. "We all know how you feel about it; but as long as Berrydown's a bachelor establishment Carol can hardly look upon it as her home."

Lady Dalberry bent forward and addressed Carol impulsively.

"Perhaps later, when you have been abroad with your friends, and we have got to know each other a little better, we might find a house that would suit us both. It would be very pleasant for me, a lonely woman with no daughter, and for you, it would mean that I could entertain for you when my year of mourning is over, and perhaps save you from this chaperon with whom you are threatened. Even when you are of age, my child, I think you will not be able to give balls and receptions without a *dame de compagnie.*—Or is it different in England?" she finished, turning to Mellish.

"I, personally, do not see how Carol is to entertain in accordance with her means unless she has some sort of chaperon," he admitted. "But then I'm old-fashioned, I believe."

"And is there no member of the family, no older lady? My husband spoke sometimes of his relations, but I cannot remember that he ever mentioned such a person."

Mellish shook his head.

"There's no one, oddly enough. Carol's sole surviving female relative on the Culver side is Miss Ellen Culver, a first cousin of her grandfather's, and she is too old and feeble for that sort of thing. Her father's people are, of course, all in America. Fortunately she has got a host of friends. Judging from the invitations she seems to have had, she could spend the rest of her life in a round of country-house visits."

"Only I happen to want a home of my own," put in Carol. She spoke with real impatience now. "It's too ridiculous. Just because of this wretched money, I'm to be made thoroughly uncomfortable. If I'd only got about twopence a year nobody would say a word against my taking up art or music and living my own life in my own way."

"I didn't know you were interested in art," commented Mellish mildly. "Of course, if you want to take a studio and give yourself up to painting, I should not dream of standing in your way. I always believe in encouraging young talent. But if you're thinking of laying down a parquet floor and giving little dances after the day's toil is over, I must insist on an adequate chaperon, I'm afraid."

Carol laughed in spite of her annoyance.

"You must have been an awful handful when you were young," she said admiringly. "It's uncanny, the way you see through my little innocent schemes. The career of an artist seems to be closed to me."

Lady Dalberry, who found herself slightly at a loss during these conversational skirmishes, brought the disputants firmly back to the matter in hand, with the calm directness which seemed to be one of her main characteristics.

"Will you consider what I have suggested," she said earnestly, "while you are staying with your friends? It is not for now. For a little while I must be alone. I am too—tired, I think."

She did not say "sad," but her wonderful voice, with its rich, beautiful inflections, said it for her. Carol felt her throat contract suddenly with emotion, and for the moment it seemed to her that there was nothing she would not do to make this woman's tragic life a shade more endurable.

"Of course, if you'd really care to have me—" she was beginning impulsively, when Mellish held up a plump hand.

"An admirable way out of the difficulty," he said, beaming approvingly on Lady Dalberry, "and one that had occurred to me, though I should not have ventured to suggest it. But we've got several months before us yet, and all sorts of things may turn up in the interval. As you say, you need time to rest and collect yourself, and Carol will know better what she wants to do when she actually takes control of her own affairs. If you take my advice, you'll let the matter rest for a while until both of you have more definite ideas as to your future plans."

For a moment it seemed as though Lady Dalberry were about to resent his interference, then her native good sense asserted itself.

"We will let it wait until we know each other better, yes?" she said, with perfect amiability. "But for myself, I do not doubt that we shall live very happily together."

Though she had shown no open resentment, she continued to address herself pointedly to Carol, and had Shand been present, he would no doubt have rejoiced in the fact that he had been witness to the first brush between Lady Dalberry and Jasper Mellish.

CHAPTER V

ON REACHING LONDON the party split up into three: the solicitor hurrying to his office and Mellish accompanying Lady Dalberry to the rooms he had taken for her at a quiet hotel off Piccadilly. She seemed tired, and obviously wished to be alone, and at Mellish's suggestion Carol and Dalberry took a taxi to Mellish's rooms in the Albany, where he arranged to join them after he had settled Lady Dalberry comfortably.

They had hardly left the station before Carol broached the subject that was uppermost in her mind.

"What on earth was the matter with you, Gillie? You were simply horrid to that poor thing in the train!"

"On the contrary, I was uncommonly nice to her! I never heard a more base accusation. At any rate, I talked to her. All you did was to squabble with Jasper!"

His indignation was not very convincing, and Carol calmly ignored it.

"What's the matter?" she asked bluntly. "Did anything happen to put your back up?"

"Nothing. You're simply fussing," he answered lightly. "What are you going to call our new-found relative, by the way? We shall have to arrive at some sort of compromise."

Carol took him up sharply.

"Why compromise? She is our aunt by marriage, after all. She signed herself 'Irma' in her letter to me, so I suppose that's what we shall call her."

"Aunt Irma," he repeated thoughtfully. "It seems unnatural, somehow."

"I don't see why. It's a perfectly good name, even if it isn't English. Don't be insular, Gillie!"

Dalberry grinned.

"All right, old thing. Let it be 'Aunt Irma,' then. After all, we've got to call her something."

But Carol did not propose to let him off so lightly.

"Why don't you like her, Gillie?" she asked, with unusual pertinacity.

"My dear girl, you're talking nonsense. I've got no earthly reason either to like or dislike her. I know no more about her than you do."

"But you do dislike her, all the same. I've only once seen you behave like that before. Do you remember that horrid little man who came to Berrydown to paint Uncle Maurice's portrait? You were hateful to him."

"Well, he richly deserved it. Honestly, I thought I behaved quite normally this afternoon. You must admit that the whole situation was a bit trying. I was perfectly polite to her."

"You were! That's the trouble. I never saw you so pompous in my life. It was devastating. Even she noticed it. Why couldn't you be decently nice to her?"

"I did as much as I could. You could hardly expect me to hold her hand and pat it. Come to that, that was your job!"

"I felt awfully sorry for her," said Carol soberly. "But she's not easy to get on with, is she? All the same, I think she's rather a wonderful woman, Gillie."

"Is she? She struck me as very like any other Swedish-American."

Carol slid a swift, mocking glance in his direction.

"I suppose you've known heaps of Swedish-Americans, Gillie dear," she remarked ingenuously.

"You little pig! One up to you. As a matter of fact, this is the first of the species I have come across so far. But she seems quite a characteristic specimen."

Carol returned to her former charge.

"Then why don't you like her, Gillie?"

He realized that evasion was hopeless.

"Honestly, I don't know. But I admit I don't like her, if that'll satisfy you. There's something about her that puts my back up. I tried to behave decently, and I did think I'd succeeded."

"Oh, you were quite polite to her. But I think she guessed you had no use for her. She's clever, Gillie, and there's something fascinating and unusual about her. I believe she could be rather horrid, though, if she liked. Her voice is lovely. Did you notice it?"

Rather to Gillie's relief, the arrival of the cab at the Albany put an end to the discussion. He wasn't in the habit of yielding to unreasonable prejudices, and he felt shy of discussing them. Also, he was too essentially kind-hearted not to feel a little ashamed of his behaviour to Lady Dalberry.

Jervis, Mellish's valet, who had been with him for years, and had known Carol and Dalberry since their nursery days, opened the door to them.

"Isn't Mr. Mellish with you, my lord?" he inquired, almost reproachfully, as though he held Dalberry responsible for the safety of his master when he was out of his keeping.

"It's all right, Jervis, we haven't lost him," Carol assured him gaily. "He's seeing Lady Dalberry to her hotel, and he'll be here in a minute."

"A trying day for everybody, miss, if you'll allow me to say so," remarked Jervis. "And I'm hoping Mr. Mellish won't catch cold to-morrow. Very tricky things, funerals, in this weather."

Gillie's mouth twitched, and he did not dare to look at Carol.

"You're quite right, Jervis, they are," he assented gravely. "I'll keep an eye on Mr. Mellish for you and bring him back safely in the evening."

"Mr. Mellish will not be staying on at Berrydown, I understand, my lord," ventured Jervis primly, as he led the way into Mellish's comfortable study.

"No. We're all coming up again to-morrow evening. It didn't seem worth while to open up the house for such a short time, and Mr. Mellish thought Lady Dalberry would prefer to be in town."

"I understand that her ladyship is a foreigner," remarked Jervis, with the freedom of an old servant, as he pulled an armchair up to the fire for Carol and helped her off with her fur coat.

"It seems a pity, miss."

There was such acute disapproval in his tone that Carol could not resist casting a mischievous glance at Dalberry, who firmly declined to meet it.

Jervis moved softly about the room, placing drinks at Dalberry's elbow and a small table bearing cigarettes and ash-trays between him and Carol.

"The cigarettes you liked last time you were here are on the right, Miss Carol. Mr. Mellish ordered some more on purpose. The Virginians are on the left. Is there anything else you would like, miss?"

Carol shook her head.

"You've made us deliciously comfy, Jervis. This is just the sort of fire I dreamed of all the way up in the train."

Jervis beamed discreetly.

"I thought it best to make it up well, miss. Very chilly things, journeys I always think, especially in winter."

He seemed to vanish into the shadows, and they heard the door close almost noiselessly behind him.

"And so hot in summer," murmured Gillie drowsily, giving himself up to the warmth and comfort of the blazing fire. "But not so tricky as funerals, mind you. Dear Jervis!"

"He seems to share your prejudice against foreigners," remarked Carol. "Now you know how silly you sounded in the cab just now."

"Not at all. It's the attitude of all right-minded Britons. You forget that Jervis can always be relied on to behave with absolute correctness on the most trying occasions. I've simply risen in my own estimation."

They relapsed into silence, watching the smoke of their cigarettes curl lazily upwards. After the cold discomfort of the train Mellish's room, with its cunningly shaded lights and glowing fire, was delicious. Carol was half asleep when Gillie spoke again.

"I say, Carol," he began, with surprising energy, "we're pretty good pals, aren't we?"

She turned to him, wondering.

"Of course. Why?"

"Has it ever struck you that we've rather taken each other for granted till now?"

"I suppose we have, but then we were almost brought up together. One does rather take one's relations for granted."

"I know. Only we're not relations at all. It's not as if you were Aunt Marian's daughter."

"That's true, of course. It's funny to think that we're not even cousins; but, somehow, it's never seemed to make much difference. You see, my mother died when I was born, and the only person I can remember is your aunt. She looked after me till I was ten, and I always called her 'mother.' Then I came to England to live with Uncle Maurice, and he and you and the boys seemed just like my own family. When they were drowned it was just like losing one's own people. I think I minded just as much. Of course, I've always known I wasn't really any relation, but I never seemed to realize it properly, somehow."

"Neither did I, till just lately. But, what with Uncle Maurice's death and various other things, it seems to have been rather brought home to me. So long as you were at Berrydown with the others, and I knew I should find you there whenever I ran down, it was different, somehow. Now that everything's broken up, it's rather rammed things into me."

"Poor old Gillie," she said, with quick sympathy. "It's hit you harder than any one. After all, as you say, I'm not really one of you, even if I did feel like it, and, though I've had to give up Berrydown, it hasn't changed my life as it has yours. I believe you were happier with your old engineering firm really."

He nodded.

"I was," he agreed soberly. "I hated giving that up, and though I do care a lot for the old place I don't want it; at least, not at the price I've had to pay for it. I've been feeling pretty blue about the whole thing lately, Carol. And I've been doing some hard thinking. I got myself into a pretty muddle, too, over it, but I managed to straighten things out to this extent. It's you that's the matter."

"Gillie! Why, what have I done?"

"You haven't done anything," he explained carefully, "except just be yourself, I suppose. It isn't so much the old life and all that I've been missing. It's you. Carol, I'm getting more desperately afraid of losing you every day."

Still Carol remained blind to the real significance of what he was trying to convey to her. If he had been any other man she would have seen at once what he was driving at, but Gillie, with whom she had alternately played and fought for years!

"But, my dear old thing, you're not going to lose me. We shall see each other almost as much as ever. After all, you'll still be in London most of the time, and even if I do go abroad, it won't be for long."

"Supposing I was to go abroad, to India, say, for a year or two, would you miss me, Carol?" he asked, in desperation.

She gazed at him in astonishment.

"Of course I should! But you're not going to India!"

He threw away his cigarette and took up his stand squarely in front of her.

"That's what I mean. You'd care, in a way; but if I knew for certain that you were going away for any length of time, going somewhere where I couldn't get at you, I simply shouldn't know what to do with myself. I expect it sounds pretty silly to you after all the years we've known each other."

For once in her life Carol was speechless. At last she understood and was trying in vain to adjust her mind to this amazing state of affairs. Gillie went on, speaking very simply and directly.

"I know I ought to have waited. Given you some sort of warning, as it were. But, somehow, all sorts of things have happened to-day which seem to have brought matters to a head. And now there's so little time. Jasper will be back in a minute, and I must get this off my chest first. Carol, I want you most awfully. Won't you marry me?"

Carol was still conscious only of dismay. In a flash it came to her that the old happy intimacy between her and Gillie was over for ever, and faced with its loss, she realized for the first time how much she valued it. And at the moment she could not estimate correctly this infinitely more precious thing he was offering her instead. She tried to answer him honestly, and was conscious only of her own incoherence.

"My dear, I don't know. I've never thought of—us—like that. We've been so happy together. If only we could go on in the old way!"

She tried to smile, but there were tears of distress in her eyes.

He dropped down on to the arm of her chair and took her hand in his.

"I know. Only the old way isn't enough for me any more. That's the worst of it. You do care for me a little, don't you?"

She did not answer for a minute. She was doing her best to deal fairly with him.

"I don't know, Gillie. I see now that I've always been fonder of you than of either of the others. If poor Dick or Morry had been still alive and had asked me this, I should have said 'no' at once. But you're different. And yet I can't bring myself to think of you in that way. And, Gillie, I don't want to marry. At least, not yet. I'm only just at the beginning of things."

"You're just at the point where you need some one to look after you," he pointed out sombrely.

She looked up at him with swift suspicion.

"You're not just doing this because you feel you ought? Because you think I need protecting, or some nonsense of that sort?"

Gillie rose to his feet and stood looking down at her.

"I'm doing it because I love you. I realize now that I've loved you for years."

For a moment she could not answer, and when she did her voice was full of compunction.

"I'm so frightfully sorry, Gillie dear. I wish this had never happened. I do care for you, but I can't feel like that about it. And I know I don't want to marry, yet, at any rate. You must give me a little time, please. I can't say anything definite now."

"I'll give you as long as you like, if you'll only think seriously over what I said. But you will remember that it means a lot to me, won't you?"

She nodded.

"I feel I've been such a pig," she said. "I do appreciate your wanting me. It's only that it's so surprising, somehow, that I don't seem able to grasp it. And then, there's my own life. It sounds silly, I suppose, but I have been looking forward so much to being on my own. You see, in a way I've seen less of life than most girls of twenty. It was lovely at Berrydown, and I was extraordinarily happy there, but, except for hunt balls in the winter and a few shooting parties, there was nothing very exciting. We used to come up for the theatres, but we never did a London season and I never 'came out' like all the other girls I know. Then there was the awful accident to Uncle Maurice and the boys, and since then, of course, I've been in mourning, and till now I haven't wanted to go anywhere. And now I'm not really heartless, honestly, but I can't help thinking of the things I shall do when I come of age and am my own mistress. I expect you think it's horrid of me," she finished miserably.

Gillie's eyes met hers with their usual frank honesty.

"I don't. It's only natural. But you've brought one thing home to me that I ought to have seen for myself. It wouldn't be fair to bind you now, before you've had time to look round. I didn't realize how much you'd been cut off from things. I don't wonder you want to have a bit of a fling before you settle down for good."

Carol rose and stood by his side, slipping her arm into his.

"Give me a year," she pleaded. "I shall know for certain then. I can't tell you now. But, please, Gillie, can't we be friends as we used to be? Don't let this spoil it all. And, of course, you're free, absolutely free. I mean, if you were to meet some one you liked better."

Gillie smiled down at her, a curious, twisted little smile very unlike his usual wide-mouthed grin.

"There won't be any one," he said, "so don't count on that. I'm sorry I bothered you. I was a fool to rush things like that. Of course I'll wait, and we won't speak of this again until the year's up. Meanwhile I shall be hanging round, so to speak, just as I've always been."

As he spoke they heard the sound of a latch-key in the front door.

"It's Jasper," murmured Carol, subsiding swiftly into the big armchair.

Gillie bent over her.

"I say, Carol."

"Yes, old thing."

"If you do meet anybody in the course of the next twelve months, you'll tell me, won't you? It'll be a bit of a facer, you see, and I'd rather hear it from you."

"Of course, Gillie dear."

"And if you should change your mind about this?"

She had only time to nod as Mellish came into the room.

Dalberry saw her home to the house of the friends with whom she was staying, and they met next day at the funeral. Almost immediately afterwards she left for Yorkshire, going straight from there to the south of France, and he did not see her again till she got back to London in the middle of the last week in February.

Meanwhile that hard-working officer, Chief Detective-Inspector Shand, was not idle, though it was not till just before Carol's return to town that he was able to bring his plans to a head. But his methods, though occasionally slow, were very sure, as a certain lanky individual who, after a prolonged absence abroad, had spent the better part of a week enjoying the pale February sunshine and watching the heterogeneous crowds that drift slowly along the Front at Brighton, was to discover.

He did not start as a hand was laid on his shoulder, but the somewhat cynical smile with which he was observing the unwieldy progress of a fat matron faded as though it had been wiped out with a sponge, and the silver-headed cane, balanced between his long, very supple fingers, gave a twitch and then was still. For a second he sat motionless, then he turned slowly and his upward gaze met that of Chief Inspector Shand.

"Coming?" asked Shand gently.

Henry Piper, sometimes known as Long Peter, nodded.

"You've got me," he said laconically, as he rose to his feet.

Later, when they had boarded the London train, he permitted himself to smile.

"How did you like Buenos Aires?" he asked artlessly. "I heard you'd been there."

"Interesting place," was Shand's urbane rejoinder. "Brighton's more handy, though, for my purposes."

"I'll let you have a card next time. Too bad we should have missed each other. You're a sticker all right. I'll say that."

He took a handsome crocodile case from his pocket and chose a cigar with the care of one to whom cigars will soon be only a wistful memory. Its quality was such that Shand hastily produced a pipe in sheer self-defence. For a time the two men smoked in silence, then Shand leaned forward.

"Piper, what do you know about Smith?" he asked quietly.

Long Peter's face became, if anything, a trifle more bland than before.

"I seem to know the name," he admitted, with exaggerated candour. "Any particular Smith? Or are you just looking up the family?"

"This particular Smith was found dead on board the *Enriqueta*, and we've reason to believe that he'd been seen with you in Buenos Aires."

Shand did not mention the fact that Smith had been in possession of several of Piper's most convincing forgeries, and had passed them off successfully almost immediately before he was killed. He knew that any attempt to elicit information about the murdered man's associates would meet with a blank wall should the forger suspect that any admission on his part might be used against him. As it was, it became evident that he was giving nothing away.

"I work alone, and everybody knows it; that's to say, I did in the old days before I began to go straight. I've been looking after my old mother at Brighton for the last month, and I can prove it."

Shand did not argue the matter.

"I don't want you for anything that's happened at Brighton, though I admit that I'd like to meet that old mother of yours. Just at the moment it's Smith I'm interested in."

"I can't call to mind any Smith, though, of course, one runs up against them now and then. You can't help it with a name like that. What's his graft, anyway? If it's passing slush, I don't hold with it."

"That's just what I'm asking you."

Long Peter shook his head.

"I'm no 'nose,' and you know it," he announced virtuously. "As for who killed him, I tell you honestly, Mr. Shand, I don't know, and I haven't come across anybody that does."

Shand, tactfully ignoring the fact that a few minutes before Long Peter had denied any knowledge of the associates of the man in question, continued to pursue his patient inquiries.

He was aware that, for all his protestations, Piper would have no compunction in telling what he knew, provided it did not affect his own safety.

"Was he the sort of man to make enemies?" he asked.

"Everybody makes enemies," answered Piper sanctimoniously. "I can imagine somebody having a grudge even against you, Mr. Shand. As for Smith, I don't know, and I wouldn't tell you if I did. I did meet him once, but I didn't know him, if you understand me. He was introduced to me."

"By whom?" snapped Shand.

Long Peter looked hurt.

"How you do take one up," he said plaintively. "We were introduced, as I said, but the man that did it was no friend of mine. Strelinski, I think his name was, but I wouldn't be sure. He seemed to be a pal of Smith's."

"A pal of Smith's, eh? What did he look like?"

"Fair, middle-sized chap, with very light hair. Looked like one of those dance-hall lizards. He and Smith were pretty thick at one time, so I was told."

"Was there any rumour of a quarrel between him and Smith?"

Long Peter shook his head.

"Not that I ever heard of."

He gave himself up to the enjoyment of his rank cigar, and Shand, convinced that there was nothing to be gained by further questioning, let the subject drop. After a pause, however, his prisoner suddenly volunteered a statement.

"I'll tell you one thing," he said meditatively. "Strelinski wasn't in Buenos Aires when Smith was killed. He left shortly after I did."

"By sea?"

But Long Peter was not to be drawn so easily.

"That's for you to find out, Mr. Shand. How should I know? But he left all right."

"How do you know?"

A slow grin spread across Long Peter's saturnine face. "From information received, Mr. Shand," he vouchsafed demurely.

CHAPTER VI

MELLISH, comfortably ensconced in front of the fire in his study, cocked his head and listened. As he did so it became increasingly evident that he had been right in his diagnosis of the disquieting sound that had reached him from the far regions of the pantry. He could hear Jervis's discreet tread in the hall, then the click of the latch of the front door as he opened it.

Mellish's usually placid face clouded with annoyance. He had breakfasted late, according to his custom, and, after a glance at the bleak March day outside, had decided to devote the morning to a careful revisal of his collection of etchings. He had come to what was, for him, a momentous decision. If he were to buy the Rembrandt he coveted, some of the small fry would have to go. There was a demand for them in America, and the price they would fetch would place the Rembrandt easily within his reach. But he hated parting with even the smallest item in his collection, and as he sat there in his most roomy armchair, a huge portfolio on his knees, and an ever-growing pile of discarded proofs by his side, he was in one of his rare fits of thorough bad temper. Jervis, who showed a positive genius for anticipating his master's moods, opened the door.

"Miss Summers, sir," he announced gloomily.

Mellish finished his examination of an etching, decided that he could not bring himself to part with it, and returned it to the portfolio.

"Show her in," he said testily. "And, Jervis, take this."

Jervis relieved him of the portfolio, and Mellish heaved himself out of the chair and made his ponderous way to the door to greet Carol.

"Now, what do *you* want?" he growled, eyeing her with mingled affection and irritation.

It was exactly a week since Carol had returned from the south of France, and she had spent most of that week in baiting Jasper Mellish, a pastime which afforded them both a good deal of innocent pleasure. But in spite of his readiness to make a joke of the whole thing, Mellish was genuinely worried about Carol's future. In a month's time she would come of age and be her own mistress, and he had tried in vain to persuade her to look out for a suitable house in which to spend the spring and early summer, and, a thing still more important in his eyes, make a selection from among the several very eligible ladies who were prepared to live with her and pilot her through the intricacies of a London season.

Instead of listening to his unanswerable arguments, she had met them with the most fantastic and, in his eyes, outrageous schemes of her own. But a few days before she had announced her intention of hiring a motor caravan and taking it over to France and thence to Spain; the alternative to this, he gathered, being an expedition to some island off the extreme north coast of Scotland, where a friend, whose sex she discreetly omitted to state, was conducting archaeological researches.

Mellish played up to her, and having argued the matter with zest, told her to go her own wicked way. One stipulation, however, he did make: March 28th was to find her in London for the celebration of her coming of age. On that date he proposed formally to hand over to her the property which would make her one of the richest women in England.

So far she had taken no steps towards the carrying out of any of her wild schemes, and he had enough trust in her common-sense to feel fairly certain that she would do nothing exaggeratedly foolish. To-day, however, he was in no temper for badinage, and Carol, who could gauge his moods to a nicety, knew that she would have to go warily. Therefore she came straight to the point, though she would have dearly loved to tease him a little first.

"Nothing, Jasper dear," she said sweetly: so sweetly that he at once became suspicious. This time, however, he was to find that he had done her an injustice. "I've only come for a moment," she went on. "A few kind words of praise and appreciation and your blessing, and I propose to fade away in the odour of sanctity. In a few minutes you'll be back among your etchings, so perfectly happy about me and my future that you won't have to give me another thought." Mellish observed her with cynical interest.

"Intense, not to say smug, self-satisfaction, but none of that beatific radiance which betokens true love. It's inconceivable that you should be marrying for money, so that I conclude you're not engaged. The only explanation is that you've evolved another plot. What devilish scheme is it this time?"

"Considering that I've followed your advice to the letter, I call that abominably ungrateful. I've got half a charming flat, and a chaperon that even you can't take exception to. Of course, I should be much happier wandering innocently and peacefully across Spain; but rather than see you fuss yourself into the grave, I am willing to sacrifice myself."

"Hum, I'm not worried about Spain. You haven't met the fleas or the cooking. I have. You'd be back in a fortnight. Do I understand you to say that you've found a permanent home?"

Carol nodded.

"And a chaperon," she exclaimed. "Don't forget that important item. Unless she and I quarrel hopelessly, I am settled for good."

Mellish collected the discarded etchings and arranged them in a neat pile.

"I do think you might show a little interest, Jasper!" she said at last, exasperated by his slowness.

He seemed even sleepier than usual, but when he looked up his eyes were very keen behind their heavy lids.

"Lady Dalberry," he said. It was a statement rather than a question.

She nodded.

"She suggested it in the train on the day of the funeral, do you remember? When I went to see her the other day she asked me if I'd thought it over, and said she was horribly lonely now that all the excitement of furnishing was over. I'm sorry for her, Jasper. She's had her whole life knocked to bits at one blow, and she *is* plucky. I think she's honestly anxious to have me, and it'll be far less embarrassing for me than having a paid companion."

"When do you move in?" asked Mellish.

He showed neither pleasure nor disapproval at the announcement, and Carol felt vaguely disappointed.

"The day after to-morrow. Aren't you pleased? I've done exactly what you've always wanted."

Mellish declined to commit himself.

"We'll see how it works," he said cautiously. "I suppose you're free to break off the connection whenever you like?"

"Yes. We agreed to try it for a couple of months, and then, if we're happy together, we shall probably go on with it. It's a perfectly gorgeous flat, and I've got a bedroom, sitting-room, an extra bedroom, if I need it, and my own bathroom. Aunt Irma's furnished the rooms quite beautifully."

"Aunt Irma, eh? Have you got your own telephone?"

Carol looked surprised.

"I don't think so, but there's one in the hall, and I suppose we shall share the expense, so that I can use it whenever I like. Why?"

"I don't know," said Mellish vaguely. "You can always have one put in if you want it. Keep me posted as to how you get on, will you?"

"Of course. I shall be in and out as much as ever. You needn't think you've seen the last of me!"

After she had gone Mellish did not return to his etchings. Instead he lighted a cigarette and stood for a long time staring thoughtfully into the fire.

He was interrupted by the arrival of Lord Dalberry. This time he merely shrugged his shoulders. He was resigned by now to the loss of his quiet morning.

Dalberry showed none of Carol's complacency.

"I say, has she been here?" he demanded.

"It depends what you mean by 'she,'" returned Mellish, with his usual exasperating slowness.

"Carol, of course. She said last night that she was coming to see you. To consult you, she called it," he finished bitterly.

Mellish's eyes twinkled.

"'Consult' is as good a word as any," he said. "In any case, I don't see that I could have taken exception to her plan. As she sapiently remarked, it was only what I had been suggesting myself all along."

"You'll let it go on, then?"

Mellish shrugged his shoulders.

"My dear Gillie, why not? It is a perfectly satisfactory arrangement. Carol needs a home, and though Lady Dalberry's not a poor woman, it will be an advantage to her to share expenses with some one. It's amazing what she has managed to spend on this flat. I'm her trustee, as you know, so that I have to keep an eye on things."

"Has she been selling out?" asked Dalberry, in surprise. Mellish nodded.

"Her jointure reverts to the estate eventually, and you're the head of the family, so there's no harm in telling you. There were certain Argentine stocks she had a right to realize according to her husband's will, and she has realized them."

"But what has she done with the money? She's got a perfectly adequate income for a woman in her position."

"I don't know. She may have reinvested it for all I know. In any case, if she has been gambling with the money and is a bit hard pressed, it's just as well that she has decided to share expenses with Carol. What objection have you got to the arrangement?"

"Every possible objection!" exclaimed Dalberry hotly. "You know as well as I do, Jasper, that that woman's no friend for Carol. I'd rather she went off on one of her wild-goose-chase expeditions than think of her, even for a week, in the house of that painted adventuress!"

Mellish raised a protesting hand.

"My dear Gillie! If we were to rule out every woman in London who paints her face, we should have some difficulty in finding a suitable chaperon for Carol, even if she'd consent to put up with one. And remember, this is the first time she's shown the smallest inclination to meet us half-way. For heaven's sake, don't antagonize her now."

Dalberry exploded.

"You're simply sacrificing Carol to your own peace of mind! You're so confoundedly lazy that you'd accept any means of disposing of her provided it was outwardly respectable. You're not a fool, Jasper, and you haven't the face to tell me that you either like or approve of Lady Dalberry!"

"By the way, you'll have to call her 'Aunt Irma' sooner or later, so you may as well make up your mind to it now," was Mellish's placid rejoinder. "My dear chap, it's no use casting vague aspersions on a woman who has absolutely nothing against her. You don't like her, that is obvious, and, to tell you the truth, I'm not in love with her myself, but that's no reason for concluding that she's a wrong-un. Carol's no fool, and if she doesn't like the look of things she can always clear out. There's nothing to be gained by trying to coerce her at this juncture."

"I wish to goodness—" began Dalberry, and pulled himself up abruptly.

"*I* wish to goodness you'd shown a little ordinary *savoir faire* when you proposed to her," put in Mellish curtly. "I don't know when or how you did it, but I'm fairly certain you *did* do it, and I haven't the smallest doubt that it was done at the wrong moment and in the wrong way."

Dalberry crimsoned at this shameless and wholly unprovoked attack.

"I say, Mellish—"

"Don't 'Mellish' me!" snapped the fat man testily. "When a girl comes back to London after an absence of nearly two months, and pointedly refrains from asking after a man she has known from childhood, and then gets scarlet at the mere mention of his name, it's pretty obvious what has happened. I stand *in loco parentis* to Carol, and apart from that, I'm very fond of her. In less than a month's time she'll be the legitimate prey of every fortune-hunter in the country. I'd give a great deal to see you two make a match of it. I've always hoped for it. And I'm confoundedly disappointed!"

He had risen from his chair and was ambling up and down the room, literally spluttering with annoyance. Dalberry smiled in spite of himself. When Jasper was at his most offensive he was least easy to quarrel with.

"You're not half so disappointed as I am," he observed drily. "As you've ferreted out this much, I may as well tell you the rest. Carol hasn't turned me down altogether. We are to wait for a year, and then I'm to try my luck again. It's no affair of yours, but I'm not sorry to have you on my side."

"It is my affair," grunted Mellish. "I'm the girl's guardian, and I'm responsible for her safety until she comes of age. If I'm on your side, as you call it, it's solely because you're the one man in London who cannot, for any conceivable reason, be after her money."

Dalberry's smile broadened into a grin.

"So long as I've got your blessing, I don't mind what your reasons are for giving it," he said meekly.

Mellish glared at him and snorted, then suddenly his face broke into a thousand wrinkles.

"Been a bear, have I?" he growled, with a fat chuckle. "The truth is I'm fond of you both, and I want to see you happy. If I thought you'd listen to me, I'd give you some good advice."

"I'm grateful for anything at this juncture."

"Then make the best of your new-found aunt. She *is* your aunt, whatever you may choose to feel about her; and I can assure you you might have fared a good deal worse. How your uncle met her I don't know, but I understand that she comes of good middle-class Swedish stock. She appears to have made him an excellent wife, and to have mourned him sincerely when he died. She's a woman of the world, perfectly presentable, and no fool. Has it ever occurred to you that she might have been infinitely worse?"

"I don't like her," was Dalberry's stubborn rejoinder.

"I daresay you don't, but your personal antipathies have nothing to do with it. And let me tell you this. Your only chance of keeping an eye on Carol and seeing that she does not fall too much under the influence of the wrong people lies in standing well with Lady Dalberry. If you take my advice you will keep on as good terms with her as possible, and cultivate the habit of running in and out of the flat."

It was obvious that this suggestion did not appeal to Dalberry.

"It's not a very inviting programme," he said disgustedly. "You can hardly expect me to force myself on the hospitality of a woman I dislike simply to gain my own ends. I'd do a good deal for the sake of keeping in touch with Carol, but not that!"

"I'm not suggesting that you should go to the flat merely to keep in touch with Carol."

Dalberry stared at him.

"What other reason could I possibly have for going?"

"To keep an eye on Lady Dalberry," was Mellish's surprising answer.

"Then you've been bluffing all this time, and you don't trust her!"

"I trust her as much as I trust anybody in this wicked world, and, as I've said, I've got nothing against her. What I don't trust is this sudden desire for Carol's company just as the girl is about to come into her money. I may be doing the woman an injustice. Very likely she has merely taken a fancy to Carol, and is really, as she says, lonely and in need of companionship; but the fact remains that Lady Dalberry has been spending money like water since she arrived in England. Where that money has gone I don't know, but I'd give something to know who her broker is, and still more to meet him. And I don't want Carol dragged into that sort of thing. I consider that, for her sake, there ought to be some one on the spot to see that she does not fall too much under the influence of Lady Dalberry and her friends."

It was unlike Mellish to be either verbose or explicit. He usually preferred to sow a seed here and there in his sleepy way, and then, apparently, leave the matter to Providence. Dalberry knew that to have spoken so freely, he must have felt more strongly about the matter than he chose to admit. He still shrank from the idea of deliberately trying to ingratiate himself with his uncle's wife, but he salved his conscience by reminding himself that he had not yet called on her in her new flat, and that, in common courtesy, he owed her a visit. The day after his conversation with Mellish he went to see her.

He took an instant and quite unreasoning dislike to the great block of flats in which Lady Dalberry had taken up her abode. Ten years before it had been the Escatorial Hotel, one of the maddest of the wild ventures of a Swiss ex-waiter with a genius for organization and more than a touch of megalomania, who made and lost three fortunes before he ended his career by committing suicide in the lounge of one of his own palatial hotels. In the Escatorial he had tried to realize his dream of what a perfect residential hotel should be, and for a time it looked as though he had succeeded. Then, owing no doubt to the ruinous charges, the tenants began to drift away in search of cheaper quarters, and the management found itself obliged to cater to a less wealthy and more transient type of guest. In spite of admirable food and excellent service it failed to appeal to the right people, and it was slowly degenerating into a second-rate hotel when the "Urban Flats Company" bought it and added it to their long list of "desirable town residences." As regards comfort, position, and general magnificence, the Escatorial was undoubtedly one of the finest blocks of residential flats in London, and if Dalberry took exception to the spacious white and gold vestibule, with its banks of palms and superfluity of uniformed porters and page-boys, it was no doubt because his own tastes were almost eccentrically simple.

Lady Dalberry's flat was on the fourth floor, the bedrooms and Carol's sitting-room looking on to the large garden which formed one of the chief attractions of the Escatorial, the other rooms facing the street. The room into which Dalberry was shown reminded him of nothing so much as the stage setting of an American super-film. Perhaps this impression was due to the incongruous mixture of Chinese embroideries and heavy Jacobean furniture and the overpowering mass of heavily scented flowers with their accompanying gilt pots and baskets; but the embroideries, if out of place, were genuine, and the furniture was good. Either Lady Dalberry had been lucky in her advisers or she possessed an unusual flair for such things; certainly she had not been cheated, and Mellish, had he been there, would have recognized the fact that, whatever she may have done with the rest of her money, in her furniture she had made an excellent investment.

She greeted Dalberry with a warmth that struck him as a little exaggerated, for he had a growing conviction that she did not like him. Carol, who had got over the slight constraint of their first meeting after her long absence, was frankly delighted to see him. She introduced him to the only other visitor, a stocky little man with very pale blue eyes and a voice so low as to be almost inaudible.

"Captain Bond knew Uncle Adrian in America," she explained.

"Before I left the Service," put in Captain Bond in a voice hardly above a discreet whisper. "War Office job. Buying horses."

"He stayed with us on the ranch," said Lady Dalberry, "and liked the life so much that he very nearly decided to remain in the Argentine."

"Wish I had," murmured Captain Bond. "They've no use for an ex-soldier in the old country. Since I sold out I've had to take what I could get."

"He is secretary to one of your London clubs," explained Lady Dalberry.

"Not a very grateful job, I'm afraid," said Dalberry sympathetically.

"Not what I've been accustomed to, but beggars can't be choosers," was Bond's rather lugubrious reply.

A depressing little man, Dalberry thought him, and a bit of a snob. After all, the secretaryship of a good club was a reputable enough job from a social point of view. It was Carol who shed an unexpected light on the situation.

"Do let's go there one night, Gillie," she exclaimed enthusiastically. "Captain Bond says it's the best in London, and they've got a magnificent band."

"No need to join first," explained Bond significantly. "Pay your money at the door and no questions asked, what?"

"I didn't realize you meant a dance club," said Dalberry. "Which of them is it?"

"The 'Terpsychorean.' And I flatter myself, though I say it as shouldn't, that there's not a better run show in London."

"It's certainly enormously popular," said Dalberry noncommittally.

He knew the "Terpsychorean" well by name, though, as it happened, he had never been there. It was one of the few night clubs that could boast of never having been raided, a distinction which did not go far towards sweetening its rather unsavoury reputation.

"Why not bring Miss Summers along one evening," insisted Bond eagerly. "If you settle a date now I'll see that a table's reserved for you. There's a good show next Monday. A couple of dancers from Monte Carlo. Come now, why not make it Monday?"

Carol supported him enthusiastically.

"Do, Gillie! Or are you doing anything else? If not, let's go. It's ages since we danced together, and Aunt Irma says there's no reason why I shouldn't go to that sort of thing, even if I am in mourning."

"They tell me that, here in England, it is different," said Lady Dalberry. "Even in New York they are more strict about mourning, and in the foreign colony where I was raised we do not go out at all for a long time. But here she could go to such a place, I think."

"There's no reason why she shouldn't," admitted Dalberry. "After all, her mourning's largely complimentary. Uncle Maurice wasn't her real uncle."

He was no frequenter of night clubs. Being essentially an open-air man, stuffy rooms and late hours did not appeal to him; but he welcomed the chance of dancing with Carol, and, after all, if she wished to sample that sort of life, it was better she should do it with him than with comparative strangers. He wondered if Aunt Irma had many more friends of the Bond kidney, and was thankful that her deep mourning prevented her from getting up a party for Carol herself.

"Then let's settle to go on Monday," insisted Carol. "Or does the idea bore you too hopelessly? You don't look very keen!"

"Perhaps he does not approve of these clubs," put in Lady Dalberry gently. "I am not sure that I do not agree with him. For young girls it means sometimes too much freedom."

Dalberry winced. He was being made to look an insufferable prig before Carol, and he could feel her astonished eyes on him.

"Good heavens! I've nothing against night clubs," he exclaimed, "provided they're properly run. I was trying to remember whether I'd let myself in for anything on Monday, that's all. As far as I know, I'm free. Shall I call for you here, Carol? We can dine somewhere first. You're moving in at once, aren't you?"

"To-morrow," she said. "Aunt Irma, may I show Gillie my new rooms?"

"Of course, my dear. I've had the light altered in the bedroom. See if you like it."

Dalberry was obliged to admit that the rooms were charming. Lady Dalberry had contented herself with making them as fresh and bright as possible, with the result that they had escaped the curious, rather theatrical atmosphere of the drawing-room.

"I was rather amused at Aunt Irma's denunciation of night clubs," said Carol confidently. "I think she must have done it to impress you with her suitability as a chaperon! I happen to know that she's fright-fully keen on this one."

"On the club or on Captain Bond?" asked Dalberry.

Carol laughed.

"I don't think she's got much use for poor Captain Bond. She snubbed him frightfully the other day, and he took it like a lamb. But after he'd gone I asked her if she thought he was making a success of his job, and she said she hoped so, because he had persuaded her to put some money into it."

So that, at any rate, was where some of the money had gone! It looked uncommonly as if Mellish were right.

CHAPTER VII

PUNCTUALLY at four o'clock on the following Monday a taxi drew up before the marble steps of the Escatorial, and Mellish climbed pon-derously out. He had decided that it was about time he saw Carol's new quarters for himself, and as he stood in the hall waiting while the porter telephoned to Lady Dalberry's flat, his blandly benevolent eye travelled thoughtfully down the list of names inscribed in Gothic characters on a satinwood panel set into the wall close to the porter's lodge.

"Lady Dalberry is out, sir," said the man, as he hung up the re-ceiver. "But Miss Summers is at home, and would be very pleased if you would go up."

Mellish, accompanied by two pages in skin-tight grey and silver livery, made a dignified entry into the lift, and was shot up to the fourth floor. He noticed that one of the boys carried a pass-key on a chain, and wondered how many people had access to these keys and what steps the management took to insure the honesty of the staff. A foolish, risky arrangement at best, he considered, and was glad that he had seen to the insurance of Carol's jewellery himself.

In the old days of the Escatorial Hotel two long corridors, with rooms opening out of them on either side, had run to right and left of the broad main staircase. To convert the hotel into flats, it had been necessary merely to close in each of these corridors with a door, making two large flats on each floor of the building, their front doors immediately facing each other.

As Mellish stepped out of the lift a man issued from the flat opposite to Lady Dalberry's and came swiftly towards him. He was slightly built and walked with the short, light step peculiar to dancers and boxers, but the quiet elegance of his clothes was more suggestive of a man of leisure than of one of the professional classes, and he gave the impression of being lithe rather than muscular. He carried his hat in his hand and was dressed with the meticulous neatness and finish that is characteristic of the well-to-do Latin. Indeed, with his clear olive skin, dense black hair, and unusually small hands and feet, he was noticeably un-English. Mellish put him down as secretary to one of the smaller Latin legations. He vanished into the lift as Mellish followed the boy through the door of Lady Dalberry's flat.

Carol received him in her own little sitting-room.

"I'm sorry you've missed Aunt Irma," she said. "But it's nice to have you to myself. Besides, I want to show you everything. Isn't it charming?"

Mellish cast an appreciative eye round the room. He liked its fresh, bright colouring.

"Who's responsible for this? You or Lady Dalberry?"

"Aunt Irma. She took any amount of trouble over it. If I'd been her own daughter, she couldn't have been keener on making me comfortable."

"Happy here, eh?"

"I should be a pig if I wasn't," she said gratefully. "She's kindness itself, and the whole place is extraordinarily convenient. The restaurant downstairs is first-rate, and we can have our meals sent up if we like, and there's none of the bother of housekeeping. Honestly, I think I'm in clover."

Mellish nodded.

"It's got its advantages, but I prefer more privacy myself. I don't know what the staff is in this place, but practically every member of it must have a pass-key to this flat. I should keep my private correspondence and all my valuables under lock and key if I were you. You've got a dispatch-box, haven't you?"

Carol laughed.

"What a suspicious old thing you are!" she said. "As a matter of fact, I've not only got a dispatch-box, but a steel deed-box! I bought it when I first came out, because it seemed such a grand, business-like sort of thing to have, but I've never used it, except for a few private letters which really anybody might read."

"Well, use it now. You'll have some important documents to put in it soon. And I should add what jewellery you're not wearing at the moment."

She consented, though she thought him unnecessarily fussy.

"I'll get a small safe, if you like," she said. "I suppose after the 28th I shall have all sorts of papers that will need taking care of."

"You can keep the bulk of them at the bank. I don't think a safe will be necessary, unless you're going to invest largely in jewellery."

She shook her head.

"I don't hanker after that sort of thing. I've got my mother's pearls, you know, but they're at the bank."

"Better leave them there for the present, unless you're very anxious to wear them."

During tea the conversation drifted to other things. Carol mentioned that she was dining with Dalberry and going on to the Terpsychorean with him afterwards.

"Why don't you come, Jasper?" she suggested. "You're getting into an awful groove. A little dissipation would do you all the good in the world."

"Do you suggest that I should dance?" he asked, glancing ruefully down at what was once his waist.

"It would be uncommonly good for you, you know," laughed Carol. "And you'd probably love it."

"You may not believe it, but I'm a very good dancer. All fat men are. But it's more pain than pleasure nowadays, alas! I'll dine with you, though, if you and Gillie can put up with me, and I'll drop into the Terpsychorean with you afterwards for a few minutes. I'd rather like to see the place."

"It's quite good, isn't it?"

"Quite bad would describe it more accurately, but I suppose you like it all the better for that. By the way, do you know anything about your next-door neighbour? He was coming out of his flat as I arrived, and I see he's down on the notice-board as Juan de Silva. Do you suppose he's an embassy man?"

Carol looked up quickly.

"It's funny you should have seen him. He worries me to death."

"Has he been pestering you?" demanded Mellish sharply.

Carol laughed outright.

"Jasper dear, how you do fear the worst!" she mocked. "I don't mean in that way—he's an entirely harmless person. But I can't place him. I've never seen him before—that I'm sure of—but he reminds me of some one, and I cannot think who it is."

"I only saw him for a moment. How did you come across him?"

"He's a friend of Aunt Irma's. A South American, I think. Anyhow, she knew him out there. It was through him that she heard of this flat. They're difficult to get, you know, and this one happened to fall empty. I believe he's something in the City."

"Stock Exchange, eh?"

"I don't know, but I fancy he's invested some of Aunt Irma's money for her. The day I arrived here I found him waiting for her with some papers he wanted her to sign. She was out, so we introduced ourselves to each other and got quite friendly. He's not a bad little man, if he'd only realize that I don't really care for a lot of silly compliments that mean nothing."

"Lays it on thick, does he?"

"I think all foreigners do—at least the Latin kind. I got fed up with it on the Riviera. They ought to give one credit for a little sense. It's an insult to one's intelligence."

Mellish regarded her thoughtfully and rather sadly. She was extraordinarily unsophisticated for her age, and he wondered how soon she would realize the part her money was bound to play in her relations with men, and how long it would be before her frank acceptance of all that life had to offer would turn to bitter disillusionment. He wished with all his heart that she were safely married to Dalberry.

"They may possibly admire you," he suggested mildly.

"I hope they do," she said honestly. "I like being admired, but not for things I know I haven't got. When they tell me I speak French like a native, for instance, I know they're lying. I hadn't been in France five minutes before I discovered the truth about my French! And that's only one of the silly things they say."

"Turn 'em down if you don't like 'em, that's the best plan," advised Mellish.

"Who is to be 'turned down'? Not some of my friends, I hope!" said a voice behind him, and he swung round quickly to find Lady Dalberry standing in the doorway.

She had evidently just come in, and Mellish's appreciative eye rested with approval on the quiet perfection of her closefitting black hat and admirably cut coat and skirt. The furs she threw carelessly on a chair by the door were unostentatious, but perfect of their kind. He heaved himself out of his chair and went forward to greet her.

"We were talking of the crowd on the Riviera," he said. "Carol seems to have suffered rather at their hands."

She nodded.

"Those hands would soon have been in her pockets if she had given them the chance," she replied, her eyes full of meaning. "We must take care of her, Mr. Mellish, you and I."

She slipped off her hat and passed her hands over her smooth, fair hair. Mellish noted, with a certain secret amusement, that she had followed the prevailing fashion and had it cut short. It was too thick to shingle, and clustered round her head in natural waves. He had to admit that it suited her, and added character to the well-shaped head and straight features.

"May I share your tea, Carol dear?" she asked. "The fire is out in my room and you are so comfortable here. I shall not disturb you?"

"Of course not," answered Carol. "Sit down and talk to Jasper while I make some fresh tea."

The conversation ran easily enough, but a more finished psychologist than Carol might have discerned the reserve that lay behind the apparently innocent small talk of these two able fencers. Antagonism would be too strong a word for their attitude towards each other; caution would, perhaps, be nearer the mark. Lady Dalberry, in spite of her almost disconcerting bluntness and lack of subtlety, was too astute ever to give herself away, and Mellish, bland and imperturbable, was always difficult to fathom. He was there, in his capacity of trustee, to spy out the land, and Lady Dalberry was perfectly aware of the fact. Whether or not she had anything to hide from him made very little difference to the fact that each was subtly aware that the other was on the defensive. Only once was she betrayed into giving a hint of her true feelings, and then the indication was so slight that Carol missed it entirely. It did not escape Mellish, however.

He had asked Carol what time Dalberry was going to fetch her for dinner, casually letting drop the information that he intended to join them. As he spoke he happened to catch sight of Lady Dalberry's face, and he knew in a flash that the news had not pleased her. While listening to Carol's answer he watched the other woman, covertly but intently, and waited anxiously for her to speak. When she did so her voice was just a shade too uninterested and casual.

"You are going on to the club?" she asked. "I did not imagine you would care for such frivolities!"

"I'm not such an old fogey as all that," he answered good-humouredly. "Besides, I shall only drop in for a few minutes to see how the children are enjoying themselves."

He thought he detected a flicker of relief in her eyes, but she answered naturally enough.

"Carol must persuade you to stay, once you are there," she said, with a pleasant smile. "A little dissipation is good even for us too, sometimes."

If he was tickled at the graceful way in which she bracketed herself with him in point of years, he did not show it.

"I trust you will have many years of dancing before you yet," he said courteously. "At least you will be saved my fate. 'Fat and scant of breath' will never apply to you."

She took his complaint with characteristic seriousness. "You should do exercises, Mr. Mellish," she assured him earnestly. "It is wonderful how much they help. Exercises and massage. Those are things my country understands."

"If I did exercises I should die," was Mellish's calm rejoinder. He spoke with such conviction that even Lady Dalberry was impressed.

He certainly looked singularly out of place as, some hours later, he made his majestic entry into the crowded supper-room of the Terpsychorean and let himself carefully down on to a little gilt chair that trembled beneath his weight.

Carol, her elbows on the table, her chin in her hands, took in the scene before her with eager curiosity.

"Like it?" asked Dalberry, his eyes on her flushed face.

She nodded.

"It makes me feel as if I'd still got hayseed in my hair," she said ruefully.

"Hullo! here's our friend," put in Mellish.

Carol looked round quickly. Lady Dalberry's next-door neighbour was coming towards them, picking his way among the throng of dancers with an ease and dexterity that suggested long practice. In evening clothes he looked sleeker and more perfectly groomed than ever.

He halted at their table and bowed over Carol's hand.

"It is a great pleasure to see you here," he said. Except for his accentuation of the letter *r*, and a certain neatness and finish in the rounding off of his words, his English showed very little trace of a foreign accent. "Captain Bond asked me to say that he has reserved a table for you near the orchestra. He will be with you in a moment. If you will come with me—"

Carol introduced him to the two men, and together they followed him to a larger and more comfortable table, decorated with trails of smilax and a great bowl of hot-house roses.

He did not offer to join them, and, having seen them settled, excused himself gracefully and melted into the crowd of dancers.

A few minutes later Bond appeared, profusely apologetic.

"I was kept," he whispered. "Some trouble in the kitchen. De Silva tells me that you did not find your table. I'm so sorry. I left special directions with that fool of a head-waiter."

At Dalberry's invitation he pulled up a chair and joined them, and for the next ten minutes or so made himself useful, pointing out people whom he thought might interest Carol.

"You see those two?" he said, indicating two of the best dancers in the room. "They're one of the mysteries of the dancing world. Barring their names, nobody knows anything about them, except that they apparently do nothing but dance all the year round. They've been away till about a month ago, probably in the south of France, and now they'll come here night after night till London empties, when they'll move on to Munich or some other big town where the bands are good and the night clubs worth going to. They always stay at the best hotels, and, apparently, have plenty of money, though I fancy the lady supplies the funds. They are not husband and wife, and, so far as one knows, their relations are quite platonic; they are never seen in the daylight, and seem to have no friends. At night they come out and dance. They've been a familiar feature of every well-known dance club in Europe for the last two years."

Carol watched them with interest. The woman was thin to emaciation, with blue eyes set beautifully in a colourless face and a close-fitting cap of shingled auburn hair; the man was of a more ordinary type, tall, well-built, with fair hair and moustache. His face was almost as colourless as that of his partner. They both looked fit, trained to a fine point, but it was the fitness attained by dancers and acrobats, people who take their exercise between four walls.

Mellish watched them too, his fingers tapping gently on the table in time to the music. He was trying to remember. Ever since his retirement he had made it a habit to drop in occasionally at New Scotland Yard. Only a week ago he had been there and had looked idly through a collection of photographs which had been brought to Shand's room from the record office. This man's portrait had been among them. Of that he felt certain, and in a moment he would remember the report that went with it. Bond was speaking again.

"You'll try our special cocktail, won't you? We're rather proud of it. You won't get another like it in London."

Mellish rose.

"Not for me, thank you," he said, with his fat chuckle. "I'm too old to face the morning after, and in any case, my bed calls me. Bless you, children, and enjoy yourselves."

Bond accompanied him to the door.

"I'm sorry you missed the exhibition turn," he said. "It'll be on in another ten minutes."

"I'm conscious of being something of an exhibition turn myself," remarked the fat man, as a couple collided heavily with his great bulk and recoiled laughing. "This is no place for the likes of me!"

In the cloakroom he ran into a friend, a stockbroker, a thin, wiry little man, older than himself, who had lately fallen a victim to the universal craze for dancing. Mellish beamed on him paternally.

"Lucky chap!" he said. "As long as a man can still see his own feet he can dance, I suppose. What do you feel like in the morning?"

"Twenty years younger than I did six months ago," responded the other cheerfully. "Try it yourself."

They chatted for a few minutes. As they parted Mellish suddenly bethought himself.

"Know anything about a man called de Silva?" he asked. "A slim, dark chap."

"I know one thing about him," laughed his friend. "He's kept it mighty quiet, too, but things get out in the City."

Then, in answer to Mellish's glance of interrogation:

"He owns this place. It was bought in Bond's name and it's registered as his, but the money was de Silva's. Bond's merely his paid man."

In the cab going home Mellish's brain played him a trick well known to those who have tried in vain to pin down an illusive memory. He had completely forgotten the two dancers who had engaged his attention at the Terpsychorean, and was meditating on the information he had just gleaned about de Silva when, inconsequently, he found himself in full possession of the facts concerning the man whose photograph he had seen in Shand's room. He remembered him now as a confidence-man and card-sharper, well known to the police, who had "worked" the continental trains and the big London stations for a time until a term of imprisonment put a stop to his activities. On his release he had "gone straight"—in other words, had become an "informer." That, at any rate, was his job in London, and probably he performed the same service for the continental police. The woman was no doubt in the same line of business.

After Mellish's departure Carol and Dalberry gave themselves up to dancing. They found both the floor and the orchestra first-rate, and when they got back to their table, just before the exhibition turn of the couple from Monte Carlo, they were more than ready for the cocktails Bond had suggested.

They had hardly sat down before he brought them himself, full of apologies for the delay.

"The poor little beggar always seems to be making excuses for something," reflected Dalberry, as he took the glass the other handed him. "Must be a dog's life, this secretary-business."

But the drinks needed no apology, and Bond's eulogy was amply justified. The exhibition dancing, too, was good of its kind. After it was over Carol and Dalberry danced once more, and on their return to their table they found de Silva waiting for them. He held a glass in his hand.

"May I join you for a little?" he asked. "My friends have gone, and soon I must go home myself. But perhaps, before I go, Miss Summers will do me the honour of dancing with me."

Dalberry sat down opposite to him and tried to look more pleased than he felt. He did not like the man, and he had an uneasy conviction that he was going to turn out to be a far better dancer than himself. Also he suddenly became conscious of the fact that he was very tired—so tired that it was all he could do to sit upright in his chair. While he was dancing he had not noticed it, but now an immense fatigue seemed to have descended on him, and he would have given anything to put his head down on his arms and let himself drift into the slumber that he craved with all his being. He put his sudden exhaustion down to the fact that he had been motoring all day, and had grown unaccustomed to late nights and a vitiated atmosphere.

He passed his hand over his damp forehead and squared his shoulders resolutely. As he did so, de Silva looked across at him.

"Let me order you one of these," he said, indicating the tall glass at his elbow.

Dalberry accepted the offer. He was beginning to realize that without the help of some sort of stimulant he would not be able to get through the evening.

With a word of excuse to Carol the Argentino rose and made his dexterous way through the crowd to the bar. In a few minutes he was back again.

"If you want a thing done, do it yourself," he said with a smile, putting a glass down in front of Dalberry. "The waiter would have taken half an hour to get this."

Dalberry thanked him and drank thirstily. He was feeling more seedy each moment. If the whisky did not pull him round he would have to go home. It was idiotic, he told himself angrily, to go to pieces like this. He put down the empty glass.

"I say, this is pretty strong!" he said, with a laugh that even in his own ears sounded vague and unnatural.

The Argentino shrugged his shoulders.

"Not stronger than one needs in this atmosphere," he answered carelessly. "It is drink that keeps all these people going night after night, far into the morning, and drink, and the profit on drink, that makes it possible for places like this to keep open at all. In fifteen minutes the bar will close for the night, and you will see the people getting more and more fagged, until at last they drift out to private houses where no license is needed, and where they can dance to a gramophone and drink what they like. Before the bar closes you will do well to order another, my friend!"

Dalberry did not answer. He was watching the dancers with almost unnatural absorption, and Carol found herself criticizing him a little impatiently. He looked sulky, she thought, as if something had happened to annoy him, and it occurred to her that he might have resented de Silva's intrusion on their privacy. But it was unlike Gillie to be so stupid. She was roused by de Silva's voice. "Shall we dance?" he suggested.

She glanced at Gillie, but he did not even turn his head, and with a little flush of resentment on her cheeks she nodded to de Silva and rose.

He was, as Dalberry had suspected, a beautiful dancer, and it was some time before they returned to the table. They found Dalberry sitting much as they had left him, turning an empty glass slowly round in his fingers, his eyes still fixed on the dancers.

"So you had your second drink, as I predicted," said de Silva, laughing. "You were wise. It's too late for another now—the bar is closed."

Dalberry stared vacantly at the glass in his hand. He knew that he had only had the one whisky and soda, but it did not seem worth while to say so. Nothing seemed worth while, except to get out of this place as soon as possible.

He rose unsteadily to his feet.

"I'm sorry, Carol," he said, speaking very slowly and in a curious, thick voice that sent a thrill of mingled surprise and apprehension down Carol's spine. "But I've got to go home. At once, I mean. We've both got to go home. Sorry—sorry to spoil your evening—"

His voice trailed off into silence. He swayed towards Carol, and would have fallen if de Silva had not caught him under the arms and lowered him into a chair. He sat there, speechless, his eyes fixed stupidly on Carol. His skin was livid, and she could see the perspiration glistening on his forehead.

"Gillie!" she exclaimed, in consternation, fighting against the conviction that was slowly being forced upon her.

At the sound of her voice he smiled foolishly, evidently trying to reassure her, then, suddenly, his face became a blank.

"It's no good," he murmured. "Sorry."

Then, without warning, he toppled forward across the table, dropped his head on his folded arms and went to sleep.

De Silva cast a swift glance in the direction of Carol.

"I think it will be best if you will let me see you home," he said gently. "I will speak to Captain Bond; he will, ah, take care of Lord Dalberry. He is accustomed to situations of this sort. You need not be anxious—Lord Dalberry will be all right with him."

Carol hesitated, looking down at the helpless figure before her.

"I don't think we ought to leave him," she said anxiously. "He looked horribly ill."

Even as she spoke she knew that he was not ill, and that it would be kinder to him to go.

"Believe me, he is not ill," de Silva assured her. "When I get home I will telephone to his valet to expect him. Bond will see him home. He will be all right."

Carol flinched before the bitter contempt in his voice, and for a moment, angry as she was beginning to feel with Dalberry, she loathed de Silva more. What right had he to judge Gillie, who, whatever he might do, was worth a dozen of him? Her glance swept round the crowded room, resting at last on Dalberry's head, pillowed on his arms on the untidy table. She laid a hand on his shoulder.

"Gillie!" she said softly.

He did not move. She might not have existed so far as he was concerned.

Until now her ever-growing indignation had been tempered with a pity that was half contempt. Now, as she realized how utterly he had let her down, it flamed suddenly beyond control.

She turned to de Silva, her eyes ablaze, her cheeks scarlet.

"Will you please take me home?" she said.

Then, without another glance in Dalberry's direction, she left him.

CHAPTER VIII

IN THE TAXI on their way back to the Escatorial Carol and de Silva tacitly refrained from discussing the events of the evening. The girl's cheeks still burned with humiliation, but she had herself well in hand, and forced herself to talk easily and naturally to the Argentino, who, in his turn, showed himself an adept at dealing tactfully with a difficult situation.

It was a relief to hear from the hall porter that Lady Dalberry, who was an inveterate bridge player, had not yet come back from her club. All the way home Carol had been dreading the inevitable explanation she would have had to make of her early return without Dalberry.

De Silva accompanied her to her door, and it was not until he said good-night, and was about to cross the landing to his own flat, that he referred to the subject they had both avoided so carefully.

"I shall find Lord Dalberry's number in the telephone book, I suppose," he said. "I had better ring up his rooms now and tell his man to be ready for him."

"It's in the book," answered Carol gratefully. "But I can give it to you, if you'll wait a minute."

"Do not trouble yourself—I can find it easily."

He hesitated for a moment, then:

"Miss Summers!"

She stood waiting with her hand on the latch of the door. "Please do not think me interfering," he said earnestly. "I know it is no affair of mine. But do not judge Lord Dalberry too hardly. It is the sort of accident that can very easily happen to a man when he has had a hard day, and is tired, and has, perhaps, got into the habit of pulling himself together occasionally with the help of stimulants."

Carol met his gaze squarely. There was a cold glint of anger in her eyes. Annoyed though she was with Gillie, this man's facile excuses for him, and all that they implied, struck her as insufferable.

"I don't understand about to-night, Mr. de Silva," she said bluntly. "But Lord Dalberry does not drink, if that's what you mean."

He shrugged his shoulders.

"I did not mean to imply that he drank. That would be a gross exaggeration. But everybody nowadays is burning the candle at both ends. It is not surprising if people are forced to resort to stimulants. I am sure he could not help what happened to-night."

Suddenly Carol's nerves betrayed her. She felt her eyes fill with tears, and, furious with herself for this exhibition of weakness, she drew hastily back into the dimmer light of the hall.

"It's no good discussing it, is it?" she said, keeping her voice steady with an effort. "Good-night, and thank you."

Then, as he opened his mouth to speak, she managed to get the door shut between them before her composure deserted her entirely.

The Argentino waited for a moment, listening intently, then, instead of going into his flat, turned and ran lightly down the stairs without waiting for the lift. He passed swiftly through the hall into the street, hailed a passing taxi, and drove back to the Terpsychorean.

Bond met him in the hall.

"I've had him moved into the ante-room," he whispered. "What are you going to do?"

He looked badly rattled for a man who, if de Silva's words to Carol were true, was accustomed to dealing with cases like Dalberry's.

The Argentino brushed past him without a word and made his way up the stairs and through the closed bar. The dancing was still in full swing, and no one noticed him as he opened a small door to the right of the bar and passed through it, followed silently by Bond. In front of him, at the end of a short passage, was a heavy oak door. He unlocked this and pushed it open, and as he did so there was not one among the players who stood or sat round the baize-covered tables that filled the big, brilliantly lighted room that did not look up with a quick spasm of alarm, and then, in relief, return to the absorption of the game.

De Silva paused for a moment, while Bond was relocking the door behind him, and ran his eye over the room. It was characteristic of him that in that swift and ostensibly careless scrutiny he missed nothing.

"The man standing next to Captain Green, who is he?" he jerked over his shoulder.

"His brother," answered Bond. "He brought him along last night."

"Have you looked him up?"

Bond nodded.

"He's all right. I went round there this morning with a scarf some one left in the cloakroom. He's Green's brother. Been staying with him for a week."

De Silva strolled slowly through the room, nodding to an acquaintance here and there. To the majority of the players he was merely a friend of Bond's, a gambler like themselves, who dropped in occasionally for an hour, but who was not looked upon as an habitue. The truth was that he preferred to leave the management of this, the most paying and at the same time the most dangerous, branch of the establishment in the capable hands of Bond. Some day, he told himself philosophically, the place would be raided. Bond would have to face the music—that was what he was paid for—and the club would be closed down. It was an extraordinary piece of luck that the cardroom, cunningly built out over the kitchen at the back of the house, had not been discovered before by the police.

He drew aside a heavy *portiere*, unlocked a small door, and passed through into the ante-room, closing the door carefully behind him.

Dalberry was stretched on a couch by the window. He was sleeping heavily, and his face had lost its first ashen pallor. Bond had taken off his collar and tie and unfastened the neck of his shirt.

De Silva stood looking down at him thoughtfully.

"What are you going to do with him?" muttered Bond at his elbow.

"Send him home, of course. He cannot sleep it off here. I will telephone to his man, and you must take him. I can keep my eye on things here while you're gone."

Bond swallowed nervously once or twice, then:

"What's the matter with him?" he asked, in his curious, muffled voice.

De Silva turned on him.

"Soused, of course. Do you not know a drunken man when you see one? You may be sure this is not the first time he has been taken home like this. What do you think is the matter with him?"

Bond quailed before the cold menace in his eyes.

"Nothing," he said hastily. "He keeled over a bit suddenly, that was all. He won't be easy to move."

"You will move him all the same, my friend," snapped the Argentino, then broke off suddenly as the other gripped him by the arm.

His mouth gaping, his face white as chalk, Bond was staring at the door through which they had come. On the other side of it an electric buzzer whirred insistently.

Before he could move, de Silva was at the door and had wrenched it open. Some one on the other side had already torn aside the *portiere*, and was trying to force his way through the doorway. The card-room was in a state of indescribable confusion. A few of the players stood motionless, knowing that all the exits were closed by now, and philosophically ready to let things take their course; but the rest, under the impulse of a blind instinct for self-preservation, were fighting their way towards the narrow opening that gave on to a flight of steps leading to the kitchen below.

De Silva was struggling with the man in the doorway. One glimpse of the card-room had been enough; he had no desire to enter it, but neither did he propose to admit any of the club "members" to the ante-room from which he had just come.

"Get back, you fool!" he gasped, exerting all his strength to force the man back. "You cannot get out this way. Here, Bond!"

The doorway was so narrow that Bond could give him very little assistance. Between them, however, they managed to throw the man back into the card-room. Bond followed him. As nominal proprietor of the club he would gain nothing by evasion. De Silva slipped back into the ante-room and slammed the door behind him.

As he did so the heavy door on the far side of the card-room burst open with a crash, and a plain-clothes officer appeared in the opening.

Bond, mechanically adjusting his tie and pulling his coat into position, went to meet him. He did not notice that the man he had helped de Silva to eject had taken his opportunity, and, opening the door quietly, had slipped through it into the ante-room.

Once inside, the intruder stood hesitating on the threshold. De Silva had switched off the lights, and the little room was in darkness. Then he caught sight of a black silhouette against the pale light of the open window. So that was the bolt-hole!

In a second he was across the room and had his leg over the sill of the window. De Silva had already climbed through and dropped lightly on to the flat roof of the scullery below. The other man followed, but just a fraction too soon, for, in his anxiety to get away, he dropped full on to the top of the Argentino, and the two rolled, clutching wildly at each other, almost over the edge of the narrow roof. They were on their feet almost at once, and stood glaring at each other in the light that still streamed from the card-room window, then the Argentino stooped swiftly, so that the light no longer fell on his face.

But he was too late. The other man gave an exclamation of amazement.

"Kurt, by all that's holy!" he exclaimed. "Now, what do you think of that!"

De Silva's only answer was to slide, like an eel, over the edge of the roof and drop into the yard below. He landed on his hands and knees, picked himself up, and ran. The rest of the flight was easy—across a low wall into the next yard, and from there, through a flimsy apology for a door that yielded to the pressure of his shoulder, into the mews that ran behind the house.

Here he was in luck, for two of the stables had been converted into studios, and the occupants had combined in giving a party. The guests were strolling up and down the mews and standing about in groups. Some were in fancy dress, a few in tweeds, and one or two in dinner jackets. The sight of a man in evening clothes roused no comment, and de Silva was able to make his way safely enough to the corner of the mews, where he stood for a moment taking his bearings before venturing into the open street.

He was not surprised to hear a voice behind him and feel a hand close firmly on his arms. He had known that his pursuer would not allow himself to be shaken off easily after that one illuminating moment on the roof, and all through the physical strain of his flight from the club his alert brain had been dealing rapidly and adequately with this new situation. He turned quickly.

"See here," he said, speaking in an urgent whisper, "it is impossible for me to stop now. And it will not do for us to be seen together. We shall be lucky if we get away at all. Tell me where I can find you."

The other man laughed softly.

"Tell me where I can find *you*!" he retorted derisively. "I'm not such a sucker as all that, Kurt! I'll come and see you at your own place, my son!"

De Silva only hesitated for a moment. He never wasted time or strength in fighting the inevitable.

"To-morrow morning at eleven-thirty at the Escatorial," he said briefly. "You will see the name, de Silva, on the board in the hall. Though what you think you will gain by it I do not know. I have nothing in your line."

For a moment the other eyed him suspiciously.

"Right-o," he said, relaxing his grip of the Argentino's arm at last. "I'll chance it."

He turned on his heel and vanished, and de Silva, after another cautious glance down the road, departed hurriedly in the opposite direction. He went on foot and chose the less frequented thoroughfares, for he had no desire to add a taxi-driver to the already inconveniently long list of people who had seen him in the vicinity of the club that evening.

Once inside the hall of the Escatorial he felt at liberty to indulge the curiosity he had kept sternly within bounds all through his walk home. He stepped softly to a small window to the right of the front door and peered out into the street. And as he looked he laughed softly to himself.

The man who had shared his flight from the Terpsychorean had not "chanced it." Having seen de Silva safely home and verified the address he had given, he was now, in the full light of the street lamp opposite, turning to depart, presumably with a quiet mind.

Carol, who had gone to bed and was trying in vain to read herself to sleep, was startled by a knock at her door. She answered languidly enough, for her head ached, and Lady Dalberry was the last person she wished to see at the moment.

"You must have spent a very dissipated evening," she said, trying to speak lightly and naturally. "I've been home for ages."

Her effort was wasted, for Lady Dalberry was far too agitated to be observant.

"You are all right, then? I have just met Juan de Silva on the stairs, and he declared to me that you were safe, but I had to see for myself. Thank goodness you left that place in time!"

Her voice was warm with solicitude. Evidently she had only just come in, for her fur coat hung loosely over her shoulders, and she was dressed in the high black dress she affected for quiet evenings at her club.

Carol's first feeling was one of indignation against de Silva for having given away Dalberry to her aunt; but with Lady Dalberry's next words her anger turned to bewilderment.

"Did Gillie suspect something?" she asked. "Was that why he brought you away so early? How did he know, I wonder?"

Carol stared at her.

"Know what? Aunt Irma? I haven't the remotest idea what you are talking about."

"How stupid of me! Of course you would not know! I was so distressed at the thought that you might not have got away in time. For you to be mixed up in such a thing! And all my fault, I thought, for letting that silly little Bond man have his way and persuade you to go to such a place. When de Silva told me I was beside myself."

"Aunt Irma, what did Mr. de Silva tell you?" urged Carol, in desperation.

Lady Dalberry drew her fur cloak closer around her.

"My dear," she said, with an intensity that was almost tragic, "the Terpsychorean was raided to-night. De Silva only just got away in time. If you had stayed you would now be in the hands of the police."

For a moment Carol was conscious only of relief. Then the Argentino had behaved decently after all! He had not betrayed Gillie. Perhaps the sudden reaction, coming after all she had gone through that night, made her a little hysterical, or it might be that Lady Dalberry's tragic attitude, combined with the sudden vision of herself and Gillie "in the hands of the police," would have upset her gravity at any time. The fact remains that, after a vain effort to treat the announcement with the seriousness it deserved, she lay back on her pillows and laughed till she cried.

Lady Dalberry stared at her in blank astonishment.

"My dear," she said severely, "I do not think that you realize what Gillie saved you from when he took you away just in time."

Her words had the desired effect. Carol's laughter died on her lips. Long after Lady Dalberry had left her she lay staring up into the darkness. For it was de Silva who had saved her, while Gillie, whom she could have sworn would never fail her, was lying helpless in a drunken stupor.

CHAPTER IX

IT WAS CLOSE on midday, nearly ten hours after the raid on the Terpsychorean, that Dalberry, in company with twenty-eight other chastened and bedraggled victims of circumstance, found himself at liberty to return home.

Mellish, hastily summoned by telephone, had sat listening with an impish gleam in his eyes while the magistrate admonished the delinquents and expressed the somewhat vain hope that the experience would prove a lesson to them. He had then dealt imperturbably with the necessary formalities to be gone through before Dalberry was finally rescued from the clutches of the law. Being still uninformed as to the circumstances in which he had been taken, he was disposed to treat the affair with a certain sardonic humour. How Carol had been kept out of it he had no idea, but he felt fairly certain that it was to her adventurous spirit that this ignominious end to an apparently harmless evening was due. He could imagine Bond's whispered invitation, Carol's enthusiastic acceptance of it, and her delight at finding herself in what she had read of in books as a "gambling hell." It was hard luck that the immediate result of this innocent attempt to see life should have been a night in the cells for Dalberry, followed by an ignominious appearance before a magistrate in the morning. Mellish had good reason to hope that this morning, at any rate, she was in a condition to appreciate the advantages of a well-ordered life.

He was chuckling as he climbed into a taxi with Dalberry, but his mirth was short-lived. Dalberry, hollow-eyed and unshaven, hatless, his coat collar turned up to hide his soiled dress-shirt, was in no mood for laughter. It did not take him long to put Mellish in possession of the facts, and by the time he had finished he had no cause to complain of the fat man's attitude. Mellish knew him too well to question his statement for a moment.

"What it's all about, I don't know," insisted Dalberry doggedly; "but both those drinks were doctored, of that I'm quite certain. I felt pretty rotten after the first, but the second was a knock-out. I didn't know a thing till I woke up at the police-station in the early hours of the morning, and even then I couldn't keep myself awake, and it was all they could do to rouse me four or five hours later. There's something damned fishy about the whole thing. As for playing, I never saw the card-room; hadn't an idea there was such a thing. You're sure Carol's all right?"

"Quite," said Mellish. "She telephoned from the flat this morning." He looked at his watch. "I'll drop you at your rooms. Get a bath and a change, and come on to the Albany in about an hour's time. I'll try to get on to Shand. He'd better hear about this."

He dropped Dalberry and went on to his own rooms. Once there, he rang up New Scotland Yard. Here he was in luck. Chief Detective-Inspector Shand was in his room, and both ready and willing to come round. He knew Mellish too well to doubt the real urgency of the summons.

Lunch was on the table when he arrived, and Dalberry, looking considerably more human than he had been an hour before, followed close on his footsteps. While they were eating he put the facts before Shand. When he had finished the inspector glanced at him shrewdly.

"Ever been drunk before?" he asked bluntly.

Dalberry laughed.

"Of course," he answered frankly. "Who hasn't? But I don't make a habit of it. You'll have to take my word for that."

Shand nodded.

"Ever been knocked clean out like that before?" he went on.

"Never. I must have been absolutely dead to the world for about four solid hours, and when I woke up at the station I was still half doped."

"Who brought those drinks? The waiter?"

"That chap de Silva brought the whisky. He fetched it from the bar himself, and, now I come to think of it, Captain Bond brought the other, the cocktail. He gave Miss Summers one at the same time."

"Bond faced the music all right this morning," said Shand thoughtfully. "He's done for. He won't get another licence, but no doubt the club will crop up again under new management."

"De Silva's?" inquired Mellish blandly.

Shand looked up sharply, then he smiled.

"Now I wonder where you picked up that bit of information, Mr. Mellish," he said. "We've known, of course, for some time that Bond was only acting under de Silva, but he had us in a cleft stick. We've been waiting for this opportunity, though I must say we never expected to get him under the Gaming Act. I didn't think he'd be such a fool."

"And even now he's slipped through your fingers."

"We've nothing on him whatever," admitted Shand. "The premises were hired by Bond and the licence taken out in his name. De Silva never appeared at all in any of the transactions. I doubt if he'll have the face to open the club again under his own name, though. He must know he wouldn't get a licence."

"Who is de Silva?" asked Dalberry.

"A wealthy Argentino, by his own account, who's come over here to spend his money. He turned up in England a few months ago. As far as is known, that was his first appearance in this country."

"You heard nothing of him when you were out in Buenos Aires the other day?" asked Mellish.

Shand shook his head.

"Nothing; but you must remember I wasn't looking for him. He had nothing to do with my man."

He rose to go.

"There's one thing of which you can feel certain," he said, addressing Dalberry. "If you were drugged that night, and from your account I think you were, it was done at de Silva's orders. Bond's just a tool—he'd never act on his own initiative."

"There's one person who might give you some information about de Silva," suggested Mellish. "He was at the Terpsychorean on the night of the raid, dancing with a very pretty lady. A useful couple, I should imagine."

Shand's eyes twinkled.

"You don't miss much, Mr. Mellish," he admitted appreciatively. "You were looking at his portrait the other day, I remember. Conyers, his name is. It took him six weeks to get into that card-room. No, he knows no more about de Silva than we do."

How far this last statement was from the truth he was to find out later. Dalberry and Mellish went with him to the door.

"By the way," Mellish asked idly, "what about that murder on board the boat you and Lady Dalberry came over in? There was a short notice in one of the papers about it, and I've always meant to ask you what really happened."

"That's a thing a good many people would give something to know," returned Shand ruefully, "myself included. Roughly speaking, a man called Smith (which, by the way, seems to have been his real name) was found strangled. That's about all there is to it."

"How did the affair end?"

"There was an inquest, with the usual verdict. Then, as no relatives turned up, the man was buried in Liverpool by the parish. There were the usual advertisements, but no one answered them. He was a bit of a black sheep, I fancy, and his people weren't anxious to claim him."

"You've no theory yourself as to who killed him?"

"You can have my theory for what it's worth, Mr. Mellish," said Shand, with a rather wry smile. "Smith was killed by a fair man, dressed in green pyjamas, and, unless I'm much mistaken, the man's name was Strelinski."

"And you couldn't hold him? Not enough evidence, I suppose?"

"The man disappeared on the night of the murder, and I have no proof that Strelinski was ever on the *Enriqueta*. Unless the murderer went overboard with the pyjamas, which I very much doubt, I don't know what happened to him. He was seen by a steward, after which no one set eyes on him again."

"Annoying business," commented Mellish mildly.

He knew his Shand, and could guess the state of mind in which he had landed at Liverpool. He had also had practical proof of the detective's tenacity, and knew that he would never rest until he had ascertained whether Smith's assailant had gone overboard or not.

"Very," assented Shand drily. Then, as he picked up his hat: "By the way, how did Miss Summers get away last night? She wasn't among that crowd this morning."

For once Mellish was caught napping. He had been congratulating himself on having kept Carol's name out of the business, and had no reason to believe the police had been aware of her presence at the club.

"What makes you think that Miss Summers was there?" he asked evasively.

"She was seen," answered Shand, with equal vagueness, "with Lord Dalberry. You've no idea what happened to her, I suppose?" he asked, turning to Dalberry.

"She must have left before the raid," answered Dalberry curtly. It was not a pleasant question to have to answer. "Mr. Mellish heard from her this morning, I believe."

"She telephoned at about eight o'clock this morning," admitted Mellish, in answer to Shand's inquiring glance. "She merely said that the news of the raid had reached her through Lady Dalberry after she got home last night. How Lady Dalberry heard of it I don't know. Miss Summers was afraid that Lord Dalberry might be in trouble, and asked me to ring him up."

"She didn't say how she got home?"

"Not a word. She was mainly concerned about Lord Dalberry. Five minutes afterwards I got his message."

"She was no doubt taken home by Bond or de Silva," reflected Shand. "Probably the latter, as he was observed going back into the club again later. She wasn't seen at all later in the evening."

"Good workers, those friends of yours," commented Mellish drily. "I suppose it was they who reported on Miss Summers?"

Shand nodded.

"The woman's the brains of the combination. She's seen the inside of Aylesbury all right, but she's kept Conyers straight for over two years now. They're getting a bit too well known on this side, though, for our purposes."

After he had gone Dalberry lingered on in Mellish's rooms. The fat man watched him throw away his third half-smoked cigarette, then stretched out an arm and quietly placed the box out of his reach.

"It will save time and some of my best tobacco if I tell you at once that Carol didn't leave any message for you when she telephoned this morning," he remarked gently.

Dalberry turned on him with a rather sheepish smile.

"You're a beast, Jasper!" he said; but he did not try to conceal his eagerness. "What did she say?"

"Nothing, except that she had left you at the club and was afraid you might not have got away. She gave no reason for having gone away without you, and when I questioned her she rang off. But her tone, I may tell you, was that of one performing an unpleasant, but necessary, duty. You're in for a bad time, Gillie, and the best thing you can do is to see her as soon as possible."

Dalberry rose.

"I'm going now," he said. "I was only waiting to find out how I stood with her. She must think me a pretty average swine."

Carol's attitude was brought home to him before he had been five minutes inside the hall of the Escatorial.

"Miss Summers is very sorry, but she is not well enough to see any one," announced the porter, as he turned away from the house telephone.

"Thanks," said Dalberry, taking out his case and choosing a cigarette with elaborate care.

"Might just as well 'ave said 'damn' and 'a done with it, by the look on 'is face," reflected the porter, as he went back to his lodge.

Dalberry hesitated. There seemed nothing for it but to go home and write to her. He was just about to leave, when the lift doors opened and Lady Dalberry stepped out. At the sight of him she hurried forward.

"Gillie, I am so glad I caught you," she exclaimed. "I guessed it was you on the phone, and I could not help hearing what Carol said. I was just going out, and I hurried a little in the hope to catch you."

"I'm sorry Carol isn't well," said Dalberry formally.

"Carol is just so ill or so well as she pleases, my friend," remarked Lady Dalberry in her quaint English. "Are you walking? Yes? Then we will go together and then we can talk."

They left the building in silence. Lady Dalberry was the first to speak.

"I do not know what has happened," she said, with her usual bluntness, "but I am not blind, neither am I deaf. Carol seems to have returned home very early last night, with you, as I supposed, until I heard her telephoning to Mr. Mellish this morning. The telephone is in the hall, and it is impossible not to hear what is being said. In this way I discover, for the first time, that she left you at the club last night. When I ask her she tells me only that she came home with Mr. de Silva, and that she does not know what happened to you. I do not wish to interfere. This matter is between you and her; but I tell you this, Gillie, my friend, she is mad with you, through and through. I do not think she will see you, however often you call!"

She looked troubled, and her deep, warm voice was full of real sympathy.

"If you have any message for her I will try to give it," she went on. "But I warn you it will not be easy to get her to listen. She is angry, deeply angry. I did not think the little Carol could be like that."

"She's got good reason to be," said Dalberry. "But she's got hold of the wrong end of the stick. I'll write to her, but if you can get her to see Jasper, do. He will explain better than I can, and she'll listen to him."

Lady Dalberry placed a sympathetic hand on his arm.

"I will do what I can. I should be very sad if anything came between you. I was so happy myself in my married life, and I want to see those I care for happy too. And you two have known each other for so long."

She waited, hoping, no doubt, for further confidences, but Dalberry merely thanked her for her offer and left it at that.

"It's very good of you," he said vaguely. "I'll tell you what happened some day, if I may. It wasn't quite so bad as Carol thinks. If you can make her believe that, and persuade her to give me a chance to explain, I should be very grateful." They parted, Dalberry feeling less antagonistic towards her than he had done in the past, but unable, even now, to treat her with ordinary frankness. He could not forget, either, that it was through her that Carol had met both de Silva and Bond. He remembered Carol's suggestion that Lady Dalberry had put money into the club, and wondered if she were very hard hit now that it was closed down. He reflected grimly that that, at any rate, would put an end for a time to the activities of Bond and the Argentino.

His satisfaction would have been short-lived if he could have been present at the interview between these two which had taken place some hours earlier.

But Bond was not de Silva's only visitor. He was preceded by the man with whom the Argentino had made an appointment, very much against his will, the night before. The interview ran, more or less, on the lines de Silva had foreseen, and did not last long.

"See here, Conyers," he said frankly, as he led the way into his study. His tone was conciliatory, indeed it remained so, with the exception of one lapse, throughout the interview. He was helpless, and he knew it. "I do not mind telling you that what happened last night gave me a bad knock. The Terpsychorean is closed down for good, and, as you may have guessed, I had a large interest in it. I was out to make big money, too, if it had run long enough. As it is, I am badly hit financially."

Conyers cast an appraising eye round the room.

"You're not so hard hit that you won't make a little loan to an old friend when he asks for it," he declared, with cheerful conviction. "I'll go easy with you, but you must realize that that little slip last night pretty well tore it. It's a damn good make-up, and I should never have spotted you if we'd met casually in the card-room. You'll have to divvy up, Kurt!"

"You will drop that name if you wish this deal to go through," said de Silva curtly. "How much do you want?" Conyers named a sum considerably larger than he hoped to get. He had guessed that de Silva would not dare to risk the revelation of his real identity, and had gambled on the fact; but, unfortunately for his plans, he had no idea as yet what his silence might be worth. He hoped later, by dint of perseverance, to find out what the Argentino's little game was. Then he might have a chance to tighten the screw.

To his surprise de Silva showed no inclination to bargain. "You understand that this is the limit, Conyers," he warned him smoothly, as he unlocked the drawer of his writing-table. "If you think you are going to bleed me, you make a bad mistake, my friend. I have my own reasons for wishing to tie your tongue at this moment, but I shall be finished with my business here in a month or so, and your information will not be worth twopence to the police or any one else after that." The other man's face changed colour, but he let the implication pass. He knew the value of silence, supposing, as he suspected, de Silva was merely making a shrewd guess at his connection with the events of the night before.

The Argentino took a bundle of notes out of the drawer and counted them swiftly.

"I will give you fifty on account—that is all I have in the flat. You will have to wait a day or two for the rest."

Conyers stretched out a greedy hand, and then, with an effort, drew it back.

"Nothing doing. It's all or nothing, Kurt."

"Keep that name off your tongue, or it will be nothing," snarled de Silva, for the first time letting his temper get the better of him.

"It'll be 'Kurt' till the money's paid over, so you'd better get a move on," answered Conyers, with the calm insolence of one who knows he has the upper hand.

But de Silva's outburst of anger was over, and he had himself well in hand.

"See here, Conyers," he said smoothly, "I am doing the best I can for you. I have got the winding up of this infernal club on my hands, and it is absolutely impossible for me to raise a cent till things are straightened out there. As it is, I am offering you all the spare cash I possess, and putting myself to great inconvenience. Give me ten days, and I will undertake to pay you. The money is not there, I tell you."

Conyers thought for a moment, then he picked up the notes.

"All right," he said. "Only remember, it's no good trying any funny business with me."

De Silva laid a friendly hand on his shoulder and propelled him towards the door.

"Good," he said. "I knew you would see reason. We have always worked well together, old chap. To-day is the 10th. Make it the 19th. That will give me time to get things straight. Clear out now, like a good fellow. I am too busy to talk."

"Where do we meet? Here?"

Conyers was on the other side of the front door by now, and it was closing gently behind him. De Silva smiled at him through the crack.

"I have your address. I will let you know. Good-bye, old man!"

Before he could expostulate, the door was shut in his face.

De Silva went back to his room, humming a little tune softly to himself. He had been blackmailed shamelessly, and by a man he not only disliked, but despised, and yet he seemed singularly unperturbed. When Bond arrived, half an hour later, he found his employer in the best of spirits.

In depressing contrast, Bond was even more peevishly gloomy than usual.

"Well, the fat's in the fire now," he whispered, as he entered the room. "I've paid the fine, and that pretty well clears us out. And even if we sell, we shan't get a brass farthing for the goodwill of the place now. And if you open again anywhere else you'll have to get a new manager. I'm through as far as another licence is concerned."

"What is so encouraging in you is your *joie de vivre*," remarked de Silva acidly. "It is a comfort to have you round when things go wrong."

"Well, if you'd spent the morning I have, being bully-ragged by a brute of a magistrate in a stinking court, you wouldn't feel like a little ray of sunshine. If you think I enjoy getting all the kicks while you rope in the halfpence, you're mistaken. Little enough I made out of the beastly place, goodness knows!"

"And little enough you are losing over it!" snapped de Silva. "*Madre de Dios*, any one would think it was you who had put up the cash. What does it matter to you if the club closes down?"

"It matters this much to me. I'm a marked man from now on. I'm dead, as far as any other job of that sort's concerned. If you've lost money, you can damned well afford it, but I'd like to know what's going to happen to me!"

"Nothing is going to happen to you, if you are a good little boy and keep your temper," answered de Silva. The biting contempt in his voice made the other writhe. "If you had not begun your lamentations so early I should have told you that I have every intention of keeping you on at the same salary. If you can get more elsewhere, you are at liberty to go."

Bond stared at him, his pale eyes bulging with amazement. "You're not mad, are you?" he inquired. "If you'd heard the magistrate this morning you'd know better than to suggest anything so preposterous. You're not in the Argentine now, de Silva. I don't know how far palm-greasing will take you there, but it's a wash-out in this country. You can't do it, you know."

"I am not trying to do it, my impetuous friend. I said that I would keep you on at your old salary, but I did not say in what capacity. It has not struck you, I suppose, that I may have more than one string to my bow?"

Bond continued to stare at him in silence.

De Silva chose a cigarette and lighted it. He did not offer one to Bond.

"Ever heard of the Onyx preparations?" he asked quietly.

Bond's eyes opened still wider. "The stuff you see advertised?" he queried. "Judging from the money they've spent on 'ads,' I should say every one's heard of them. Face-creams, hair-wash, depilatories, and all that sort of thing. Is that what you mean?"

"All based on a marvellous receipt discovered in the tomb of Tutankhamen, or words to that effect," supplemented de Silva appreciatively. "Extraordinary how the public love that sort of thing. The face-cream is worth its weight in gold already, and it is sold in half-pound pots and costs slightly under sixpence a pound in ingredients. Have you ever been inside the shop?"

Bond shook his head.

"Don't even know where it is," he said.

"Then you had better find out, my friend. Turn to the right as you leave this building, and take the second to the right again and you will see it. The Onyx Beauty Parlour. Inside you will find a mint of money, all in little pots, six quite unusually pretty girls, and a fat lady with the smooth, unwrinkled skin of a girl of seventeen. It is remarkable how many fat ladies have beautiful skins," he reflected. "That is why they are so often to be found in beauty parlours. Go and look at her, Bond. You will find your office on the ground floor behind the shop."

Bond looked even sulkier than usual.

"I suppose I can take it that you own the place," he said. "What do you suppose I shall do there? Isn't your fat lady capable of running the show by herself?"

"She does not run it, my friend. She sells the little pots. The show is run by an elderly spinster of repellent aspect, who, by the way, is one of the most efficient accountants I have ever met. May you prove a worthy successor. She leaves at the end of the week, and before she goes she will have time to show you round."

Bond hesitated.

"Look here," he said at last. "I don't see myself getting mixed up with anything fishy of that sort. The Terpsychorean was all in the day's work, but I draw the line at shady massage establishments."

De Silva turned on him with such venomous swiftness that he shrank.

"You draw the line!" he exclaimed, and his voice cut like a whip-lash. "Since when, I should like to know, have you been in a position to do any such thing? If there is a line to be drawn, I will draw it, when and where I please. Understand that?"

Bond's pasty face crimsoned.

"You can be as confoundedly insulting as you please, de Silva," he whispered furiously. "You may think you've got me in the hollow of your hand, but let me tell you, once for all, that there's a point beyond which I won't go. That business of Lord Dalberry the other night—"

"Well, what about that business of Lord Dalberry?"

De Silva's voice was like silk now.

"There was something confoundedly fishy about it. It's the last time I'll allow myself to be mixed up with anything of that sort, and I want you to realize it."

He had begun well, but, like all weak men, he lacked staying power. Already his words were ceasing to carry conviction.

"And if I ask you to undertake some little job for me which, let us say, does not meet with your approval?" asked de Silva gently.

"I shall refuse, that's all. I warn you that unless this Onyx business is straight I'll have nothing to do with it."

"You'll refuse? And then, my friend?"

"You can do your damnedest."

Bond's voice shook a little. He knew only too well what de Silva's damnedest might be. He knew, also, that he would never face it. De Silva read him easily.

"Listen to me," he said simply. "You are in my hands, and you will do whatever I choose to tell you, neither more nor less, for the simple reason that you are a coward and a bully, and stick at nothing to save your dirty skin. All your life you will be in the hands of some one stronger than yourself, and all your life you will bluster and talk about your honour and your word as an Englishman, and quote worn-out tags that mean nothing to you any more. And all your life, I tell you, you will give in in the end. There is nothing too filthy for you to touch, and nothing to which you will not stoop, for a price. You can go. I have not time to listen to your scruples, because I know what they are worth. Get out!" Bond, his face livid, rose without a word and picked up his hat. There was murder in his eyes, but de Silva had summed him up justly, and knew that he was too weak to be dangerous.

"You will meet me to-morrow at the Onyx Beauty Parlour at eleven, and I will give you your orders. Go."

And Bond went.

CHAPTER X

As de Silva had foreseen, Bond came to heel meekly enough the following morning. Except when it suited his purpose, the Argentino was no bully, and, Bond having taken his medicine, he was satisfied to let the matter rest and ignore the little scene which had taken place between them the day before.

The Onyx Beauty Parlour was typical of its kind. It was, as de Silva had said, only a few minutes' walk from the Escatorial, and stood, almost within sight of the back windows of de Silva's flat, at the angle of a broad but unfrequented thoroughfare and a discreet side street, inhabited mainly by private dressmakers, hairdressers, stationers, and other modest, but respectable, danglers on the fringes of a prosperous neighbourhood.

Bond was inclined to sneer at the locality, but de Silva had chosen more wisely than a critic of Bond's calibre was likely to realize. On the opposite side of the road to the Onyx a small hat-shop had been opened about six months before by the wife of a well-known actor-manager. It had had an immediate success in the theatrical world, had supplied the hats for two big productions, and had lately been "discovered" by the ultra-smart American wife of a rich banker, since which it had been patronized by the greater part of that opulent cosmopolitan set that had its centre in Park Lane, and its outermost fringes in Bayswater. Here was a clientele after de Silva's own heart. The theatrical world would give him all the advertisement he desired, while the buyers could be relied upon to pay. Already customers had begun to drift over from the hat-shop, and, once they had been, they came again, for the astute Argentino had seen to it that each of his pretty girls was an expert in her own line. The little shop with its rather precious window display and its charmingly-decorated interior was beginning to be talked about, and his fat lady was an accomplished saleswoman. And, apart from the fact that it was rapidly becoming a paying proposition, the Onyx suited him admirably in other ways. What these ways were he did not divulge to Bond as he initiated him into the workings of the establishment, but he said enough to rouse in him a certain gloomy curiosity.

They were standing in the little room behind the shop, which was to serve as Bond's office. The hairdressing and massage departments were upstairs on the next floor, and the manicure salon was housed in a slightly larger room behind the shop.

"Well, what do you think of it?" asked de Silva.

Bond relapsed into even more settled gloom. He detested the whole atmosphere of the place, and, characteristically, could not bring himself to believe that it was being run on strictly business principles, wherein he did his employer an injustice. From de Silva's point of view the place was a purely money-making concern, and he was far too astute to jeopardize its success by permitting anything that might bring him under the eye of the police.

"It's a smart enough little place," admitted Bond grudgingly. "But how you're going to make it pay in a neighbourhood like this, I don't see, unless you're up to some fishy business, in which case, you can take my word for it, it won't last long. I've seen too much of that sort of thing not to know. And I don't want to be mixed up in it."

"It is hardly a question of what you want, my friend," remarked de Silva suavely. "However, you can set your mind at ease. I assure you, for the hundredth time, that this is a shop, neither more nor less, and it's going to be a paying one before I've finished with it. Your police, that you are so much afraid of, will not put their noses into the place, or, if they do, they will find nothing but my fat lady and her little pots. The only shady element in the whole business will be yourself, my good Bond. Try to get that into your thick head. And stop trying to be funny."

"I'm not trying to be funny," stated Bond literally, looking more lugubrious than ever. "If you say you're running the thing on the straight, I suppose I've got to take your word for it. But you won't make it pay. You're too far out. And the whole thing's on too small a scale. As it is, you're cramped for lack of space. Can't you get the whole house?"

"I have got it," said de Silva curtly. "But I'm using the top floor, and you will have to make shift with what you've got here. I'm keeping it small and select on purpose."

Bond sighed.

"Have it your own way, but if you'd take my advice you'd take the whole of the ground floor for the shop and move the face massage and all that stuff up to the attics. It'd be an immense improvement—"

"I am running this place in my own way," cut in de Silva sharply. "The top floor I want for my own purposes. I have things stored there. And, while we are on the subject, I may as well make one thing clear."

He pointed to a tall glass-fronted cupboard which stood against the left-hand wall of the room.

"The top floor of this house was once a flat, and it has its own front door, as you no doubt observed, to the left of the shop window. From there a private staircase runs up to the three attic rooms. The only inside connection between the shop and the flat is through the door behind that cupboard. I have blocked it on purpose, and I keep the key of the front door. You understand?"

Bond understood perfectly. His face cleared for the first time.

"Now I get you," he said. "If you want to use this place as a blind for something else, it's nothing to do with me. I'm paid to run the shop, and if you choose to shut off the rest of the house, it's your own affair."

"See to it that you do not make it your affair, then. Only, try to grasp one thing. This business is not a blind, as you so neatly put it, but a genuine financial undertaking, and, if I employ you as manager, I expect it to be properly run. If things go wrong, you will be personally responsible. I have some boxes stored in the flat upstairs, and I may want to get at them any time during the day or night, and I do not want my movements interfered with. That is all."

Bond nodded. After his employer had gone he settled down to inspect the books with the help of the manageress whose place he was taking. He worked till late in the afternoon; indeed the staff, including the manageress, had gone and the shutters were up before he was ready to leave.

He pulled the roll-top of the desk down and locked it. Then, stepping lightly, he looked into the shop and made sure that the place was really deserted. Having ascertained that he was alone in the building, he went over to the glass-fronted cupboard which concealed the door on to the private staircase and examined it minutely. The glass door was unlocked, and opened easily when he tried it. He took out the row of ornate powder boxes and perfume bottles which filled the lower shelf and piled them on the table. Then he ran his fingers carefully over the back-board of the cupboard. But there was no give in it anywhere, and though he pulled out the shelf, he could find no kind of latch or fastening behind it. The cupboard was what it appeared to be, a solid, unpretentious piece of office furniture. He replaced the contents, closed the doors, and stood gazing at it thoughtfully. De Silva had said that it was the only means of communication with the flat above, and, though he had been over the whole of the premises of the Onyx, he had seen nothing anywhere else resembling a door.

Struck by a sudden thought, he stepped forward and, grasping the cupboard firmly, tried to shift it. But he could not move it an inch. Either it was a good deal heavier than it looked or it was attached to the wall in some way. Evidently his employer had spared no pains to cut off the shop from the flat he proposed to retain for himself.

Bond was reluctantly obliged to confess himself beaten, but he found it hard, even now, to tear himself away. He had lived by his wits, such as they were, for so long that his mind had degenerated into a lamentable state of mingled suspicion and cunning. And he knew de Silva. In spite of the latter's assurances, Bond had never for a moment swerved from his original conviction that the Onyx was merely a shield for something very different. The fact that the business was being run on law-abiding lines was in itself enough to convince him that it had something more important behind it, and he had every intention of discovering what this was. He had not believed for a moment that de Silva had really cut off all connection between the shop and the flat, and had made up his mind that the way through lay in the back of the cupboard. And now he was obliged to confess himself beaten.

He picked up his coat and hat and prepared to leave the building. His hand was actually on the knob of the door leading from the office to the shop, when a sound reached his ears that held him frozen to attention.

Some one was unlocking the street door of the closed shop. Bond heard footsteps and the soft click of the latch as the intruder closed the door behind him, and with the sound came the realization that there was only one person, barring himself, who possessed a key to the shop. De Silva! And de Silva was the last man in the world he wished to meet at that moment.

With a quick glance round to see that he had left nothing out of place, Bond slipped silently across the room and into a small cloakroom and lavatory that had been built out over the yard behind. By leaving the door ajar he found he could command a view of at least half the office.

He waited, and from his hiding-place he saw the door open and de Silva step lightly in. He carried a suitcase and was whistling softly to himself, and his thin lips bore a smile of sheer satisfaction that made the watcher's fingers twitch with longing. He had hated his employer for a long time, and the feeling had increased immeasurably in intensity in the last twenty-four hours. He drew back still farther behind the protecting door, but his eyes never left the other man for a moment.

De Silva gave a quick glance round the office and then went swiftly to the cupboard. For a moment Bond lost sight of him behind the angle of the cupboard. Then there was a click and the whole cupboard swung out into the room with the door to which it was attached, running over the carpeted floor on castors cleverly set at an angle.

The Argentino disappeared into the passage beyond, and the cupboard rolled easily back into place behind him.

Bond straightened himself, for his position had become cramped, and adjusted the door more carefully to his line of vision. He had barely done so than the cupboard swung open again and de Silva appeared once more, this time without the suitcase, and departed by the way he had come.

Bond gave him five minutes or so after the shop door had shut behind him, then he left his hiding-place and hurried across the room to the cupboard. He ran his hand over the side, only to find that there was no protuberance of any kind, but, slipping his hand between the cupboard and the door to which it was attached, he had no difficulty in finding the catch that released the lock. The cupboard swung open and he disappeared. He was gone for about fifteen minutes, and when he came back and rolled the cupboard gently back to its accustomed place against the wall, his face had lost something of its discontent, and there was a satisfied gleam in his eyes that boded ill for his unsuspecting employer.

During the days that followed he kept a careful eye on the customers who patronized the Onyx, but there was not one among them that he could justly designate as suspicious. Nobody, to his knowledge, made use of the concealed entrance to the flat during business hours, and though he hovered persistently in the neighbourhood of the quiet street after the shop was closed, he never once surprised de Silva on his way there.

Lady Dalberry came twice in the course of the following week and purchased various of the Onyx preparations, "for the good of the house," as she explained to Bond, de Silva having begged her to patronize his new venture. On one occasion she brought Carol, who sampled the hairdressing and manicure departments and expressed herself more than satisfied. Some days later Carol came again, this time by herself, and was joined, Bond noticed, almost immediately by de Silva, who had not been near the place for several days. The little episode afforded Bond a certain malicious satisfaction, for the Argentino's unconcealed delight in the girl's company was only equalled by her obvious desire to get rid of him as speedily and courteously as possible. He was not to be shaken off, however, and insisted on showing her round the entire establishment and seeing her back to the Escatorial afterwards. It was significant that she did not visit the Onyx again.

Bond would have been even better pleased if he had known how much of her time was being spent in avoiding de Silva. In spite of Lady Dalberry's uniform kindness and real consideration, it was beginning to dawn on the girl that the joint *menage* of the Escatorial was not quite the ideal arrangement it had seemed at first. For one thing, she did not care for her aunt's friends, and she had begun to dislike de Silva definitely. Also, though she hesitated to admit this even to herself, her estrangement with Dalberry was beginning to worry her. When, in her anger, she had definitely refused to see him, she had not expected him to take his dismissal without a protest. And now, for more than a week, she had heard nothing of him, and as she had not seen Jasper Mellish, she was unaware of his efforts to set himself right in her eyes. Several times Lady Dalberry had tried to broach the subject of "that poor Gillie" and what she termed "this foolish misunderstanding," but Carol had flatly refused to discuss it, and she had been obliged to let it drop. But the girl was beginning to feel both ill-used and apprehensive, and, with her native honesty, was constrained to admit that she had only herself to thank for her anxiety.

At last, one day, finding herself in the neighbourhood of the Albany, she decided to drop in on Jasper Mellish and see if she could not pick up a hint as to Dalberry's movements.

She found Mellish at home, and in a mood that was new to her. She had learned long ago how to humour him when he was on one of his brief, but violent, fits of irritation; but in spite of their many heated arguments, she had never before come definitely under the ban of his disapproval.

He greeted her curtly.

"So you've come," he said. "To be frank with you, I'm not sure that the moment has not passed. I said 'at once' in my letter, if you recollect."

She stared at him.

"Your letter?" she repeated, quite at sea as to his meaning.

He moved impatiently.

"Yes, my letter. You're not going to tell me that you didn't get it?"

"I've had no letter from you for a long time," said Carol. "I haven't the remotest idea what you're talking about."

Mellish's manner changed abruptly.

"Let's get this straight," he said sharply. "I wrote to you nearly a week ago, asking you to see me as I had something of importance to discuss with you. I've been expecting to hear from you ever since."

Carol shook her head.

"I've had no letter," she assured him. "If I had, I should have answered it. You might have known that."

He was too absorbed in his own thoughts to take up the challenge.

"So that's it," he murmured. "If my brains hadn't been wool-gathering I should have guessed, I suppose. Where were you last Tuesday afternoon?" he asked suddenly.

After a moment's thought Carol answered:

"At the Little Theatre. Why?"

"You *were* out, then. Didn't your aunt tell you that I called?"

"Yes. She said that you'd only stayed a short time and were sorry to miss me."

"She gave you no message from me?"

Carol looked puzzled.

"Not exactly a message. She said that you hoped to see me soon, as far as I can remember."

"A half-truth is sometimes better than a lie," said Mellish grimly. "My message was that I *wanted* to see you at once, and Lady Dalberry said that you would no doubt telephone to me. When you didn't ring up, I wrote."

"But I never got the letter!"

"No. I might have guessed you wouldn't. I ought to have sent it by hand. As it is, who is to say that it wasn't lost in the post?"

"Aunt Irma may have misunderstood the message," suggested Carol doubtfully. "Her English is so good that one's apt to forget that it isn't her real language."

"She might. As you say, one can hardly blame her."

Mellish's tone was very dry. He turned to Carol with one of his sudden, disarming smiles.

"I've been doing you an injustice. I apologize, my dear. You've probably guessed what I wanted to see you about. There are certain things you ought to know about that night at the Terpsychorean, things that Gillie would have explained to you himself if you hadn't refused to see him. When I got no answer to my letter I concluded that you were indulging in a feminine fit of sulks, to put it mildly, and did not intend to listen to Gillie's version of the affair. He was already under the impression that he had offended you irretrievably, and your behaviour led me to suppose that he was right."

There was a silence, then:

"Have I ever done anything to make you think me a mean little beast?" asked Carol.

Her voice was low and not quite steady. Mellish could not see her face.

"Never," he answered promptly. "It was because the whole thing was so unlike you that I resented it. Also, you must remember, you had just cause to be angry. Gillie's behaviour must have seemed inexcusable. He realizes that—otherwise he would have tried to see you."

Carol kept her head resolutely turned away.

"I wish he had," she confessed. "I've minded horribly. I couldn't understand why he didn't write or something. I came to-day in the hope—"

She broke off suddenly.

Mellish was suddenly reminded of an old habit she had had, as a child, of creeping under a certain big table with a heavy cloth when she wanted to cry. He strolled over to the cupboard where he kept her favourite cigarettes and opened a box.

"I can put the Terpsychorean business right in a few words," he said, without looking round. "Gillie wasn't drunk that night, though I admit you had good reason to think so."

There was a pause.

"He was awfully queer, Jasper," came at last from Caro.

"I know. So would you be if you were drugged."

"Drugged?"

"You'll have to take my word for it, Carol. I know what I'm talking about. He really was drugged, absurd as it sounds. It was a deliberate attempt on the part of some one to discredit him in your eyes, just as there has been an equally deliberate attempt to prevent you from seeing either of us for the past week."

He left her to absorb this statement while he crossed the room and, with his usual deliberation, placed the cigarettes by her side. She took one mechanically.

"But I don't understand, Jasper. Who would do such a thing? And why?"

"That's what I'm hoping to find out. Let me tell you the whole story, then you can draw your own conclusions."

In as few words as possible he gave her Dalberry's version of what had happened at the Terpsychorean. He also told her of de Silva's connection with the club. She was quick to grasp all that the information implied.

"If Captain Bond put anything into that first drink of Gillie's, he must have been carrying out Mr. de Silva's instructions," she exclaimed. "Captain Bond couldn't have any possible reason for trying to get Gillie out of the way."

"But de Silva might? What makes you think that?" asked Mellish sharply.

She reddened.

"A week ago I should have laughed at the idea," she said frankly. "And it seems ridiculous now. It's only that, during the last few days, Mr. de Silva's been—well—rather forthcoming. It isn't that he's said or done anything any one could possibly take exception to, only he's always turning up, and, once he's there, I simply can't get rid of him. If I liked him I shouldn't object to it in the least, but I don't. And the fact that he's such a friend of Aunt Irma's makes it so much more difficult. I don't want to be rude to him."

"He did nothing to annoy you that night he drove you home from the club, did he?"

"Nothing. He couldn't have been more considerate. I ought to be grateful to him, really. It was a horrid situation, and he got me out of it very neatly."

"Having got you into it in the first instance, that was the least he could do. I shouldn't waste gratitude on him if I were you."

"You can't really believe he had anything to do with what happened to Gillie! It's unthinkable!"

"Gillie did not feel ill till after he'd had those two drinks at the Terpsychorean," Mellish pointed out. "And those drinks were undoubtedly mixed by either de Silva or Bond. Add to that the fact that de Silva is, or was, the proprietor of the club, and that Bond is in his employ, and I don't see what other conclusion you can come to. I'm afraid you've added yet another to your long list of admirers, my dear, and a determined one at that. At any rate he's invented an original method of getting rid of his rivals!"

He spoke lightly with a purpose. He did not want to alarm the girl more than was necessary to put her on her guard against the Argentino.

"But what was the point of it all?" she exclaimed. "He must have known he couldn't keep us apart for ever!"

Mellish decided to tell her frankly the conclusion he had come to.

"I think he made a bad side-slip over the Terpsychorean business. You must remember he's a Latin, and he probably let his jealousy of Gillie get the better of his judgment. Also, he bungled badly over the drug itself. If he had given Gillie a slightly smaller amount, it would have been far more difficult for him to prove that he wasn't simply the worse for drink. Drugs are tricky things to play with. They react quite differently on different people. I don't suppose, for a moment, he meant him to lose consciousness. The suppression of the letter was simply a blind attempt to postpone the consequences of his blunder. I should have given him credit for more sense myself, from what you tell me of him."

"Anyhow, he'll hardly dare to show his face after this. I can't tell you what a relief it is to feel that I needn't always be avoiding him."

"I shouldn't count on that. He doesn't know how much we may have guessed. He's been making hay while the sun shines, from your account, and he's not likely to relinquish the position easily. When you say he's always turning up, do you mean that he comes to your aunt's flat?"

"It isn't his coming to the flat I mind, it's the exasperating way he has of dropping in when Aunt Irma's out. He's done it three times now, and each time I've opened the door to him myself, thinking that it was Aunt Irma and that she had forgotten her key. That's the worst of a service flat. Ordinary visitors are shown up by one of the pages, but Mr. de Silva comes out of his own flat opposite and just knocks, and, so far, I've been caught every time. When he finds Aunt Irma out he asks if he may come in and wait in her sitting-room, and, as he's an intimate friend of hers, I can't very well refuse. Last time I was literally driven out of the flat. I was determined not to give him tea, and I saw he was going to ask for it, so I invented an appointment and cleared out myself."

"Have you spoken to Lady Dalberry about it?"

"How can I? Apart from the fact that they seem to do a lot of business together, they are old friends, and the flat is as much hers as mine."

"Do you think she knows he comes to see you?"

Carol smiled rather ruefully.

"I don't even know it myself," she said honestly. "As I say, he hasn't done or said a thing I could possibly complain of, and, for all I know, it may have been just bad luck that he came when Aunt Irma was out. But I don't think so. He has got a queer way of turning up and waylaying me on the stairs or catching me just as I am going out of the flat. I don't believe it can be altogether accidental. There's something about the whole thing that bothers me, and I'm nervous about Aunt Irma. I believe he's getting hold of her money in some way. She's always going over to his flat with bundles of papers, and I'm sure she consults him about all her investments. He belongs to the bridge club she goes to, and I know she lost heavily to him the other night. She was talking about it next morning. And now there's this business of Gillie's illness and the disappearance of your letter. It does look as if he'd got round Aunt Irma. Do you think he's got some hold over her, Jasper?"

"It certainly looks as if she'd had a finger in the pie," said Mellish evasively. "Though, of course, the loss of the letter and the bungling of my message to you may be a sheer coincidence. As you say, it might be due to her bad English, and, after all, letters do get lost in the post. What do you want to do? Leave the flat? I daresay we should have no trouble in terminating any arrangement you made with Lady Dalberry." Carol shook her head.

"I can't leave her in the lurch like that, after all the trouble she's taken to make me comfortable. She had the rooms done up on purpose, and she's really been a brick. And, after all, we've no proof that she's mixed up in this business at all. If the de Silva man gets really troublesome, I shall have to go, and I shall tell her frankly why I am leaving. But, for the present, I think I'd better stay."

Rather to her surprise Mellish did not question her decision.

"You may be right," he said. "There's more in this business than meets the eye, and we've undoubtedly got a better chance of finding out what de Silva's object is if we can keep in touch with him. So long as you are on your guard, I don't see any reason why you shouldn't stay where you are, unless you feel nervous, in which case you had far better leave at once. Do you feel equal to meeting de Silva and, possibly, Bond, without betraying the fact, either to them or Lady Dalberry, that your suspicions have been aroused? If de Silva annoys you in any way, ring me up here."

Carol hesitated for a moment.

"All right, I'll do my best," she said. "And I'll post any letters I write myself, though, honestly, it seems too absurd! I feel as if I were acting in a cheap melodrama."

"No harm in being on the safe side, all the same," said Mellish easily. "And, by the same token, don't mention the fact that you have seen me or Gillie. Meet him outside, if you can. I'll ring you up at intervals."

"Aunt Irma nearly always goes round to the club in the evening. She's got a mania for bridge. Unless I'm out you'll find me alone after dinner, if you telephone then."

"Shall I tell Gillie that?" asked Mellish innocently. "He's about due to ring up now. He drops in or telephones on an average of every three hours nowadays."

Carol fell into the trap.

"Why are you seeing so much of him all of a sudden?" she asked.

"I'm not," answered Mellish blandly. "His visits are unflattering-ly short. He merely asks whether I have heard from you, and then, the answer being in the negative, removes himself till next time. He hasn't seemed in the mood for conversation lately. You may find him more chatty when you meet. Have you any message for him?"

Carol, her cheeks a shade pinker than usual, was on her way to the door. She turned.

"No, thank you," she said demurely. "I shall be writing to him in any case."

"Then take my advice and post the letter yourself," called Mellish after her as she disappeared.

When she had gone he rang for Jervis.

"In the future, whenever I go out I shall leave an address that will find me," he said. "If Miss Summers should ring up at any time her message is to be telephoned on to me immediately, wherever I may be. If, at any time, I should forget to mention where I am going, I shall expect you to remind me, Jervis."

"Very good, sir. Lord Dalberry is on the phone."

Mellish settled himself luxuriously in his chair.

"Tell him that I am asleep and have left orders that I am on no account to be disturbed, but that Miss Summers is writing to him. Have you got that, Jervis?"

"You are asleep, but Miss Summers is writing to Lord Dalberry. Very good, sir."

And Jervis departed on his errand of mercy.

CHAPTER XI

ON LEAVING Mellish's rooms Carol hurried back to the Escatorial, impelled by a quite shameless desire to get hold of Dalberry as soon as possible. She tried to ring him up from a public call-office on her way home, but the line was engaged. If she had known that she had missed him on the telephone at Mellish's flat by a few minutes she would have bitterly regretted the pride that had prevented her from asking if she might ring him up from there. She knew that Lady Dalberry was probably at home, in which case she dare not call up from the Escatorial. There seemed nothing for it now but to write to him. One thing was quite clear to her: she could not rest in peace until she had put things right between them.

She swung quickly into the big hall of the Escatorial, her mind so full of the letter she was about to write that she did not notice a dumpy, thickset figure which had just emerged from the lift. The sound of her own name, spoken in a curious husky whisper, caused her to turn, and, to her annoyance, she recognized Captain Bond. He carried a suitcase and a heavy motor coat slung over his arm.

Her first instinct was to ignore him, then she remembered Mellish's instructions and her undertaking to obey them. She realized now that the task was not going to be an easy one. The mere sight of the little man's pasty, querulous face brought back the Terpsychorean and his share in what had happened there.

With an effort she greeted him pleasantly. He dropped the suitcase he was carrying with a sigh of relief, and shook hands.

"Have you been calling on us?" she asked. "I hope you found my aunt at home."

"I've had to deny myself that pleasure," he explained elaborately. "My time was too short. I'm leaving for Paris tonight, and have been getting my final instructions from Mr. de Silva."

"You'll have a lovely trip. Paris ought to be delicious now, in spite of the cold."

"I'm afraid I shall have no time for frivolities," he grumbled, delighted, as usual, to be able to voice a grievance. "I shall only have two days, and those will be spent in stuffy warehouses, sampling scents and face-creams and all the things you ladies love."

Carol persisted nobly in her determination to be pleasant.

"I'm not sure that I don't envy you," she said, with something of the sprightliness she felt that he expected of "you ladies."

"It's not a man's job," he assented gloomily.

He stood staring at her in silence until, having waited in vain for him to move on, she was driven to holding out her hand in dismissal.

"Well, I hope you'll have a good crossing and a pleasant time when you get there," she said, with cheerful banality.

He shook hands with her absent-mindedly, picked up his suitcase and then stood with it in his hand, barring her way to the lift.

"What do you think of our preparations, Miss Summers?" he asked suddenly.

She could not help smiling at the inconsequence of the question.

"The Onyx things? I think they're excellent."

He nodded.

"You're right. They're about the best of their kind. Quite pure and all that. You know that quite a lot of the big places stock them now? Garrods and Hammidges, for instance. You can get all our things there."

There was another pause. Then, with an involuntary glance at the deserted staircase, he finished hurriedly:

"If you want any of the Onyx preparations, Miss Summers, go to one of the big stores for them. Don't get them from us. You'll find them just as good elsewhere."

And with that he turned and hurried away, leaving Carol staring after him in mixed consternation and astonishment.

In the light of what she had learned that afternoon, his intention was obvious. He was trying, in his bungling way, to warn her against the Onyx.

On reaching the flat she went straight to her room and wrote her letter to Gillie. Then, without waiting to see whether her aunt was at home, she rang for the lift and went down and posted the letter herself at the little post office at the corner of the street.

On her return to the flat she opened the door of her aunt's sitting-room and looked in. Lady Dalberry was sitting by the fire, reading.

She looked up with a smile.

"I thought I heard you come in just now. Did you go out again?"

Carol nodded.

"I found I'd got no stamps, so I ran out to the post office to get some."

"My dear, how troublesome for you! Why did not you let the porter fetch them? It is what he is here for."

"It wasn't any trouble, really," Carol assured her. "I hadn't taken off my hat when I discovered there were none in my drawer."

Lady Dalberry laughed.

"This seems to be our unlucky day," she said. "The same thing happened to me, only I was not dressed to go out. I was going to send the porter, but, if you have just bought some, perhaps you would have pity on me. I only need one."

There was a glint of humour in Carol's eyes as she opened her bag. Lady Dalberry could hardly be expected to know that, among other fittings, it contained a special leather case for the little stamp-books issued by the Post Office. The case had had a book in it when the bag was given to her some months before, and it had remained untouched ever since. If, as she suspected, Lady Dalberry was trying to test the accuracy of her statement that she had been to the post office to buy stamps, she was ready with her proof.

She produced the case, opening it in such a way that her aunt could see that the book was an unused one.

"Is one enough?" she asked. "I've got a whole book here."

"Plenty," said Lady Dalberry, as she took it. "I will fetch my letter."

She rose and left the room. Carol waited until she heard the door of her bedroom close behind her, then she went swiftly to the writing-table and looked into the little inlaid box in which she knew Lady

Dalberry kept her stamps. She had been right in her suspicions. The box was well stocked. Evidently it was not going to be so easy as she had imagined to attend to the posting of her own letters.

She made her way slowly to her room, deep in thought. In the passage she met Lady Dalberry, carrying a letter in her hand.

"Thank you, my dear," she said gratefully. "Have you anything more for the post? I am going to ring for the boy."

"I'm afraid not. My letters aren't written yet. I wish they were!"

She had almost reached her room when Lady Dalberry called her back.

"By the way," she said. "Have any of your letters gone astray lately? Juan de Silva was complaining of the carelessness of the people here and asking whether we had had any trouble. I told him that, as far as I knew, we had missed nothing. He says that they leave the letters lying about in the porter's room downstairs."

For the moment the audacity of the attack took Carol's breath away, then she was conscious of a cold touch of fear at her heart. Until now she had been unable to bring herself to believe that Lady Dalberry was really actively concerned in the plot against Dalberry. But this last move, coming on the top of the illuminating little episode of the stamp-box, brought the truth forcibly home to her, and she realized that the situation was not only awkward, but alarming. She answered naturally enough, however.

"I don't think so," she said. "I certainly haven't missed anything. The whole place seems to me extraordinarily well run. I should be sorry if either of the porters got into a mess. They're so nice, both of them."

Safe inside her room, she pulled herself together and faced the situation. She realized now that she was frightened, and made a determined effort to steady her nerves. It was absurd, she told herself, to yield to panic now. After all, when she had decided to stay on at the flat, she had been aware that Lady Dalberry was, to put it mildly, under the influence of de Silva, but she knew now how half-hearted her own suspicions had been. Such things, she had felt, simply did not happen to people like herself. It was disconcerting in the extreme to discover that they did, and still more disquieting was the realization that there was no one in the flat to whom she could turn in a moment of emergency. It was one thing to assure Mellish that she would face the music, sitting in the comfortable security of his room at the Albany, and quite another to contemplate her own complete isolation in this flat, without even a servant within call, for the staff of the Escatorial was housed far away in the basement. She was suddenly overwhelmed by the sense of her own loneliness and inadequacy, and was actually on the point of packing a bag and going to the nearest hotel for the night, rather than spend another hour under the same roof as Lady Dalberry, when in a flash her imagination, which had so nearly been her undoing, saved her.

She pictured herself on the morrow going to see Mellish and confessing to him that her nerve had failed her after all. That he would be sympathetic, she knew. Indeed, he could be relied upon to treat her with the greatest kindness and consideration, and, unbearable thought to one of her generation and temperament, he would not be surprised. It would be only what he would naturally expect from a sex he had been brought up to look upon as both timid and inconsistent. Ever since her uncle's death she had been asserting her independence, and had scoffed at Mellish's endeavours to hedge her round with the conventional restrictions he considered necessary for her safety; and, now that he had given her a chance to show that she was of different mettle to the Victorian women he professed to admire, she could hardly bring herself to go to him and confess herself beaten.

With a characteristic little jerk of her shoulders she turned and switched on the lights over her dressing-table. With the swiftness of reaction she had made up her mind to stay and see the thing through. She was dining with friends, and did not expect to be back till late, a fact for which she was thankful, for, in spite of her determination, she did not feel equal to facing a long evening in Lady Dalberry's company. She was too fundamentally honest to take kindly to deception of any sort, and she felt that, for one day, she had done more than her share of lying. The words had come easily enough to her lips, but, looking back on her last interview with Lady Dalberry, she realized that she was a mere beginner at a game the other woman played to perfection, and that the fewer encounters she risked the better.

She had just finished dressing for dinner when the telephone bell rang in the hall. She opened her door and listened, but there was no sign of life, either from Lady Dalberry's bedroom or the sitting-room. She concluded that her aunt had already gone down to the restaurant for dinner.

She crossed the hall and took down the receiver.

"Is Miss Summers at home?" asked a voice. For a moment she was puzzled, then she realized that Jervis was speaking.

"Who is it?" she asked. "I am Miss Summers."

"Will you hold the line a minute, miss? Mr. Mellish would like to speak to you."

She glanced round her apprehensively, the receiver at her ear, but there was no movement from either of the two rooms across the hall. All the same, she wished she had ascertained definitely that the flat was empty before answering the telephone. Then she heard Mellish's voice, with its slow drawl.

"I took a chance of catching you alone," he said, "because I wasn't sure of finding you later. Are you alone in the flat?"

"I think so," she answered, speaking as low as she dared. "Is it anything important?"

"Only this. I've been thinking things over, and I've come to the conclusion that it will be wiser for you to clear out. I don't imagine, for a moment, that you are in any danger, but that fellow may make himself unpleasant, and I don't feel that, after what has happened, your aunt is sufficient protection for you. I ought never to have given in to your suggestion in the first instance."

There was a moment's pause, then:

"I think I'd better stick to our first plan," she said undecidedly.

"Nonsense!" came sharply from the other end of the wire. "If there's no one you care to go to, I'll take a room at a hotel for you for a night or two, and then we can settle whether you'd like to leave London for a time or make other arrangements. Get your things packed and be ready to leave to-morrow morning."

His voice was peremptory. In his anxiety he had adopted a tone he generally knew better than to use when dealing with Carol, and the girl was quick to resent it. A moment earlier she had been more than inclined to accede to his suggestion; indeed her hesitation had been only to save her face. Mellish's assumption that she would fall meekly in with any arrangements he might think fit to make roused her to immediate opposition.

"I'm sorry," she said, keeping her voice low and selecting her words carefully. "I'm afraid it's no good. I've decided to stick to our first arrangement. I'll explain why when we meet."

"Has anything fresh happened? If not, let me beg of you—"

She cut him short.

"I can't argue about it now, but please let things remain as they are for the present."

A sudden suspicion seized Mellish.

"What's the matter?" he asked. "Is anybody listening?"

"Possibly. I don't know."

"Very well, then. I'll ask you a few questions that can be answered by 'yes' or 'no.' Has anything important happened since I saw you?"

"No."

"Has anything at all happened? Anything you would like to tell me?"

"Yes."

"You have quite made up your mind to stay on for the present?"

"Yes."

"Can you meet me on the bridge by the Powder Magazine in Kensington Gardens to-morrow morning at eleven?"

"Yes. That will suit me perfectly."

"Excellent. We will thresh the matter out then. Meanwhile, you're all right?"

"Quite."

He rang off, and Carol, after fetching her cloak and bag from her room, telephoned to the porter for a taxi and left the flat.

She slammed the front door behind her, and then, following a sudden impulse, slipped her latch-key into the lock and turned it carefully. Very gently she pushed the heavy door ajar and looked through the chink.

Lady Dalberry's bedroom door was open and she stood on the threshold. She was staring at the telephone, and on her face was a look of mingled curiosity and annoyance that confirmed Carol's suspicion that she had been listening to her one-sided conversation with Mellish and had gathered nothing from it.

The girl felt deeply grateful for the instinct that had warned her to be careful in her answers.

With infinite precautions she closed the door. Then she ran swiftly down the stairs and into the waiting taxi.

CHAPTER XII

AN AMUSING dinner-party and an evening spent in the society of people she had known for years, and on whose friendship and integrity she knew she could rely, went a long way towards dispelling Carol's fears. She returned to the Escatorial a very different person to the nerve-racked girl who had left it only a few hours before. Though she was still conscious of a sense of insecurity that made her lock her bedroom door carefully before settling down for the night, her self-reliance had returned to her and she slept like a log and woke feeling refreshed and confident in the morning.

Lady Dalberry breakfasted in her room and Carol did not see her before leaving the flat to keep her appointment with Mellish. She found him, a peaceful and reassuring figure, meditatively observing the boats on the Serpentine, and the first thing he did was to hand her a note from Dalberry, written in answer to her letter.

"He rang up this morning, and when he heard that I was meeting you, he entrusted me with this. We decided that it was wiser not to send it by post."

He turned his back and displayed a fatherly interest in the ducks while she read it and scribbled a pencilled answer, accepting Dalberry's invitation to dine that night, on the back of the envelope. Mellish undertook to see it delivered, and slipped it into his pocket. Then he began to tackle her in earnest on the score of her obstinacy in insisting on staying on at the Escatorial.

But he was unfortunate in the moment he had chosen. The fine, bracing weather, her own sense of physical fitness, and the added stimulus of Dalberry's letter, had effectually banished her fears of the night before, and she was filled now with a high spirit of adventure. Mellish soon realized that nothing he could say would alter her decision, and abandoning what was obviously becoming a futile discussion, he asked what had happened after her return to the flat the day before.

She told him all that had passed between her and Lady Dalberry, and his mouth hardened as he listened.

"This only confirms me in my decision that you ought to leave that place at once," he said emphatically.

"If you take that line, I shan't report to you any more," she countered. "I must stay on for a bit, but I promise that, if anything really unpleasant happens, I will clear out at once. Meanwhile, I shall keep my eyes open and try to find out what hold this wretched man has over Aunt Irma. I can't help feeling sorry for her, and I'm sure she has been dragged into this in spite of herself."

She and Lady Dalberry lunched together, and Carol found it easier than she had expected to keep up at least a semblance of their old friendliness. Dalberry's letter and the knowledge that she was to meet him that evening prevented her from dwelling unnecessarily on what had passed, and at the moment she felt more than prepared to meet whatever might lie in the future.

She told Lady Dalberry that she was dining out and would probably not be home till the small hours. Fortunately for her, her aunt took it for granted that she was spending the evening with some friends who had recently arrived in London from abroad, and beyond saying that she would be at her club until fairly late, and would not sit up for her, did not pursue the subject further. Thus it was that, secure in the knowledge that her aunt was still unaware that she was in communication once more with Mellish and Dalberry, Carol, in her most becoming frock, set out with a light heart to keep the appointment she had been looking forward to all day, little dreaming that, during her absence, the Escatorial was to achieve an unenviable, if brief, notoriety as the scene of a tragedy as grim as it was mysterious.

Just over an hour before her return—to be exact, a few minutes after eleven-thirty—the night porter of the Escatorial strolled out on to the steps to "cast an eye on the weather," as he expressed it. As he did so, a taxi, coming from the direction of Park Lane, drew up opposite the door. According to his custom he ran down the steps and opened the cab door.

The occupant made no move to get out, and, after waiting for a moment, he peered into the interior of the cab, expecting to find that one of the tenants of the building had dined, not wisely but too well. The light was bad, but it was good enough for him to see that the passenger, who was huddled in the corner of the cab as though asleep, was a stranger to him.

The taxi-driver twisted himself round so that he could see into the interior of the cab.

"Anything wrong, mate?" he asked. "I was told the Escatorial."

The porter turned to him.

"'E's not one of our lot," he said. "Drunk, isn't 'e?"

"'E ain't no drunk."

The driver climbed out of his seat and came round to the door of the cab.

"'E was sober all right when I see 'im last," he stated. "'E and the other gentleman was walkin' along Regent Street when they stopped me. They was both steady enough then."

He climbed into the cab and shook the occupant gently by the arm.

"'Ere, sir," he said. "You wanted the Escatorial, didn't you?"

There was no response, and he bent lower and peered into the man's face, with the result that he backed out of the cab in a hurry on to the porter's toes.

"Somethin' wrong in there," he said briefly. "Take a look at 'is face!"

The porter went round to the other door and opened it. Then he shut it again hurriedly. He was an old soldier and quite capable of keeping his head in an emergency. He had his duty to the flats to consider, as he expressed it afterwards, and he saw no reason why the fair name of the Escatorial should be sullied by a sordid affair of this kind.

"If you take my advice, you'll drive 'im round to the police station round the corner," he said decisively. "'E don't belong 'ere."

The driver hesitated and, by so doing, effectually ruined the porter's neat scheme.

"This was the address I was given," he insisted obstinately.

"I can't help that. 'E don't belong 'ere. You cut off with 'im to the station."

But it was too late. A policeman had just turned the corner, and at the sight of him the cabman's face cleared. He gave a shrill whistle and signalled to him to come over. The policeman did not hurry himself as he strolled across the road towards them, but after a brief glance into the interior of the cab, his manner changed considerably.

With the help of the taxi-driver he got the man out of the cab, and together they carried him into the Escatorial and laid him down on the floor of the porter's room.

The policeman knelt down by his side.

"He's gone," he announced, after a brief examination. "Anybody know who he is?"

"'E doesn't belong 'ere," asseverated the porter earnestly. "And, what's more, 'e's never been 'ere to my knowledge. The day-porter may know 'im by sight; I don't."

The constable went to the telephone and called up the police station. In less than ten minutes the station inspector arrived, bringing with him a constable and the divisional surgeon, whom he had picked up on the way.

Now it so happened that the inspector was an old associate of Chief Detective-Inspector Shand. It also happened that Shand had dropped into the local police station for a chat only a few days before. His visit had not been entirely without an object.

"Know anything of a chap called de Silva?" he had asked casually.

The inspector shook his head.

"That's a new one on me," he said. "Who is he?"

"He's in your manor, anyway. Got a flat at the Escatorial. I'm interested in him, that's all."

He left it at that, but the inspector knew him well enough to take the hint. While the surgeon was making his examination he called up New Scotland Yard and got on to Shand. Shand listened to his report in silence.

"Give me ten minutes and I'll be with you," he said, when the other had finished.

He was as good as his word. The surgeon had barely finished his examination when Shand joined the little group gathered on the threshold of the porter's room.

His eyes narrowed automatically as they fell on the distorted features of the dead man, but he made no comment. He was not entirely unprepared, however, for the surgeon's verdict.

"Strangled?" he echoed. "Looks as if it might have been a fit."

For answer the surgeon pointed to the man's throat. On either side of it, below the ears, were two well-defined bruises. The swollen, blackened features and the protruding eyes spoke of asphyxiation.

"Strangled!" repeated Shand softly to himself. "He was found in a taxi, you said."

The taxi-driver stepped forward.

"That's right," he said. "'E was all right enough when 'e and the other gentleman got in in Regent Street; that's all I know."

Shand turned on him sharply.

"There was another man, then. Where is he?"

"'E's gone all right. Stopped the cab at the corner of Lifford Street and got out as cool as you please. 'Drive to the Escatorial,' 'e says. 'You know where it is?' And then I come on 'ere."

"Was that all he said?" asked Shand.

"No, it wasn't," answered the taxi-driver irately. "Took me in proper, 'e did! Stood with the door in 'is 'and and talked to the chap inside, the cold-'earted devil! That was 'ow I didn't suspect nothing. 'Good-bye, old man,' 'e says. 'Don't forget to let me know 'ow you get on.' Then 'e goes off, carryin' 'is 'at in 'is 'and, as cool as you please."

"He was carrying his hat? Then you must have got a good look at him."

"Oh, I see 'im all right. And I'd know 'im again, too. Slim sort of chap, not too tall, with very light 'air. I see it in the light from the lamp. Almost white it was."

Shand's memory switched suddenly back to the story of the steward on board the *Enriqueta*. Fair hair that might have been white, seen in the light of a lamp. That was his description of the man bending over Smith. And this man, too, had been strangled!

"Would you put him down as a foreigner?"

The taxi-driver hesitated.

"I don't know as I would," he said at last. "And yet, now you come to speak of it, 'e might 'ave been. Spoke very clear and precise like, but I didn't notice no accent."

"And he gave this address?"

"As clear as anythink. 'You know where it is?' 'e says to me."

Shand cut him short or he would have gone over the whole scene again.

"Better see if there's any one in the building who can identify him," he said to the inspector. "The porter doesn't know him, you say?"

"Never seen him before. He certainly isn't one of the tenants. We haven't searched his pockets, though."

"Time enough for that later," said Shand. "I'll go through the flats while you're getting the ambulance. Don't move the body till I come back."

While he was speaking he had stepped out into the hall. The sound of a woman's voice made him turn suddenly, and he found himself face to face with Lady Dalberry. He recognized her at once, though he had not seen her since that day on the station platform at Liverpool.

She stopped as her eyes fell on the policemen and the little group of people behind them.

"Is there anything the matter?" she asked quickly, in her deep, rich voice.

Shand explained briefly that a man, apparently on his way to visit one of the flats, had died suddenly in a taxi and that he was anxious to get him identified.

"You would wish me to see him?" she said at once. "Where is this poor man? But it is not likely, you know, that any one would visit me at this time of night."

Shand hesitated.

"I ought to warn you that it will not be very pleasant," he said.

Lady Dalberry looked at him with a hint of contempt in her eyes.

"I am not a child," she said simply. "Where am I to go?"

He led the way into the porter's room. As he stood aside to let her pass in he glanced at her face. Her make-up, as usual, was heavy, but he had a suspicion that she had paled under her rouge, and the lines about her mouth had certainly deepened. It was an unpleasant ordeal for any woman, he reflected, especially for one who, not so long ago, had looked on the mutilated body of her husband. For the second time since he had first set eyes on her he found himself paying an unwilling tribute to her courage.

She bent over the body.

"No, he is not known to me," she announced, as she straightened herself. "I have never seen him before."

She seemed glad to get out of the little room, and Shand did not blame her. He escorted her to the lift. On the way she paused and turned to him.

"Miss Summers, who lives with me, is still out," she said. "She will be coming in soon, but I am sure she does not know this man. Mr. de Silva, our neighbour, might be able to help you. He sometimes has visitors late in the evening."

Shand thanked her and, having seen her on her way, went back to speak to the porter.

"I'd better begin with this floor," he said. "You may as well give me the names of the tenants."

"There are no flats on this floor," the porter answered. "You'll find nothing but the restaurant and kitchens here and some of the servants' bedrooms. The flats begin on the floor above."

Shand ran his eye down the names on the board in the hall, then he told the porter that he would not need him and got into the lift.

The boy stopped it at the first floor, but Shand told him to go on.

"On second thoughts, I'll begin at the top," he said, "and work down. I won't keep the lift. It's a job that will take some time, and I can use the stairs."

"There's only Lady Dalberry and Mr. de Silva on the top floor, sir," volunteered the boy.

"Is this Mr. de Silva in?"

"I ain't taken 'im down, not since I've been on duty."

"They keep you up a bit late here, don't they?" asked Shand sympathetically.

"The lift closes at twelve, and we take it in turns to do night duty, two nights a week, each of us. It ain't so bad. If it 'adn't been for 'im, down there, I should be off 'ome by now."

"Long hours?" inquired Shand.

"Not so dusty. I didn't come on till eight to-night."

"The tenants of the flats can use the stairs, I suppose?"

The boy nodded.

"They mostly ring for the lift, though. Here you are, sir."

As Shand pressed the bell of de Silva's flat he glanced at the door opposite. The light still shone through the transom. Evidently Lady Dalberry had not yet gone to bed.

We waited for a minute or two, and then rang again. This time he heard a movement behind the door. He stood listening, his hand on the bell. He was just about to ring again when the door opened a few inches and a head appeared tentatively in the crack.

"Who's there?" demanded the owner, with all the irritability of a man just roused from his first sleep.

"Mr. de Silva?" inquired Shand smoothly.

The door opened wide and revealed the Argentino, clad in a rather gaudy silk dressing-gown, his usually smooth hair ruffled and on end. Evidently he had come straight from his bed.

"That is my name. What do you want?" he said impatiently.

"I am an inspector of police," said Shand briskly. "Sorry to disturb you, but I'm afraid I must ask you to come downstairs with me. A man has died suddenly in a cab on his way to these flats, and we are anxious to establish his identity. We have reason to believe he intended to call at this flat."

He was watching the other keenly as he spoke. His last statement had been pure bluff, but he had his own reasons for wishing to confront de Silva with the man who lay in the porter's room downstairs.

The Argentino stared at him perplexedly.

"It is very unlikely that he was coming to see me," he said slowly. "I certainly was not expecting anybody. Of course, if you insist, I will come down."

He glanced significantly at his attire. The dressing-gown had fallen open and the rich silk pyjamas beneath were plainly visible.

"Much obliged," said Shand heartily. "Don't bother about your clothes; there'll be nobody about now but my men and the porter."

De Silva drew the dressing-gown closer round him.

"Very well," he said. "Just wait while I get my key."

A moment later he joined Shand, and the two men made their way down the stairs together. De Silva took it for granted that the lift had stopped working, and Shand did not disabuse him. He was not sorry to have a few words with him out of range of the interested gaze of the lift-boy.

"You didn't happen to see a man hanging round the flats earlier in the evening, I suppose?" asked Shand, trailing his red herring shamelessly.

De Silva stared at him.

"I haven't been out of my flat since I came up from the restaurant about half-past eight. I was tired and went early to bed."

Shand gave an apologetic laugh.

"I'm afraid I shall be unpopular all round to-night," he confessed. "I don't enjoy dragging people out of their beds, but I must find out where this man was going, if I can."

"Well, I am not likely to be able to help you," said the other shortly.

Shand led the way to the porter's room. The ambulance had arrived, and the dead man had already been placed on the stretcher and covered with a blanket. As Shand drew this down, leaving the face exposed, he watched de Silva closely. He was not disappointed.

The Argentino was staring at the still figure on the stretcher with mingled surprise and horror.

"Do you know him?" asked Shand.

The Argentino nodded. He seemed genuinely shocked.

"I have known him slightly for a good many years," he said frankly. "First in the Argentine, and then in London. He called himself Conyers, but ..."

He stopped, as if he did not wish to say more.

"Not a very reputable character, eh?" suggested Shand. "Have you any reason to suppose that Conyers was not his real name?"

"None," de Silva assured him. "And I should be very sorry now to say anything against him. Indeed, I know of nothing definite, except the fact that he was in very low water and had been trying to raise money."

"When did you last see him?"

The answer came promptly enough.

"One day last week. He came to borrow money, and I was obliged to refuse him. I had lent him a small sum a short time before, on the strength of our acquaintance in South America, but, as I told him, I am not a rich man, and I could do no more for him. We parted on quite friendly terms. Indeed, it is very probable that he was coming to see me to-night to make another effort to persuade me. As far as I am aware, I was the only person he knew in this building."

"Have you any idea what he did for a living?"

De Silva gave an expressive shrug of his shoulders.

"I should say that he lived by his wits, but I do not know. How did he die? An epileptic fit?"

"We shall know more about that at the inquest," said Shand evasively. "Do you happen to know whether he was subject to fits?"

"I have never heard that he was, but, as I told you, I did not know him very well."

"Could you tell me anything about his associates?"

De Silva shook his head.

"I know nothing about his private life. He got my address from a man I had done business with in the Argentine, and I only saw him on the two occasions he came here."

Shand thanked him and let him go.

"That's all for to-night," he said to the inspector. "The ambulance men can come now. We've got all we're likely to get."

"He was giving it to us straight, I suppose?" queried the inspector, with a jerk of his head in the direction in which de Silva had gone. "He seemed a bit glib with his information."

"He was right about the name, anyhow," commented Shand thoughtfully. "He's Eric Conyers right enough. I recognized him myself. It's less than a week since he called on me at the Yard, poor chap."

He stood looking down at the quiet figure lying on the stretcher.

"I say, Fletcher," he said suddenly. "Do you sleep in your wristwatch?"

"No," answered the inspector, with an appreciative glint in his eye, "but there's some that do, I understand. But then, I don't wear a dandy little gold and platinum watch-bracelet like our foreign friend there."

Shand nodded absently. He stood watching the ambulance men as they lifted the stretcher and edged it carefully through the narrow doorway.

"Are you coming?" asked the inspector.

Shand picked up his hat.

"Not at the moment," he said. "I've got another job here first."

He followed the stretcher into the hall, and arrived there just in time to meet Carol.

She had been seen home by Dalberry from the Savoy, where they had spent the evening, but they agreed that it would be wiser not to drive up to the door together, so she had dropped him at the corner of the street and come on alone to the Escatorial.

She was startled to see an ambulance standing at the bottom of the steps. Her taxi drew up immediately behind it and, seized with an indefinable sense of foreboding, she hurried into the hall to find herself confronted by the stretcher-bearers and their grim burden. It was completely covered by a blanket, and her apprehension increased at the sight of the shrouded form.

Behind the little group stood a man whose appearance struck her as vaguely familiar.

He stepped forward at the sight of her.

"Miss Summers, I think," he said. "There is nothing to be alarmed about. There was an accident in the street and they brought the man in here."

There was something comfortingly reassuring in his quiet voice and straightforward, steady eyes.

"Who is it?" she asked anxiously.

"Nobody connected with these flats," he said. "I am sorry you should have come in just at this moment."

He beckoned to the lift-boy, who was standing in the little group on the steps, watching the departure of the ambulance.

"Take Miss Summers up to her flat," he said. "And see her in before you bring the lift down."

Then, to her surprise, he drew her aside, out of earshot of the boy.

"I saw Mr. Mellish to-day," he went on, in a voice so low that it only reached her ears. "He spoke to me about the state of things here. If you are in difficulties at any time, you have only to ring up this number and ask for me—Detective Inspector Shand of New Scotland Yard."

He scribbled a number on a plain card and handed it to her, then, having put her in charge of the lift-boy, went on his way, leaving her with an added sense of security.

CHAPTER XIII

MELLISH was lunching at his club two days later, when he was told that Miss Summers wished to speak to him on the telephone. Moving with surprising quickness for one of his ponderous build, he hurried from the dining-room, and, as he went, he blessed the foresight that had caused him to leave his address with Jervis whenever he was away from his rooms.

"Anything wrong?" he asked, before Carol had time to speak.

"Nothing to make a fuss over," she answered. "But I've had rather a curious interview. I'd like to tell you about it."

"Are you alone this afternoon?"

"Yes. Aunt Irma's lunching out and going on to a lecture. She said she probably wouldn't be back to tea. I was wondering whether you could come round."

"Is it urgent, or can I finish my lunch first? It's a good lunch!"

The fat man's voice was so plaintive that Carol laughed. "My poor dear! You can lunch as slowly as you like, if you'll have your coffee here afterwards. I'll make it for you myself and it will be good! That's the one thing Aunt Irma *has* succeeded in teaching me."

She was as good as her word, and Mellish told her so as they sat over their coffee and cigarettes in her little sitting-room at the Escatorial.

"I'm not sure that you won't make an excellent wife to some one after all," he concluded, as she refilled his cup. "Now, what's it all about?"

Carol regarded him meditatively, a shrewd twinkle in her eyes.

"I suppose you're picturing me as a placid matron in a lace cap, with a bunch of keys in a little bag," she said appreciatively. "I think you must be what they call 'a survival,' Jasper dear."

"I'd rather be a survival than an elderly clothes-peg with a henna top," he retorted stoutly. "That seems to be the best this generation can do in the way of matrons, and the old men are worse. Stop flouting my grey hairs and tell me what excuse you've got for dragging me out of my peaceful and respectable club at this hour of the day."

"You'll apologize for that in a minute," said Carol calmly. "I shouldn't wonder if I was about to make your hair stand on end."

She leaned forward impressively.

"You remember that night at the Terpsychorean?"

"Have I ever been allowed to forget it?" groaned Mellish. "Go on."

"I don't suppose you remember a couple who were dancing there. Captain Bond pointed them out to us."

"Curiously enough, I do," answered Mellish dryly. "I am also perfectly aware of the fact that the murdered man whose photograph has been in the papers for the last two days is the man we saw that night. I, too, read the Daily Press. Don't behave like a writer of cheap detective fiction."

Carol looked frankly disappointed.

"I didn't suppose you'd noticed him at the club," she said. "What a bore you are, Jasper, spoiling all my best effects. All the same, I *will* make you sit up and take notice! I met his dancing partner yesterday."

She had the satisfaction of seeing that she had scored a point. Mellish turned to her with real interest in his eyes.

"Met her! Where?"

"On the landing outside this flat. I had just come in, and, as I got out of the lift, I saw her come out of Mr. de Silva's door. I didn't want to run into him, so I stayed where I was. Besides, they were having the most frantic row, and I didn't feel inclined to burst in on it. He was standing in the doorway and she was screaming, literally screaming, at him. I couldn't see his face, but his voice, when he answered her, was utterly hateful. Jasper, I was bored with him before, but I'm afraid of him now. I didn't know he could be like that."

"What was she saying?" asked Mellish.

There was nothing for Carol to complain of in his attitude now. Her eyes widened and there was a note of horror in her voice as she answered:

"She was accusing him quite openly of having murdered Conyers, the man in the cab. She kept on shrieking 'You foul murderer!' at the top of her voice. It was horrible! I wonder the lift-boy didn't hear her, though he was half-way down to the hall by then."

"What did de Silva say?"

"He was brutal! After all, the poor creature was beside herself. He told her to clear off, and said that if she came near him again he would put the police on to her. He accused her of being drunk. I'm sure she wasn't that."

"Did he say any more?"

Carol's eyes twinkled with mischief.

"I'm sorry to shock your Victorian ears, Jasper dear," she said demurely, "but he called her a common streetwalker. I'm sure she isn't that either," she finished thoughtfully.

Mellish snorted.

"Let me tell you that the Victorians were quite capable of calling a spade a spade, and far better able to recognize one than you are. However, in this instance, I agree with you. There was another accusation that de Silva might have levelled at the lady with justice. As he didn't do so, I think we can take it for granted that he knows very little of her past history."

"What do you mean? Don't tell me that you know all about her too!"

"I know very little except the fact that she has served a term of imprisonment, and that, according to the police, she has run straight ever since. I gather that she's a lady with a good deal of character."

"I like her," said Carol thoughtfully. "At least, I did, after I'd had a chat with her. And I was awfully sorry for her."

Mellish's eyebrows shot up.

"Am I to understand that you broke in on this pleasant little exchange of amenities and invited her to tea?"

"On the contrary, I kept very carefully out of the way while Mr. de Silva was there. Fortunately he went in fairly soon and slammed the door, and I was hesitating as to what to do when I saw the woman flop up against the wall. In another minute she'd have been flat on her back on the carpet. I had to lend a hand."

"She might have been drunk," suggested Mellish.

Carol gazed at him with pitying contempt.

"She might have been, but she wasn't. Anybody could see that she wasn't. She was simply all in. I believe it was only rage and excitement that had kept her on her legs till then. She wasn't fit to be about at all. She must have been terribly fond of that Conyers man!"

"I apologize," said Mellish meekly. "What happened next?"

"I grabbed hold of her and got her to the window on the landing. Fortunately it was open. I must say, she's got plenty of pluck. She pulled herself together and said she was sorry to have made a fool of herself. The funny thing was that she recognized me."

Mellish, remembering how he had tried to keep the fact of Carol's presence at the Terpsychorean from Shand and how signally he had failed, was not surprised.

"Yes?" he said.

"She talked a lot. I think she'd got to a stage when she had to have the whole thing out with somebody. I was terrified that Mr. de Silva would come out of his room, but he didn't. Aunt Irma heard me talking to some one, though, and she was furious when I told her who it was. I had to tell her, because she opened the door and saw me. That was when the whole thing was pretty well over, though."

"You couldn't tell your story more connectedly, I suppose," was Mellish's plaintive comment. "What did the distressed lady tell you exactly?"

"She declares that Conyers told her, more than a week before he was killed, that he had got a hold over de Silva and was going to skin him, as she put it. She is sure, from what he said, that he was going to see de Silva on the night he was murdered. She didn't actually say so, but I suppose he must have been blackmailing him. Anyhow, she is absolutely convinced that de Silva killed him."

"De Silva dined here at the Escatorial in the public dining-room, and was not seen to leave the flat afterwards. He was in bed when the police called to interview him. Besides, the taxi-driver had a good look at the man who got into his cab with Conyers, and I happen to know that they arranged for him to see de Silva passing through the hall here one day and he stated emphatically that he was not the man. No, with the best will in the world, I don't see how anybody is to bring it home to de Silva."

"All the same, I wish you could have seen that poor woman. There was something terribly convincing about her. I can't get her out of my head. I asked her if she knew of any other enemies Conyers might have had, and she said, quite frankly, that there were a good many people who had no cause to love him, but that de Silva was the only person who had anything to gain by his death. She declares that Conyers told her that he had de Silva in the hollow of his hand, and that de Silva would give a good deal for the opportunity to put a knife between his shoulders some dark night. She's beside herself, Jasper. I'm so afraid that she'll do something foolish. He'll be absolutely merciless if she does."

"She didn't say what Conyers's hold over de Silva was, I suppose?"

"She doesn't know. He never told her. I suppose the police are certain that de Silva didn't go out again that night?"

"He can't prove it," Mellish admitted. "But they are inclined to believe his story. You see, he went straight to his flat after dinner. The boy who took him up in the lift has verified that. The porter was in the hall all the evening, and there are always one or two of the boys hanging about. It seems very unlikely that he could have gone out and come in again without being seen by any one."

"The porter isn't in the hall all the time," Carol pointed out. "For one thing, he very often posts the letters himself. I've seen him. It would be possible to wait on the steps until the coast was clear and slip out when the porter's back was turned. You can't see the stairs from the lift."

"It would be very risky, to say the least of it, and, remember, he would have to get back. Say that the porter did go to the post and de Silva waited in the street to see him go, he couldn't possibly be sure that one of the boys wouldn't be in the hall. You can't see inside the hall from the street."

"All the same, he might have risked it and carried it off, through sheer luck," said Carol obstinately. "I don't want to think that he did it. The whole thing's horrible enough without that; but if you'd heard that poor woman, you'd feel as I do, that it can't be all imagination on her part."

"The police have gone into it pretty carefully, I fancy, but it might be worth their while to ascertain the porter's exact movements during that evening, if they haven't already done so. I'll see Shand about it. By the way, he spoke to you the other night, didn't he?"

Carol nodded.

"He was awfully nice. He said he knew you. I've got his telephone number in case I need it, but I don't think there's much fear of that. For one thing, I took the bull by the horns and spoke to Aunt Irma about Mr. de Silva."

"Has he been making a nuisance of himself again?"

"He will lie in wait for me, and yesterday he literally pushed his way into the flat. I'm sure he knew that Aunt Irma was out. At first it was only a case of silly compliments and that sort of thing, and I thought it was just his way of being agreeable. But yesterday—"

Her colour deepened.

"What happened?" snapped Mellish.

"I think he lost his head altogether. I had a hateful time with him, but I made him understand at last that I simply wouldn't be pawed. He saw then that he'd gone too far and tried to make me say I'd forget it and all that sort of thing, but I told him to get out and never speak to me again. He went like a lamb. I think he was afraid I'd tell Aunt Irma. I did, the moment she came in, and she said she'd speak to him."

She laughed rather ruefully.

"The ridiculous thing is that I had all sorts of romantic ideas about him and Aunt Irma. I couldn't imagine what she could see in him, but I really did think they were going to make a match of it. So that it was a complete surprise when I found that I was the attraction."

"Do they seem really intimate with each other?"

"I don't know. You see, he never comes unless he knows I'm alone in the flat. I believe they play bridge at the club together a lot, and Aunt Irma's always going over to his flat with prospectuses and things. She consults him about everything, and I'm sure he's got a hold over her financially in some way."

"I don't care what hold he's got over her," said Mellish emphatically. "I won't have you subjected to annoyance of that sort. The thing's intolerable! I'll wait and see Lady Dalberry myself."

"It'll give the whole show away if you do," Carol reminded him. "She doesn't know that I've been seeing you and Gillie. Honestly, I'm sure it will be all right now I've spoken to her about it. She took it quite well, and said she was awfully sorry he'd been such a fool."

"All the same, I'll see her myself. It's just as well she should know that I've got my eye on things. I don't like the situation at all. You'd better make some other arrangements and get out of this place at once."

"I will if it gets impossible, but I don't believe he'll dare to speak to me again. I told Aunt Irma quite plainly that I wouldn't see him or have anything more to do with him, and she quite saw my point."

"All the same, she may just as well see mine, too," insisted Mellish stubbornly.

He settled himself down comfortably to await Lady Dalberry's return, telling Carol to go out and leave him if she had other engagements. She refused, saying that it was seldom enough that she got him to herself nowadays, and that she was going to make the most of the opportunity.

He was more pleased and flattered than she realized. She had captured his heart in her nursery days, and confirmed bachelor though he was, he liked nothing better than to sit and watch her face light up with interest as he rambled on in his indolent way. And he was worth listening to. Carol was astonished to find how time had flown when Mellish paused suddenly in the middle of a sentence and held up a fat forefinger.

"That sounds like your aunt," he said. "Will she come in here, or do we beard her in her den?"

Carol, who had not heard the front door open, was astonished at the quickness of his hearing. Before she could answer, Lady Dalberry entered the room.

"I came away earlier than I intended," she began. "It was so hot and I had a headache ..."

She stopped at the sight of Mellish hoisting himself out of his chair.

"But this is delightful!" she exclaimed. "We have not seen you for so long."

For a time they talked desultorily, then Mellish firmly broached the subject of de Silva and his unwelcome attentions. He did so with a deliberation combined with a suavity that made Carol's lips twitch. He was so polite and, at the same time, so inexorable.

"I'm sure you will agree with me that this must stop," he finished smoothly.

While he was speaking Lady Dalberry's face had been inscrutable. It was only when she turned to answer him that it flashed into animation.

"I cannot tell you how it has distressed me," she assured him eagerly. "That our little Carol should have been frightened! And I know now how alarmed she must have been by that mad fellow, or she would not have run to you."

There was a hint of malice in her voice, and Carol felt the hot blood rise to her cheeks as she realized the implication. She was being treated like a hysterical schoolgirl. Mellish came to the rescue.

"I should imagine that, as an experience, it was not so much alarming as unpleasant," he commented gently.

"It was unfortunate," corrected Lady Dalberry. "That, I think, is the worst you can say of it. I have spoken to Juan de Silva, and I find he is terribly distressed that he should have made so bad an impression on Carol. He was carried away by his feeling for her and forgot that he was in England, where, if Carol will forgive me, the girls are colder, less mature, than they are in South America. It is difficult for any one with southern blood to understand this. Of course, he had no right to behave as he did. He should have come to me first and told me of his feeling for Carol. He admits this and is greatly distressed. He is very anxious to see Carol and apologize to her in person. I told him that I was afraid he had offended her too deeply for that, and he begged me to intercede for him."

She paused, but Carol made no comment, and she was forced to go on.

"Having lived so long in the Argentine, I can understand a little of his feelings. I know that he did not mean to frighten Carol, and I am sure that, now he understands her feelings, it will not happen again. Like all Latins, his emotions are very strong, and he has never learned to control them. He is in a state almost of despair, and, to tell you the truth, I am afraid for him. It would be a very kind and gracious act if you would see him, Carol."

The girl threw a swift, appealing glance at Mellish.

"I'd much rather not," she said uncomfortably. "I don't want to be horrid, but, honestly, it seems to me waste of time."

"He will be in the depths of despair," said Lady Dalberry. "Everything is so exaggerated with these South Americans. Well do I know it; always we were having trouble with the men on the ranch. They are not like my people. In Sweden they live with their brains; in the Argentine, with their hearts."

She spoke almost regretfully, and Mellish was seized with a suspicion that, of the two, she inclined towards the South American method.

"Carol's right," he said firmly. "An interview with Mr. de Silva now will, at best, be an uncomfortable one, and it can lead to nothing satisfactory for either of them. Better let the matter rest."

"The truth is. Aunt Irma, I don't like Mr. de Silva," said Carol frankly. "I'm sorry, but I've always felt that way about him, long before this happened. Won't you tell him that I don't bear him any ill-will, but I'd rather not see him again? Of course, if we run into each other here, at any time, we shall meet on quite friendly terms, but I'd prefer it if he doesn't try to see me. He has been making rather a nuisance of himself, you know!"

Her words were brave, but she felt horribly embarrassed. It was not easy to say these things about her aunt's friend, and, as she spoke, she saw a swift spasm of anger pass over Lady Dalberry's face. She braced herself for the unpleasant scene that seemed inevitable, but the other woman's voice was quite mild when she answered.

"Of course, if you feel like that about it, my dear, there is nothing more to be said," was her only comment. "But I am sorry, for Juan de Silva's sake."

Carol accompanied Mellish to the door and, at a sign from him, walked with him to the lift. There was something he wanted to ask her, and he wished to make sure that they were out of earshot of Lady Dalberry.

"I suppose you didn't gather the name or address of the distressed lady you interviewed yesterday?" he asked.

"She never told me. You see, we were interrupted just at the end by Aunt Irma."

"How much did you tell your aunt? Not that she is your aunt, by the way. It's difficult to remember that you're not really related to the Dalberrys at all."

Carol gave a little involuntary shudder.

"I'm glad now that I'm not. I'm sorry for her, but I should hate to feel, somehow, that she'd got any real claim on me. I told her as little as I could because I was afraid of what she might repeat to Mr. de Silva. I simply said that I'd found a woman leaning against the wall outside his door, and that, as she seemed to be ill, I had stopped to speak to her, and that then I'd recognized her as some one I'd seen dancing at the Terpsychorean. She asked if I had any idea who she was, and I said that I knew nothing about her except that and the fact that she had been calling on Mr. de Silva. I suggested that she should ask him. That put her off, I think. Anyway she did not ask any more questions, for which I was thankful. I hate lying, and I seem to do nothing else nowadays."

"She didn't connect the woman with the murder?"

"I don't think so, but she evidently thought she was a bad lot. She was furious with her for having dared to speak to me, and said it was a piece of gross impertinence. I explained that, so far as that was concerned, I had done all the speaking in the beginning. The poor thing was too far gone then to say anything."

On leaving the Escatorial Mellish climbed into a taxi and drove to New Scotland Yard. He found Shand in his room.

"I've developed an unholy interest in that vampirish-looking lady who was associated with the murdered man, Conyers," he said. "I remember you alluded to her as the brains of the combination. Can you give me her name and address?" Shand smiled.

"I'm afraid you won't find her a very pleasant companion, Mr. Mellish," he answered. "She's been down here twice, and I'm half inclined to have her watched. She's out for blood, poor thing, and I don't know that I blame her. She got hold of Conyers when he was down and out, and literally dragged him on to his feet again. It couldn't have been an easy job, either, but there's no doubt they'd both been running straight for a long time. And now ..."

He made an expressive gesture with his hand.

"You think there's nothing in her story?"

"I'd give a great deal to believe there was," said Shand frankly. "I'm pretty sure that the Argentino's as crooked as they make 'em, and there's a good deal about his connection with Lady Dalberry that I don't like, but I can find nothing against him. And I'm inclined to accept his story that he was in his flat at the Escatorial at the time the murder was committed."

"You've been into that thoroughly, I suppose?"

"We've ascertained that he went straight to his flat after dinner, and no one saw him either go out or come in from then on. He can't actually prove an alibi, naturally, as he was alone in the flat, but there are too many people in that hall for him to have got in and out undetected."

"Miss Summers made a rather pertinent suggestion," said Mellish thoughtfully. "He might have been watching on the stairs until the coast was clear. I had a look at them myself, and it would be quite possible, if one stood just round the angle of the first bend. It gives a clear view of the hall, too. And the stairs are very little used, I understand."

"He'd have to get back," was Shand's doubtful rejoinder. "Frankly, I don't see how he would do it. You can't see into the hall without going right up the front steps, and any one doing that would be seen to a certainty."

"All the same, it might be worth while to ascertain whether the hall was left empty at any time during the evening."

"It was," Shand admitted. "Between nine and nine-thirty the night-porter went over to the post with some letters belonging to the tenants. On the way back he stopped to speak to one of the porters from the flats opposite. He thinks he was gone about fifteen minutes. Just after he left one of the tenants arrived with some small luggage, and the lift-boy took him up to his flat and had to help with the bags. He remembers the time because he was annoyed at having to do it single-handed in the porter's absence. The other boys were at supper."

"Then, so far as we know, the hall was actually deserted for about fifteen minutes during the evening."

"It was, and, as you say, our man might have got out, but that does not explain how he got in. The porter was sitting by the fire in the hall from then onwards till he went on to the steps and saw the taxi drive up at about eleven-thirty. And de Silva was undoubtedly in his flat when I called."

Mellish heaved a sigh and got to his feet.

"It seems a bit of a deadlock. I should like to see that lady, though. You might give me her name and address. No objection to my having a chat with her, I suppose?"

"None whatever, Mr. Mellish," Shand assured him. "And if you can get anything out of her except vague accusations, I shall be grateful. Mrs. Roma Verrall she calls herself."

He consulted an index card lying at his elbow and wrote the name and address on a bit of paper.

Mellish tucked it into his pocket-book.

"Thanks," he said. "Any further developments?"

"There's this," answered Shand. "We've been through the dead man's effects and discovered a telegram, making an appointment at the Corner House, Piccadilly, at ten o'clock on the night of the murder. He was coming from that appointment when he was killed."

"No chance of tracing the sender of the telegram, I suppose?"

"It was sent from a small office in West Kensington, and, by sheer luck, the clerk remembers the man who handed it in. She describes him as slight and fair, with a perceptible foreign accent. It's getting monotonous."

He gave vent to a short laugh that made Mellish look up quickly.

"In what way?"

"The man who, I'm convinced, was responsible for the death of Smith on board the *Enriqueta* was described by the steward as 'on the thin side, of medium height, with hair so fair that it might have been white.' Piper's description of Strelinski, the man he declares was an associate of Smith's in Buenos Aires, and who, according to him, sailed about the same time as Smith, was as follows: 'Fair, middle-sized, with very light hair. Looked like one of those dance-hall lizards.' The taxi-driver is quite definite about the appearance of the man who got out of his cab on the way to the Escatorial: 'Slim sort of chap, not too tall, with very light hair, almost white.' And now there's this girl at the post office. It all points the same way. If we can lay our hands on this man Strelinski, we shall clear up both murders. Both Smith and Conyers were strangled. It's the old story of the method repeating itself."

"I can only say that I hope you're wrong," said Mellish heavily, "though I must admit that it sounds convincing enough."

Shand stared at him in surprise.

"Lady Dalberry was on board the *Enriqueta* when Smith was killed," went on Mellish gravely. "And this man Conyers was on his way to the block of flats in which she lives when he met his end. I can see nothing to connect her with either event, but, taking into account her connection with de Silva and all that has happened lately, I tell you frankly, I don't like it."

CHAPTER XIV

MELLISH DROVE BACK to his rooms in a very thoughtful mood. So silent was he that Jervis's decorous comments on the weather fell on deaf ears, and that faithful adherent was driven to the conclusion that his fears were at last realized and that his master had contracted the chill that, in Jervis's apprehensive mind, always hung like the sword of Damocles over his head.

"A little hot milk and a drop of cinnamon in it, sir?" he suggested winningly.

Mellish came to himself with a start.

"Good heavens, no!" he exclaimed. "I shall want you to take a letter for me in a minute or two, Jervis."

"Yes, sir, if you're sure you're all right, sir."

"Of course I'm all right! And I should be obliged if you wouldn't treat me as if I were in my dotage. If I want any of your disgusting concoctions I'll ask for them."

"Very good, sir. I have placed the Tantalus in the study, and there is a kettle on the boil now in the kitchen."

He withdrew judiciously, just in time.

Mellish sat down and wrote a note to Mrs. Roma Verrall. In it he asked her to call on him at her earliest convenience, hinting that he wished to see her in connection with the death of Conyers, and suggesting eleven o'clock the next morning as an hour at which she would be sure to find him. Then he rang the bell.

Jervis answered it, carrying a small jug of boiling water which he placed ostentatiously on the writing-table.

"I want you to take this letter," said Mellish. "And, if possible, hand it to the lady yourself. If she is out, leave it in the hands of some one who seems competent to see that she gets it. Say it is important. And take away this object."

He pointed to the offending jug of hot water.

"Very good, sir," answered Jervis meekly, and departed with the letter, leaving the hot water still at Mellish's elbow.

Mellish had dined and had already spent more than two hours browsing happily over a catalogue that had arrived that day from an art dealer in Paris, when Jervis appeared at the door, disapproval written on every line of his usually placid countenance.

"A lady to see you, sir," he said. "In answer to the letter you sent this evening."

Mellish pushed the catalogue aside and got on to his feet.

"Show her in," he said, and stood watching the door with interest.

His visitor came in swiftly, moving with the graceful ease he had noted in her at the Terpsychorean. But whereas, when he first saw her, she was consciously controlling her movements, now the perfect balance of her walk was mechanical and she had the air of one so obsessed by one dominating idea as to be almost unaware of her surroundings. At the supper club, the startling whiteness of her face had been due largely to cosmetics; to-night her pallor was even more pronounced and her eyes more strikingly brilliant, but there was not a trace of make-up on her cheeks and her lips showed grey against her ashen skin. Her clothes were still cheaply effective, but they looked as though she had thrown them on blindly, and Mellish, noting their complete unsuitability to the chilly March evening, guessed that, in her abstraction, she had come out without a coat.

He went forward to meet her and took her hand. It was icy, and he felt her fingers jerk and quiver as he held them. Carol had been right when she said that the woman was almost at the end of her tether.

"It was kind of you to come so soon," he said, and his slow, quiet voice reacted soothingly on her jangled nerves.

As he spoke he drew her to the fire and forced her gently into an armchair.

She sat staring at him, clutching the arms of the chair.

"You said in your letter that it was about Eric," she said, in a voice that was hardly above a whisper, "so I came."

"I ought to explain," answered Mellish, speaking even more slowly than usual. He had a feeling that her brain was hardly capable of taking in extraneous things, so centered was it on one subject. "I happened to meet a friend of mine from New Scotland Yard to-day, and something he told me made me think you could throw some light on this unhappy business. So I ventured to ask you if you would come and see me. I hardly hoped you would act on my letter so promptly. I no longer hold any official position myself, but I think I may promise you that anything you may tell me will receive due consideration at headquarters."

She made a hopeless gesture.

"I've been at them till I'm sick," she exclaimed passionately, "and they won't listen!" Her voice, torn with emotion though it was, was not unpleasing, but as she became more vehement, her cockney accent asserted itself. "Even when I told them what he'd said to me with his own lips the night before he was killed, they put me off. I could see they didn't mean to do anything. And that swine'll get away with it!"

She stared at Mellish with unseeing eyes.

"After the way I've worked for him. Keeping off those beasts that were trying to get him back to his old ways. Fighting for him! And now, all those years gone for nothing and him lying dead!"

She broke down completely and sat huddled in her chair, her face buried in her hands, her shoulders shaking.

Mellish stood and waited quietly till the outburst had spent itself.

"I'm afraid nothing I can say will be of any comfort to you at this moment," he said at last, "but I should like to assure you of my very real sympathy. If you feel equal to telling me exactly what your suspicions are, and why you hold them, I can promise to go into the matter fully with you. Take your time and let me have the whole thing from the beginning. What makes you think that Conyers meant to go to de Silva's flat that night?"

"Because he as good as told me so. As much as a week ago he said that he was on to a good thing. That he'd met a man he'd known out in the Argentine and spotted his little game. Those were his words. And he was going to see to it that he made it worth his while to keep his mouth shut. He wouldn't tell me more, because he knew if it was anything like blackmail I wouldn't stand for it, but I knew him so well I could always see through him, and I wasn't such a fool as not to spot a thing like that. I told him to leave the whole thing alone. You see I was frightened. It was always the way. After he'd been running straight for ever so long, and it seemed as if I was beginning to breathe freely at last, something would crop up and it would take all I'd got to hold him back. And there wasn't an ounce of vice in him! Just weakness and the bad company he'd got into when he was a lad. If they'd only left him alone! I always knew when he was up to something he didn't want me to know. He'd sort of half tell me things and I'd have to guess the rest. But I'd always get round him in the end. This was the first time he really got away with it.

I wish to God I'd stuck to him a bit more closely that last week!"

"You think he did go so far as to threaten the man?"

"I know it. If he was alive, you might cut my tongue out before I'd so much as whisper, but I'm past caring now. All I want is to see that devil get what he deserves."

"What makes you think it is this man de Silva?"

"Because of what happened the night the Terpsychorean was raided. Of course the police didn't hold us, seeing why we were there, and, properly speaking, we should have gone home together after the raid. Instead of which Eric went to the door with me and told me he'd follow later. I didn't think anything of that, knowing he might have an appointment with one of the inspectors. When he did get home later he told me that story about this man he'd spotted. Said he was going under another name and no one but him knew what his real name was, and that he'd practically agreed to settle up. He said he'd caught him climbing out of the window and that he gave himself away somehow then. He wouldn't tell me the man's name, but he did say that he'd got a photo of him in a suitcase he left at his old lodgings, and that if he showed it to this man he'd come over with anything he liked to ask. Well, I didn't like it and I tried to get him to drop the whole thing, but there was too much money in it and I couldn't get him to listen. I worried myself sick over it, but he'd got so that if I spoke about it he'd shut up like a clam and I couldn't do anything."

"Did he show you this photograph he spoke of?" asked Mellish.

"He hadn't got it. It's at some lodgings we stayed in nearly six months ago. I was taken ill, and the doctor sent me to the country for a month. What with my lodgings there and doctor's bills and all, we were pretty hard up, and one night Eric flitted, without paying the rent. He left a suitcase and a trunk behind, and, though he was always talking of going back and settling up and fetching them, he never did. He was always careless about things like that."

"Are they still there, do you think?"

"I know they are. I met a friend the other day who lodges there, and she told me the landlady was holding them for the rent."

"We'll have a look at that photograph. I still don't see, however, what makes you connect all this with de Silva."

"One of the plain-clothes men told me that de Silva had got away through a window at the back and that they'd just missed him. They were pretty sick about it, too. Remembering what Eric had said about spotting the man getting out of a window, I made sure that de Silva was the man. And I know Eric saw him the day after the raid. He let that out when he wasn't thinking, and then shut up and wouldn't say any more. But the day he was murdered he told me he was going up that evening to collect what was due to him. I tried to stop him and told him to let well enough alone, but he laughed and said that when I'd seen what he was going to bring home to me that night I'd sing another song. And then he went off, and that was the end."

She spoke simply, but with an utter hopelessness that was tragic. For her, Mellish realized, it *was* the end. After all her efforts to keep the man straight she had failed, and, with that failure, had lost all that made life worth living.

"You did your best," he said gently. "I wish he had listened to you."

"I don't know," she said, in a dull voice. "I can't stand this climate and I'd been seedy for a long time, and, perhaps, I wasn't as much on the spot as I should have been. I feel now that I didn't try hard enough. But it was the money that tempted him. We'd had a bad winter, what with me being ill and everything."

"You can remember nothing else he said that might give us some clue as to the identity of this man?"

She shook her head.

"As I said, he was very close about the whole thing, because he knew I didn't like it. But the man was de Silva, you can take my word for it. I tell you I know it. I was sure enough of it before, but when they told me about the cab driving up to the Escatorial like that, I was dead certain. De Silva was the man he spotted at the Terpsychorean that night, and it was de Silva that did him in."

"You know that de Silva declares he was in his flat all that evening? The police have been into it pretty thoroughly, and he certainly was never seen to go out."

She looked at him with a hint of humour in her haggard eyes.

"What's an alibi? If you've been to the Yard they'll have told you that I've been in trouble. I've made a clean break with the old lot now, but there was a time when I could have got a dozen witnesses to say they'd seen me in any old place. And me never having set a foot in it! If that fellow wanted to get out without being seen, he'd do it. Besides, I don't say he did it himself. If they get this fair man they're talking such a lot about, let them find out who paid him! Eric got into that cab to go to de Silva's, that I'm sure, and he never got there."

"If what Conyers hinted to you is true, it was certainly to de Silva's advantage that he didn't," said Mellish slowly. "He might conceivably have made an appointment with Conyers and, instead of keeping it himself, have sent this man to meet him and bring him to the flat. Conyers would have gone with him, suspecting nothing. It's a far-fetched theory, though."

"It's plain enough to me," said the woman wearily. "But I might as well talk to the moon for all the notice any one will take of me. They've been ready enough to listen to me at the Yard before now, and I've never given them a tip yet that wasn't straight, and they know it. When they turned me down there I went to de Silva and told him straight what I thought of him. He tried to bluff me all right, with his talk of the police, but when I saw his face I knew. He was scared stiff, for all his talk, and, if he'd dared, I should have gone the way of Eric. Little I'd care!" she finished bitterly.

She rose to her feet with difficulty and stood clutching the mantelpiece, her whole body shaking uncontrollably.

"I'd better go," she said. "You're like the rest. I might have known it."

Mellish faced her squarely.

"You're wrong there," he assured her, with a sincerity she could not doubt. "I don't say that I accept your theory, but I'm quite prepared to consider it. So much so that I'm going to try to put you in the way to prove it. Can you get hold of this photograph you spoke of? I'll settle whatever is owing to the landlady who is holding the trunks. Does she know you? I mean, would she give up the things to you on receipt of the money?"

She nodded.

"Eric and I lodged there together till I went to the country. And, anyway, she's the sort that would give them up to any one if she saw the colour of their money. I wonder she hasn't sold them before."

"Do you know how much is due to her?"

"Ten pounds would cover it. I don't know to a shilling."

Mellish opened a drawer and took out a packet of notes. He counted fifteen.

"Here you are," he said. "This will give you a margin. Now I want you to go there as soon as you can, and if you can find the photograph, bring it to me here. You can leave it with my man if I'm out. Have you spoken of this to any one?"

"Not about the photograph. I'd have told the police, if they'd have listened to me, but they didn't give me a chance. Unless Eric spoke to any one of it, no one knows about it."

She stuffed the notes into her bag and prepared to go.

"You'll feel better about the whole thing now that you are doing something definite," he said kindly. "If we do bring this home to de Silva it will only be with your assistance, and you won't help us by brooding over it unnecessarily. Try to get a good night's rest and, if you can, keep your mind off it till to-morrow."

She took his outstretched hand mechanically.

"I can sleep all right," she murmured. "It's the dreams I mind."

Mellish, his keen eyes on hers, caught her wandering glance and held it.

"That stuff you take isn't doing the dreams any good," he said. "Take my advice and cut it out. We're going to need your brains, if there's anything in this. Keep them clear for Conyers's sake."

For a moment she was nonplussed, then, with a short laugh, she stretched out her hand and stared at the twitching fingers.

"No wonder you spotted it," she said. "Any fool can see I'm all to pieces. It's only this last week. I gave it up six years ago, but when they told me about Eric I had to have something. I'll try to drop it, so long as I can be of use, but I won't promise more than that. And you can trust me to get the photo."

It was close on midnight when she left Mellish's rooms, and he had imagined that she would go straight home and set about her search for the photograph in the morning. Astute though he was, he had not reckoned with the fact that he was dealing with a woman whose state of mind was not normal at the best, and who was still under the influence of the stuff with which she had been drugging herself ever since Conyers's death. She left him with her thoughts intent on the task he had given her, and she proceeded, blindly and instinctively, to carry it out.

Her mind was centred on her loss and the urgent need to avenge Conyers's death. Until that need was satisfied she would know no rest. But there was another influence at work in her clouded brain, an influence of which she had given Mellish no inkling, and that was fear. She had spoken only the truth when she said she would be glad to die; but she was afraid, for all that. There was a moment, during her interview with de Silva, when she knew she had gone too far, and in that second the expression on his face had terrified her. She had not been exaggerating when she said that she knew he would have killed her if he could, and ever since, hardly realizing it, she had been on her guard.

She was no sooner in the street than she cast an instinctive, furtive glance round her. She felt, rather than saw, a dark figure detach itself from the shadows on the other side of the road and slip silently across behind her. Twice she stopped, pretending to tie her shoe, and each time the shadow slowed down until she moved on again. Never did it pass her. With fear clutching at her heart she hurried on until she reached the reassuring glare of Piccadilly Circus. There, not daring to glance behind her, she boarded an omnibus. She was barely seated before a man jumped on and ran so quickly up the steps on to the top that she had no opportunity to see his face.

At South Kensington she got down and, going into the Tube, took a ticket for Earl's Court. Two or three belated theatre-goers followed her to the ticket office, and she was conscious of a man among them, but again she failed to catch a glimpse of his face. By sheer luck the lift doors were just shutting and she slipped in a second before they closed, and was borne down secure in the knowledge that her pursuer, if he existed, had not had time to follow her. When she stepped out at the bottom she could hear the other lift descending, and knew that in another moment she would be trapped. Instead of following the little crowd to the platform she turned and ran for the stairs, and was well on her way up them before the second lift had disgorged its passengers.

She emerged, panting, into the street, and literally hurled herself into a taxi that had just set down a fare at the station entrance. As she opened the door she told the driver to go to Victoria, the first name that occurred to her, and he swung round and down Onslow Place before she was properly in her seat. She peered through the little window at the back, but could see no sign of any pursuit. A group of people were entering the station, but she could see no one coming out, and she felt satisfied that, if any one had been following her, she had succeeded in putting him off the scent.

She put her head out of the window and gave the driver the address of Conyers's old lodgings. He had some difficulty in finding the right number in a dingy street off Tottenham Court Road, and there was a further delay while he fumbled for change for one of Mellish's pound notes, but the street was reassuringly empty, and while she stood waiting, her finger on the bell, for the door to open, not a soul passed down it.

The landlady, whose lodgers had a habit of forgetting their keys and returning in the small hours, opened the door herself and poked her head suspiciously round it.

"Oh, it's you," she said sourly. "And about time, too! I ain't got no bed for you, so you needn't think it, not till you've settled up what you owe me. If you haven't got it, you can just take yourself off, that's all!"

Mrs. Verrall pushed her way into the dingy passage.

"I haven't come to stay," she answered curtly.

It did not take long to settle with the woman, once she had actually set eyes on the money.

"The trunk's in the back parlour," she said, in answer to Mrs. Verrall's question. "I couldn't have it cluttering up the bedroom. You're surely not going to take it away at this time of night?"

"Where's the suitcase?"

"With the trunk, of course. What d'you think I'd done with it? Popped it? You'll want a cab if you're going to take the lot."

"I'll send for them to-morrow. There's something I want out of the suitcase. The rest can wait."

The woman led the way into a stuffy little room off the hall and lit a flickering gas jet.

"You must have wanted it pretty badly to come at this time," she remarked, eyeing her visitor's movements inquisitively.

Mrs. Verrall did not answer. She was on her knees by the suitcase, feverishly unstrapping it. At that moment the sound of a bell came pealing from the lower regions, and, with a muttered curse on lodgers in general, the landlady went to open the front door, reluctantly leaving her visitor to her own devices.

It did not take Mrs. Verrall long to find the shabby writing-case she was looking for. She sat back on her heels and turned the contents on her lap.

Among a litter of old letters were half a dozen photographs. She knew most of them by sight, and discarded them by the simple process of pitching them on the floor. Then she came on the one she was seeking.

It was a group of three men. Two of them she recognized as old acquaintances of Conyers whom she had met in his company; the third, a slight, fair man, with well-cut, rather effeminate features, she had never seen before.

She sat studying it preparatory to putting it in her bag. So absorbed was she that she did not notice the landlady's heavy tread as she descended to the basement, or the faint creak, immediately afterwards, of a loose board in the passage. She was taken completely unawares when a hand closed over her throat from behind and she was jerked violently backwards with her head against the knees of her assailant.

She struggled in vain to free herself, tearing at the iron fingers which sank inexorably, deeper and deeper, into her throat.

Then suffocation overcame her; there was a sound like the beating of a thousand drums in her ears; strange lights, that seemed to penetrate agonizingly to her very brain, danced in front of her eyes. Then the torture ended mercifully in a great wave of utter darkness.

CHAPTER XV

JERVIS HAD CLOSED the door on Mrs. Verrall with a distinct sensation of relief. She was not the sort of person he was accustomed to see in his master's company, and the more he thought about her the less he liked her. He had formed his own opinion of the type of lodging house to which he had delivered Mellish's note, and Mrs. Verrall was exactly the kind of lady he had expected to find there. Incidentally, her deshabille had been a good deal more pronounced when she had issued from her room in answer to her landlady's raucous summons than he cared to contemplate, and her reception of Mellish's letter had been hysterical, to say the least of it.

His manner was portentous as he shot the bolts home on the front door after her departure. Then, having ascertained that his master was supplied with all that he required, he made his way to bed, acutely conscious of the fact that, owing to the intrusion of this undesirable woman, he had lost nearly an hour of well-earned rest.

He was awakened out of his first sleep by the insistent ringing of the telephone bell.

His first action was to look at his watch. The hands pointed to five-minutes to two. He shrugged into a dressing-gown and made his way down the passage to the hall. To his surprise his master was before him, and had already taken the receiver off the hook.

"Hullo! That you, Carol?" he heard him say.

There was a pause during which Jervis hovered, uncertain whether to wait or go back to his room. Then he discovered that Mellish had forgotten his slippers, and was standing in his bare feet on the cold parquet of the hall. He decided to wait.

"Mrs. Verrall? Yes. You haven't got it?" There was relief rather than disappointment in his voice. He had made sure that it was Carol on the telephone, and the thought had brought him out of bed at a run.

"You were what? Mercy on us! I had no idea you'd go to-night or I should have suggested your waiting till to-morrow. Where are you? Very well, I'll come now."

He hung up the receiver and, turning, caught sight of Jervis's appalled countenance in the background.

"I'm going out, and I don't know quite what time I shall be back. Get to bed, Jervis; I shan't need you."

Jervis was engaged in facing this abrupt re-entry of Mrs. Verrall into his well-ordered life.

"Can I get you a cab, sir?" he said feebly.

"I'll pick one up as I go. Don't sit up for me."

"You'll put on your slippers, sir," he begged, obsessed by the sight of his master's unprotected toes.

"Since when have I been in the habit of going out in my night clothes? Pull yourself together, Jervis!"

It was half-past two before Mellish reached Mrs. Verrall's lodgings. She had evidently been watching for him from the window, for she opened the door to him herself. She was dressed as he had seen her last, but she had removed her hat, and her hair was rough and disordered. She looked utterly exhausted.

"Come in here," she said, speaking in a curious, hoarse voice. "They're all in bed. We shall have to be quiet."

He followed her into a depressing dining-room in the middle of which stood a table covered with a stained cloth and still littered with the remains of supper. As he closed the door behind him she seized his arm and clung to it convulsively. She was trembling violently.

Mellish put his arm round her shoulders and led her to a chair. Then he sat down opposite to her and took both her hands in his.

"There, there," he said reassuringly. "It's all over now and you're quite safe. You can trust me to see that you're properly looked after in future."

"I've lost the photo," she exclaimed piteously, almost as though she expected him to scold her. "He took it. ... I did my best!"

She put her hand to her throat and, for the first time, Mellish noticed the purple marks which were already beginning to darken into bruises.

"Good God!" he exclaimed, shocked out of his usual imperturbability. "The brute must have half-strangled you!"

She nodded.

"It hurts," she told him childishly. "And I'm afraid I don't know where to go!"

"Don't let that worry you," he said. "I'll see that you are protected. Try to tell me all about it."

She was shaken and confused, but the whole thing was still so vividly impressed on her mind that, by degrees, he got a connected account out of her.

It appeared that the landlady had found her lying on the floor, and had done her best to bring her round. It was some time before she realized her surroundings, and, when she did, her throat was so sore that she could hardly speak. Meanwhile the landlady was vociferous in her associations that she had seen no one, and that she was sure that only the lodgers were in the house when she went down to the basement after letting in the latecomer who had rung the bell while Mrs. Verrall was opening the suitcase. This she declared to be a woman who lodged in the third floor.

"Went straight upstairs to her room, she did," she insisted. "I see her with me own eyes before I went downstairs. Besides, she wouldn't do a thing like that. Whoever done it must 'ave got in after I left the 'all."

Mrs. Verrall was convinced that the woman was lying, and that she had let in a man, not a woman, as she declared. He had no doubt bribed her to go downstairs and stay there until she heard him leave the house.

"She'd do anything for money," she assured Mellish. "Besides, she'd never have left me like that, once her curiosity was aroused. She's far too inquisitive, and she was mad keen to see what I was after before the door bell rang. She was terrified for fear I should go to the police, and tried to make me promise not to. She knew her story was too thin to be believed. How he tracked me, I don't know. I could have sworn I'd thrown him off."

"Don't distress yourself about the loss of the photograph," said Mellish kindly. "You've seen it, which is half the battle. Can you describe the third man in the group?"

Her connection with Scotland Yard had taught her to be accurate, and she was able to give Mellish a very clear idea of what the man in the photograph was like. It tallied admirably with that of Shand's suspect, Strelinski.

"You've helped us more than you realize," Mellish assured her. "Now, about yourself. Will you feel safe here for another few hours? Is your landlady trustworthy?"

"She's all right. She and her husband are very decent people. They won't let any one in if I tell them not to."

"Very well, then. Will you go to your room now and try to get some rest? Which floor are you on?"

"I'm on the top, and the door's a good one with a stout lock. I shall be all right to-night, but I must get away to-morrow. I'm frightened."

"I'll see to that. I promise you'll be out of this and in a safe place by lunch time. If it's any comfort to you, I don't think the man meant to kill you. I fancy he's got enough on his conscience, and isn't inclined to take any further risk. He's got what he was after, and I fancy he'll let you alone in future."

Mellish watched her go up the staircase, and waited in the hall till he heard her door close, then he let himself softly out of the house. A prowling taxi passed him when he was half-way down the street, but he ignored it and waited until he came to a rank before getting into a cab. He was taking no risks after the story he had just heard.

At seven o'clock he rang up Dalberry, and by eight the two men were breakfasting together. While they were eating, Mellish gave Dalberry a short account of the events of the night before.

"Can you undertake to find a temporary home for Mrs. Verrall until this blows over?" he finished. "She ought to be got out of London, and if you've got a nice, motherly farmer's wife up your sleeve who'd take her in for a bit, produce her. Then we'll settle how to get her there."

"I can do that for you. Not a farmer's wife, as it happens, but one of the lodge-keepers. She asked me the other day if I'd mind if she let her room to an artist in the summer, and I know there's no one there at present. She's a thorough good sort, and can be trusted to fuss over your Mrs. Verrall and make her comfortable."

"Has she got a man on the premises, in case of any possible trouble?"

"Her son. One of the gamekeepers, an enormous chap who'd be equal to tackling any one. Give them a hint that she's to be looked after and they'll be as good as a body-guard."

Mellish's next move was to go with Dalberry to Scotland Yard. There they interviewed Shand, who showed considerable interest in this new development.

"Funny how our fair friend goes on cropping up," he said thoughtfully. "I've no doubt what Mrs. Verrall's description would have been if she'd managed to catch a glimpse of her assailant. I can understand his attack on Mrs. Verrall, but I'm blessed if I can see what he wanted to put Smith out of the way for. I wish I could get on to the link between this Conyers business and the affair on the *Enriqueta*."

"Conyers was removed because he knew too much," suggested Mellish. "It looks very much as if something of the kind may have happened in the case of Smith."

Shand nodded.

"I've been of the opinion all along that Smith did not know that his assailant was on board the boat," he said. "I shall always believe that he stumbled on him just before he was murdered. As you say, he probably signed his own death warrant when he did so. Everybody who knew him agreed that he was too loose-tongued to keep the fact to himself if he had a friend on Board, and he seems to have stated several times that he knew no one. What beats me is the length to which Strelinski seems to have been prepared to go rather than risk the discovery of his identity. The man must have a good deal on his conscience!"

"Is nothing known against this man Strelinski?" asked Mellish.

Shand smiled.

"We're taking a good deal for granted in assuming that it is Strelinski," he reminded him. "Personally, I've a curious conviction that it is, but I've nothing to go on but a chance remark of Long Peter's. As a matter of fact, we were in communication with the Buenos Aires people on another matter some time ago, and I took the opportunity to make a few inquiries. They knew nothing of any one of that name, and though they had more than one person on their books answering to the very vague description we were able to give them, there seemed to be no one who fitted into our little puzzle. I can't understand this fellow's being willing to risk his neck rather than face exposure."

"His neck's not in much danger at present," Mellish reminded him. "He's covered his tracks very neatly so far. What about de Silva? Nothing has transpired in that direction, I suppose?"

"Nothing. He's apparently leading the ordinary life of a well-to-do man about town who dabbles in little business ventures on the side. He's running a Beauty Specialist place, the Onyx, and he's put that man Bond in as manager, but there's nothing wrong with the show, so far, and, what's more, he seems to be making it pay. Probably he's trying to get back his losses on the Terpsychorean."

"He dropped a lot over that, I imagine?"

"A pretty penny, I should think. He'd barely got it going when the blow fell. Why he was such a fool as to think that he could put that gambling stunt over, I can't think. He might have known that that sort of thing always gets given away sooner or later, generally by the people who are most nervous of being caught. They can't keep their tongues still. Now, about Mrs. Verrall."

It did not take the three men long to complete their plans for her protection, with the result that, soon after half-past ten, an elderly woman, presumably a friend of the landlady's, was seen to go down the area steps of Mrs. Verrall's lodgings. Shortly after eleven a taxi drove up to the house and Mellish climbed ponderously out. When the door opened he lingered for some minutes in conversation with the landlady, standing in full view of the street, an unmistakable figure in his heavy, well-cut overcoat. Then he went in and the door closed behind him.

Ten minutes later he came out, carrying a large suitcase and accompanied by a woman, obviously Mrs. Verrall. She wore the dress and hat she had hurried out in the night before, with the addition of a heavy veil and a bulky, if inexpensive, imitation fox fur, which she held closely up to her chin. She and Mellish got into the cab and drove away.

Almost immediately the driver of a taxi that was standing outside a cabman's eating-house on the other side of the road issued from the shop, having evidently just finished his lunch, mounted his box and drove away in the direction Mellish and his companion had taken.

When Dalberry, ten minutes later, swung round the corner, driving his own car, the street was empty. Mrs. Verrall had been watching for him, and it did not take her a second to dart across the pavement and into the closed motor. She also wore a veil and had with her a small suitcase. She sat well back from the windows and did not uncover her face till the car was clear of London and spinning along the straight country road.

By two o'clock that afternoon she was safely established at one of the Berrydown lodges, and Dalberry was already on his way back to town.

Meanwhile Mellish had deposited his charge and her luggage at a respectable boarding-house near Victoria Station, kept by an ex-sergeant of police. The driver of the taxi that had followed them did not stop, though he slowed down as he passed the house and took a careful note of the number. Mellish looked after him with a twinkle in his eye; he had not missed the man's sudden diminution of speed, and he knew that a plain-clothes detective at the other end would by now have reported to the Yard and handed in the number of the cab.

He said good-bye to his companion, slipping a note into her hand as he did so, and drove away. Though he kept a sharp look-out he could see no sign of any one watching the house. All the same, he hoped devoutly that the follower would think it worth while to return and ascertain that the lady Mellish had chaperoned so carefully did not leave the premises. If he did decide to do so, Mellish felt quite at ease as to the result, the lady in question having already divested herself of her borrowed garments and settled down in the kitchen to prepare lunch for her boarders, regaling her husband with the story of her adventures the while.

Late that evening he was rung up by Shand.

"Any result?" he asked.

Shand's voice was grim as he answered.

"We've been properly sold," he said. "We've traced the taxi all right. A police constable found it abandoned in a side street in Pimlico at six o'clock this evening. It had been stolen from outside a pub early this morning, and the owner had already reported the loss at the local police station. I can't blame my man. His instructions were to take the number of the cab and he carried them out, but, since I've seen his report, I've been kicking myself for not taking better precautions."

"Did he manage to get a sight of the driver?"

"He did," answered Shand bitterly. "And he describes him as slight and fair. Looked like a foreigner. He noticed him sitting in the eating-house. It's our fair friend, right enough, and he's playing this game single-handed. We could have taken him this morning, and we opened our fingers and let him slip through."

CHAPTER XVI

FOR SOME DAYS Carol had seen nothing of de Silva, and she had begun to feel safe in the conviction that he had definitely ceased his unwelcome attention. Lady Dalberry had crossed the landing to his flat on more than one occasion, but he had not set foot across her threshold—at any rate, when Carol was at home. In consequence the girl was completely taken aback when her aunt opened the attack again at breakfast one morning.

"I want to speak to you about that poor Juan de Silva," she said. "Don't you think you have punished him enough?"

Carol stared at her in astonishment. "I thought we'd settled all that," she said. "It's ridiculous to talk of my punishing him. I simply don't want to see him any more. I thought he understood that."

"He did, and it hurt him terribly. Surely he has suffered enough, Carol. And the whole situation is impossible. Apart from the fact that he is an old and valued friend of mine, this foolish quarrel puts me in a very difficult position. I do not like to have to remind you that this flat is my home as well as yours, and that I have a right to receive my friends in it. Juan de Silva is looking after some of my business interests, and it is necessary that we should see each other. It would make life easier and pleasanter for all of us if you would consent to forget the past and give him the chance he asks to right himself in your eyes. He is very fond of you, my child, and he knows now that he can expect nothing in return."

"If he's really as fond of me as you say," said Carol miserably, "surely it would be better for him not to see me. I'm sorry that I can't like him, but there it is, Aunt Irma, and I can't help it. As for his coming to the flat, I told you that, provided he did not come to see me, I had no objection. I'm prepared to be pleasant to him if we do meet, but I can't see any reason why we should run into each other. After all, you've got your rooms and I've got mine. We needn't interfere with each other."

Lady Dalberry smiled.

"My little Carol," she said gently. "Do you really think that he would come to the flat at all under those conditions? I have told you that he cares for you and that his pride has been bitterly hurt. I have known him for many years now, and I have never seen him so humiliated. Only a very young and inexperienced girl could imagine that a man of this type would accept the sort of compromise you offer. Be generous, my child, and set his mind at ease."

"What do you want me to do?" asked Carol helplessly. "Give him a chance to plead with you himself. It is the only thing he asks, to set himself right with you. You will find him quite reasonable. He knows now that you will never return his feeling for you, and I have told him that, attached though I am to him, I should never give my consent to a match between you. You are not suited to each other in temperament, and he is not, and never could be, of your world. All he asks now is your friendship. If you would see him it would be more than generous, it would be merciful."

Carol felt trapped, but she made one last effort to resist.

"I can't see what good it would do. Honestly, Aunt Irma, it would be far better to leave things as they are."

Lady Dalberry sighed.

"I cannot force you, my dear, and, if you feel so strongly about it, I will not try. But I do feel that, in fairness to him, you ought to hear what he has to say."

"There's nothing he can say that will make any difference. It isn't that I bear him any grudge; it's simply that I don't want to have any more to do with him. I wish he would understand that."

"That is hardly a message you can expect me to give him. It would be too cruel. If that is really how you feel, I think that you should tell him so yourself as mercifully as possible." Carol realized suddenly that there could be but one end to this unprofitable discussion.

"If you make such a point of it, I will see him," she said. "But it will be a very uncomfortable interview for both of us, and I would much rather have avoided it."

Lady Dalberry rose and came to Carol's side. For a moment the girl thought she was going to kiss her, and it dawned on her that her aunt must have felt very strongly indeed on the subject of her break with de Silva. For an emotional woman Lady Dalberry was singularly undemonstrative, and she and Carol had never been on kissing terms. Even now she went no further than to lay her hand on the girl's shoulder, but there was real feeling in her voice as she answered:

"That is generous of you, Carol. I am sure you will not regret it, and you will find that my poor Juan is not so black as you have been painting him in your imagination. May I tell him that you will see him this evening?"

"Only if you are going to be here yourself," said Carol, with unusual firmness. "And he must understand, please, that I will never see him when you are out."

"He knows that already. I have told him that I will not permit you to receive him in my absence. But you must see him alone this once, my dear. I shall be in my own sitting-room next door, so there will be no breach of the proprieties."

There was a hint of sarcasm in her voice that was not lost on Carol.

"I will see him," she answered quietly, "but only if you are in the flat."

"I am not going out at all this evening. About nine o'clock, then, and he can come in to me for a little business talk afterwards."

All that day the shadow of her coming interview with de Silva hung over the girl. It was ridiculous, she told herself, to feel nervous, and she realized that Lady Dalberry's covert sneer at what she no doubt considered a troublesome attack of prudery on the girl's part was not unjustified. All the same, there was an atmosphere about the whole thing that she did not like, and she was angrily conscious that her hand had been forced very skilfully. She waited for him in her little sitting-room that evening with a restlessness that was half irritation, half dread.

He entered with a diffidence that in another man she would have found disarming. He was evidently wretchedly nervous and wholly bent on conciliating her. She noticed that he left the door open behind him.

"It was very kind of you to see me," he said gently, making no attempt to take her hand. "It is more than I dared to hope for."

"Aunt Irma said that you wished to see me. I don't want to be horrid, Mr. de Silva, but honestly I think it is waste of time. It would have been better to have left things as they were."

She spoke brusquely, partly from sheer embarrassment and part-ly because she could not control her instinctive dislike of the man.

"I know," he answered. "You were persuaded against your will, and I am very grateful to you for giving me a chance to justify myself. I will not keep you long now or trouble you in any way in the future."

He paused, and she waited in silence. There seemed nothing she could say.

"I behaved very badly," he went on at last. "I see that now, but I ask you to believe that I could not help it. I suppose this is hardly the time to say it, but I have loved you ever since I first saw you in this flat nearly a month ago. I have hoped that perhaps, some day, you might see in me something more than just a casual friend of your aunt's. I see now that there was no foundation for my hopes, and I have heard, what I did not know until the other day, that you are one of the richest women in England and destined to move in a very dif-ferent world to a humble person like myself. Your aunt has made me understand this very clearly now, but, believe me, Miss Summers, I did not know it then. In my ignorance I had hoped to ask you one day to be my wife. That is my only excuse for my folly."

In spite of the stilted, almost theatrical wording of his little speech, it rang true, and at the end it came near to achieving dig-nity. Much as she disliked him, Carol could not refuse to accept his apology.

"I'm dreadfully sorry," she said sincerely. "My money hasn't an-ything to do with it, of course. It's just that it seems, somehow, im-possible to think of you in that way. Please try to put the idea out of your head altogether. I know I could never care for you in that way."

"I know," he said gently. "I see now that I was a fool. I do not know England well, and in my country things are different. With us love is undisciplined; it is swift and passionate. Here marriage is a thing to be considered calmly, with consideration."

There was a touch of derision in his tone that stung Carol.

"I'm afraid my answer would have been the same, whatever country we had been in, Mr. de Silva," she said decisively.

He was quick to see that he had struck a false note.

"But you have forgiven me?" he insisted. "That is all that matters now. We are friends?"

He held out his hand as he spoke, and Carol took it reluctantly.

"We are as much friends as we shall ever be," she said, knowing her words to be ungracious, but unable to control her antipathy to the man.

He bowed over her hand.

"It is more than I deserve," he answered smoothly, "and I am not ungrateful, believe me. But you were more generous to Lord Dalberry, Miss Summers."

Carol stiffened.

"I don't understand, Mr. de Silva."

"Your English standards are strange to me, but his offence was surely greater than mine, and he was more quickly forgiven."

"Lord Dalberry ..." began Carol hotly, then pulled herself up with an effort. She had been on the point of betraying her knowledge of the plot against Dalberry—a plot engineered, she was now convinced, by the man who had almost trapped her so neatly into an admission. She had a sudden inkling of his true object in forcing this interview, and she blessed the instinct that had warned her just in time.

"Lord Dalberry is an old friend," she went on coldly. "As you yourself pointed out that night, Mr. de Silva, he was hardly to be blamed for what happened. You made excuses for him, if you remember, and I was sorry afterwards, when I heard his explanation, that I had allowed my temper to get the better of me and refused to listen to them."

For a moment he was taken aback, then he recovered himself swiftly.

"I am glad he was able to convince you," he answered. "I did my best. I hope I was right and that your generosity has not been misplaced."

There was no mistaking the insolence of his manner now. Carol, her temper now well under control, watched him with interest. She was convinced that he was not idly jeopardizing his own cause. He was working with a definite object in view, that of making her angry enough to reveal how much she knew.

"I don't think there is likely to be any further misunderstanding between us," she said quietly. "We have known each other all our lives, you know."

"If you will forgive me, Miss Summers, those are the people one very often knows least well. I have a feeling that Lord Dalberry must have made an even better case out for himself than I did when I tried to help him."

He waited, his keen eyes on hers and a derisive smile on his lips, but she did not take up the challenge and he was obliged to continue.

"I should be interested to hear his explanation of how he came to find himself in such a condition in the company of a lady," he insinuated.

"You must ask him yourself, Mr. de Silva," she answered. "You were present, and I understand that he was found by the police in a room belonging to you in the club, so that he no doubt feels he owes you an apology."

He raised his eyebrows in surprise.

"A room belonging to me? I had a part share in the club, unfortunately for me, but my connection with it was purely financial. I had no room there, and I had no idea, until the night of the raid, that Bond was using the club for nefarious purposes. Bond is one of my little problems, Miss Summers. He is a harmless creature in his way, and I cannot make up my mind to abandon him altogether. He would simply drift into the gutter. But the truth is that he cannot run straight. It was not easy to find a position for him where he would be kept out of mischief."

"From what my aunt tells me, he seems to be running the Onyx very well," said Carol, only too thankful that the conversation had shifted to a less dangerous topic.

De Silva shrugged his shoulders.

"He will do well there so long as temptation does not come his way. If he fails me again he will have to go."

He paused for a moment, then went on:

"You have been most generous, Miss Summers, both to me and Lord Dalberry. I only hope he feels as grateful as I do."

He moved towards the door.

"I think Lady Dalberry is anxious to see me about some shares she is interested in. I suppose I shall find her in her room?"

"She said she would be waiting for you. I want to see her for a moment myself, then I'll leave you to talk business."

She rose to leave the room, but, to her surprise, de Silva rather clumsily barred the way.

"I wonder if you will forgive me if I ask you to let me see her first," he said, with a glance at his watch. "I have an appointment I must keep, and I can only give her a few minutes."

The sight of him standing between her and the door made Carol feel uneasy.

"That's all right, Mr. de Silva," she said. "I only want to ask her a question about dinner to-night. I won't keep her."

He was obliged to stand aside, and she went swiftly down the passage to Lady Dalberry's sitting-room. To her surprise it was empty.

"My aunt must be in her bedroom," she said. "If you'll wait here I'll go and fetch her."

Before he could stop her she had gone down the passage to Lady Dalberry's bedroom. There was no answer to her knock, and, opening the door, she looked in. The room was empty.

A swift wave of anger came over her as it dawned on her that, after all her promises, Lady Dalberry had left her alone in the flat with de Silva. She remembered how anxious he had been to prevent her from leaving her room just now, and had no doubt that he and her aunt had arranged this between them.

She deliberated for a moment, then went into her aunt's room and rang the bell that summoned the hall-boy. Then she went back to Lady Dalberry's sitting-room.

"I am sorry, Mr. de Silva," she said, standing in the doorway. "But my aunt is not in the flat."

He looked surprised.

"But I know she was expecting me," he exclaimed. "That being the case, she is hardly likely to be long. I will wait here, if you don't mind."

"Certainly. I shall be in my room. But if you prefer to go back to your flat I'm sure that my aunt will let you know as soon as she gets back."

She did not attempt now to conceal the contempt in her voice, and de Silva took note of it.

"I suppose I could not persuade you to keep me company, Miss Summers?" he suggested. This time the sneer was obvious.

"I'm afraid not," she answered quietly, as she left the room.

In the passage she met the boy who had come up in answer to the bell. She asked him to get the scuttle in her sitting-room refilled, and waited on the alert for any sound from the sitting-room while he did so, but de Silva showed no signs of following her. When the boy had gone she closed the door and turned the key. She felt a fool as she did it, and all the more angry with her aunt for having put her in such a position. She drew a chair up to the fire and tried to settle down with a book, but she found her attention wandering, and when, ten minutes later, she heard a step in the passage outside her room, she was on her feet in an instant.

It stopped outside her door, and she saw the handle turn and heard the click of metal as the locked door gave slightly in answer to the pressure outside. For a moment she felt absurdly frightened at the thought that de Silva was standing on the other side of the door. Then, with a sensation of relief, she recognized Lady Dalberry's voice.

"Carol, are you there, my child? Why have you locked yourself in?"

Carol opened the door.

"Mr. de Silva is in your room," she said coldly. "He said he was in a hurry to see you."

"I know. He appears to be annoyed because I have kept him waiting. I have told him that he must contain his patience for another minute or two. I want so much to know whether you two have made it up at last. He did nothing to make a bad impression?"

"If he had done anything, it would have been a little awkward for me," Carol reminded her. "You promised not to leave the flat while he was here, and you know I wouldn't have consented to see him if I hadn't been certain that you were on the premises. You didn't play fair, Aunt Irma!"

Lady Dalberry laughed.

"My dear, do not be absurd!" she exclaimed. "I assure you I was writing letters in my room until a quarter of an hour ago, so you may rest assured that you were well protected. Though what you imagined poor Juan was going to do to you, I fail to see. Was that why you were cowering behind a locked door just now?"

Carol felt her cheeks flame.

"You were not in the flat when we went to look for you," she said positively.

"I was out of the flat for exactly ten minutes, during which time you were as safe as if you had had a dozen chaperons. Do you suppose I should have left you for a second if I had thought there was a chance of anything happening to you? Surely you are being a little ridiculous, Carol!"

"The point is that you let me think you were going to be here, and you deliberately went out and left me," said Carol hotly, her anger getting the better of her. "I know now that I can't trust you!"

"That is both foolish and exaggerated. I did not leave you deliberately, as you suggest. I was sending a parcel to America, and, as it had to be declared and registered, I thought it better to do it myself. I was out of the flat just long enough to walk down the street to the post office and back. It never occurred to me that you would take this silly attitude about it. You are becoming hysterical on the subject of poor Juan de Silva, my dear. I am sure that nothing that he said or did this evening could have given you any cause for alarm. I did not know that English girls were so easily frightened."

She had begun her speech on a note of tolerant amusement, but her temper had begun to slip towards the end and there was both anger and contempt in her voice. Carol was beginning to feel that there was some faint excuse for the other woman's attitude, and the suspicion grew on her that perhaps she had been behaving rather like a hysterical schoolgirl. For all that, she was too genuinely annoyed to capitulate easily.

"All of which does not alter the fact that you broke your word," she insisted stubbornly.

Lady Dalberry's only answer was to leave the room, closing the door behind her with the exaggerated gentleness of one who is determined not to slam it.

CHAPTER XVII

NEXT DAY Carol lunched with Dalberry. The night before she had debated long and earnestly whether to speak to him about the events of the afternoon. Her common sense told her that he would hardly be likely to take the recital quietly, and she knew him well enough to be afraid that, in his anger, he might precipitate matters and force her to leave Lady Dalberry's flat. Unpleasant as her last interview with that lady had been, she felt definitely that she did not want to go at present. Now that she was on her guard she felt safe enough to wish to stay and see the thing through, and she knew that, if she was to carry out her plan in peace, she would do wisely to wait until she could report direct to Mellish and leave Dalberry in ignorance of what had happened.

But she was finding it more and more difficult to keep things from Dalberry. Of late her thoughts had turned instinctively to him when she was troubled or worried, and she had grown to long for the sound of his voice and anticipate the queer little thrill of pleasure that the mere sight of him gave her.

Before they were half-way through lunch she had forgotten her misgivings and told him the whole story.

The result was exactly as she had feared. He was furious, and tried to insist on her immediate departure from the flat. It was with difficulty that she persuaded him to wait for Mellish's verdict, and only succeeded by promising him that, if that fat and easy-going person definitely vetoed her plan of remaining, she would abide by his decision. Determined to leave nothing to chance, Dalberry rang him up on the telephone and arranged to take Carol on to the Albany from the theatre to which they were going.

It was a stupid play, indifferently produced, but they enjoyed it as two people do who are in complete sympathy with each other. Mellish, who had seen it a few days before, and been woefully bored by it, was more than a little tickled at the bland, if vague, satisfaction with which they answered his questions regarding the performance. Things were turning out admirably from his point of view, and he was beginning to look forward to the day when, with Carol safe and in good hands, he would be able to regard his trusteeship as a mere sinecure.

His amusement faded, however, when he heard what Carol had to tell.

"Gillie's right!" he said. "That flat is not the right place for you."

Dalberry turned on Carol triumphantly.

"What did I say?" he exclaimed. "I hope that settles it!"

Carol turned pink with annoyance.

"Aren't you being rather absurd about it, you two?" she said. "After all, nothing happened yesterday except that Aunt Irma played a rather low-down trick on me. Honestly, I don't think she in the least realized what she was doing."

"Tush! The woman's not a fool," exploded Mellish. "She was perfectly aware of what she was about."

"She knew she wasn't keeping her word, of course. It isn't that I mean. The point is that she didn't realize in the least that I should really mind. When she hinted that I was being stupid and prudish, she meant it. She couldn't understand my being angry."

"I wish you'd explain why you always stick up for her," exclaimed Dalberry. "You're not going to tell me that you like her!"

Mellish caught the angry gleam in Carol's eyes.

"If you must talk, I wish you'd contrive to say something sensible, Gillie," he murmured plaintively. "Do you really want to stay on at the flat, child? If you've got a good reason up your sleeve, produce it. I don't want to play the heavy father, you know."

She turned on him gratefully.

"I'm not trying to whitewash Aunt Irma, honestly," she said slowly, "and I don't like her. I wasn't sure at first. She used to say something quite ordinary to me in that queer, deep voice of hers, and for the moment I'd forget all the things I didn't like about her. I know now that it's just a trick she's got, and it doesn't affect me any more. Now that I feel I can't trust her, I actually dislike her. I think that's why I try so hard to be just to her. After all, she is a foreigner and she doesn't understand our ways, and, you must remember, she has been very kind to me."

Mellish nodded comprehendingly.

"I see all that, but why stay on?"

Carol laughed rather shamefacedly.

"I've got my back up, I suppose. And I want to know what it's all about."

She glanced nervously at Mellish and, by the set of his mouth, knew that she was beaten.

"Not good enough," was his decisive verdict. "I'm afraid you'll have to go, Carol. Is there any one who will put you up for several days till we have time to look round a bit?"

"The Carthews would have me, I know," said Carol reluctantly. "But not till next week. They don't come back to town till to-day. To-morrow's Sunday, and I must give them some notice. But, really, it's ridiculous, Jasper."

He ignored her objection.

"I don't see why you shouldn't stay in the flat till Monday," he reflected. "This man, de Silva, is capable of going a long way in pursuit of his plans—witness his attack on Gillie—but I have a strong feeling that he won't dare to show his hand until he is sure of what he is after."

Carol stared at him, puzzled. It was Dalberry who enlightened her.

"You mean until Carol is actually in possession of her money?" he said.

"Exactly," answered Mellish. "And she comes of age on Monday next. That, I am certain, is what these people are waiting for. She must be out of the flat by then."

He turned to Carol.

"On the twenty-eighth you come into possession of your father's estate. That gives you two days from now. Can you go to the Carthews' first thing on Monday morning? I shall have to ask you to come here in the afternoon. There are certain formalities to be gone through."

"I can, I suppose. As a matter of fact, they wanted me to spend next week with them and I refused, so I know they are available."

"Very well, then. Get on to them the moment they come back, and if you use the telephone, don't communicate with them through the one in the flat. Also, say nothing to Lady Dalberry about your intended departure. I don't want to precipitate her plans, if she has any. Why not say merely that you are spending Monday with the Carthews and staying the night? Take a dressing-case and send for your other luggage later. She will simply jump to the conclusion that they have persuaded you to stay on. Will you do that?"

Carol nodded. There were moments when she knew better than to argue with Mellish, and this was one of them.

"What are your plans for to-night and to-morrow?" he asked.

"I'm dining with the Carthews to-night," she answered, openly amused at his solicitude. "To-morrow I am more or less at a loose end."

"And you are going down to Berrydown, I think you said?" he went on, turning to Dalberry.

A significant glance passed between the two men.

"I was going down for the day. I can put it off, if you like."

"No. You ought to keep an eye on things there. I'll look after this end. Ring me up to-morrow, Carol, and give me a general idea of your movements. I don't want to lose touch with you till you're out of that house."

Carol laughed outright.

"I believe you're trying to frighten me, between you," she said. "All right, I'll keep you advised. I think that's the right expression."

She found Lady Dalberry at home when she got back to the flat. She looked tired and depressed, and Carol had a feeling that something had happened to upset her.

She confessed to a headache, and said she was going early to bed.

"I've been thinking over old times," she said sadly. "It is always a mistake to dwell on the days when one was happy, and it has upset me. And, all day, I have been longing for something. I know it is foolish, but I think you will understand, Carol."

In spite of herself, Carol's quick sympathies were aroused.

"What is it?" she asked.

"I want to visit my husband's grave. I know that it will only reopen old wounds, but I cannot help it. If you had a car I would ask you to drive me down to Berrydown to-morrow; but we could hire one, if you would come with me. Or are you already engaged?"

"No. I'd like to go. I've been hankering after Berrydown myself lately. And, oddly enough, you could not have chosen a better day. Gillie's going down himself to-morrow, and he can take us in the car if we let him know in time."

Lady Dalberry hesitated.

"It would be kind of him," she said at last. "But I would rather go alone with you, if you do not mind, my dear. I shall be bad company for any one, and I cannot get out of my head that Gillie does not like me. If you will put up with my foolish moods, I should be happier with you."

And Carol, who had been looking forward to the drive with Dalberry, found herself saying that the arrangement suited her to perfection.

"But I'd rather ring him up and tell him we are coming," she suggested. "If we want him to give us lunch it won't do to take him unawares. Remember the house is really by way of being shut up."

She was on her way to the door when an exclamation from Lady Dalberry stopped her.

"I forgot to tell you the telephone is out of order," she exclaimed. "I rang up the exchange from the post office to-day and they promised to send some one, but no one has been."

She rose and went to the writing-table.

"You had better telegraph," she said. "Here's a form. Tell him we shall arrive about one o'clock."

She was leaving the room as she spoke, and when, a few minutes later, Carol rose from the table, the telegram in her hand, she found her aunt, already dressed for the street, in the doorway.

"I am going out and I will give it to the porter," she said.

Carol, who had barely time to dress for her dinner-party, handed it to her and hurried to her room.

It was close on eleven when she got back that night. It was not until she had alighted from the taxi and was about to pay the driver that she discovered that she had left her purse at the house at which she had been dining.

The loss of the bag was doubly annoying as she had her latch-key in it, and was obliged not only to borrow the money for the fare from the night porter, but to get one of the pages to fetch his pass-key and accompany her upstairs.

When she reached the flat door, however, she ceased to regret the accident that had caused her to bring the boy with her. De Silva was standing outside his flat, evidently in the act of going in.

His face lit up at the sight of her, and he made a futile effort to spin out a rather florid good-night. Unfortunately for him, the boy had already opened the door and was standing waiting, so that he was forced to cut the conversation short and go into his own flat.

Carol dismissed the boy and, her mind still full of the loss of the bag, went straight to the telephone. It was not till she had taken off the receiver that she remembered that the telephone was out of order.

In her annoyance she stood for a moment staring stupidly at the offending instrument. The light from the hall lamp shone full on it, and as she looked she became aware of something that made her catch her breath in sheer panic as she realized what it implied.

Just above the point where they connected with the instrument, the wires had been neatly severed. The damage was plainly visible to any one standing near the receiver, and the cut was too clean to be the result of any accident.

For a moment consternation held her powerless; then, as she realized that Lady Dalberry could hardly have failed to notice the cut wires, even if she had had no hand in the matter, her naturally quick temper flared, and she turned and made blindly for her aunt's sitting-room. Whether the course she was about to take was a wise one, she did not stop to consider. Thus it was just as well for her that she found the room empty.

Still intent on her mission she hurried to Lady Dalberry's bed-room. The door was standing open and she went in.

The room was empty. She looked into the dressing-room and drew a blank there. Then, seeing the curtains waving in the breeze from the open window, she even went so far as to step on to the balcony that ran past the three bedrooms on that side of the house. There was no one there. Evidently Lady Dalberry had decided to re-main at her club after all.

Carol stood for a while at the open window, looking out over the dark expanse of the garden that lay behind the flats, her mind busy with this fresh proof of her aunt's treachery. For, if Lady Dalberry had eyes in her head, she must have seen what had happened. Carol was now faced with the disquieting fact that she was definitely cut off from outside help should she require it, and the situation was made none the pleasanter by her conviction that whoever had severed the wires had done so with her aunt's connivance. With an increasing sense of foreboding she turned from the window and made her way to her own room.

She was half-way down the passage when the thing happened that put even the disablement of the telephone completely out of her head.

She heard a movement behind her. So on edge were her nerves that she turned sharply and stood, her hands clenched, prepared to find de Silva waiting for her.

To the girl's amazement Lady Dalberry was standing on the thresh-old of the empty room she had just left. She was dressed in a loose tea-gown and had evidently not been out, as Carol had supposed.

"So you are back," she said pleasantly. "I thought I heard your key in the door. Was your evening amusing?"

Carol was too bewildered to answer her question.

"But, Aunt Irma," she exclaimed, "where were you? I've just been to your room and you weren't there then! Where have you come from?"

Lady Dalberry's face betrayed nothing but mild incredulity.

"But that is impossible," she returned. "If you were in my room I must have heard you. You could not have looked very carefully, my dear."

"But I did," Carol insisted. "I found the door open and went in, and you weren't there. I even looked in the dressing-room, and there wasn't a sign of you."

"All the same, if you had called to me or looked on the balcony you would have seen me," Lady Dalberry assured her placidly. "I suppose you thought I was out when you could not find me."

Carol was about to tell her that she had not only looked, but had actually stepped out on to the balcony, when some instinct warned her not to give voice to her suspicions.

"I thought you were at the club," she answered, trying to speak lightly. "I concluded that the bridge mania had proved too strong for you."

Lady Dalberry shook her head.

"I could not face all those people at the club to-night," she said, so pathetically that, if her mind had not been full of other, more perturbing, things, Carol might have felt sorry for her.

As it was, she said good-night as quickly as possible and went to her room. Once there she sat over the fire seeking in vain for a clue to this new problem. Where had her aunt been when she was searching for her in the bedroom? Carol had a growing conviction that she had been nowhere in the flat. And yet it was obvious that she could only have come from her own room when Carol saw her, for there had not been time for her to reach the doorway from either the hall door or any of the other rooms in the flat.

When at last, chilled and stiff with sitting over a dying fire, she rose to undress, she locked the door carefully and even placed a chair behind it in such a position that it was bound to fall if any one attempted to enter the room. Then, contrary to her usual custom, she closed and locked the French windows that gave on to the balcony, pushing the heavy dressing-table across them.

Then she went to bed, but, in spite of her precautions, she slept badly and rose unrefreshed. For the first time her resolve to see this thing through was thoroughly shaken, and she admitted to being thankful that, owing to Mellish's insistence, she would spend only one more night in her aunt's flat.

CHAPTER XVIII

LADY DALBERRY'S manoeuvres had already lost Carol a sleepless night, but it would have been even more disturbed if she could have followed her aunt's movements during the early part of the evening.

When Lady Dalberry left the flat with Carol's telegram to Dalberry in her hand she did not, as the girl had imagined, leave the building. Instead, she crossed the landing to de Silva's flat. Taking a latch-key from her handbag she let herself in, and went at once to his sitting-room. De Silva had been out all the afternoon and did not expect to get back till after dinner—a fact of which she was presumably aware, for she did not make any attempt to find him, but walked straight to his desk, on which was a pile of letters which had come by that morning's post.

They had already been opened and read by de Silva, and she did not scruple to go through them until she had found the one she wanted. The first three she did not even trouble to remove from their envelopes; the fourth, a fairly long typewritten effusion, she glanced through, making some notes on a slip of paper. The printed heading to the paper was that of a well-known firm of private inquiry agents.

Then, with the letter open in front of her, she sat down to compose a telegram. The wording of it seemed to cause her some trouble. Twice she rewrote it before she got it to her liking, each time putting the discarded form carefully away in her bag. The third time she was successful.

Then she went to the window, which commanded a view of the entrance to the flats, and, screened by the curtain, waited patiently until she had seen Carol emerge and enter a taxi, on her way to her dinner-party.

Only then did she move. Throwing Carol's telegram to Dalberry carelessly on the table she made her way back to her own flat. Once there she took the crumpled telegraph forms from her bag and burned them on her sitting-room fire, watching them until they were reduced to a fine ash.

She did not trust the wire she had just written to the porter, but took it herself to the post office. On her way down in the lift she told the page to see that the fires in the flat were kept up, as she had changed her mind and would be dining in the restaurant and spending the evening at home.

She arrived at the post office just as it was closing.

"This is important," she said to the clerk. "I hope it will go to-night."

"It will be dispatched to-night," answered the girl, "but if it is a small country place, it may not be delivered till the morning."

"That will do very well," said Lady Dalberry, with a smile that betokened complete satisfaction.

As she strolled back to the Escatorial her face bore the impress of one well pleased with the way in which her affairs were progressing.

De Silva did not get back to his flat till close on nine o'clock that evening. The first thing that met his eye was Lady Dalberry's hand-kerchief, lying where she had left it beside the open letter on his writing-table.

With a queer little smile and an expressive shrug of his shoulders he pocketed it, and looked quickly round for any further traces of her visit before ringing the bell for the servant to light the fire. There were none save Carol's unsent telegram to Dalberry, which was on the table. He picked it up, and after glancing through it, stood folding and refolding it in his slender fingers, his eyes dark with thought and a smile of satisfaction hovering on his lips. As soon as the fire was well alight he burned it.

He was writing busily when, half an hour later, he heard the click of a key in the front door, and the page showed in Captain Bond.

One glance at the man's face was enough.

De Silva waited until the boy had left the flat, then:

"For God's sake, pull yourself together!" he snapped. "What has happened to make you look like that?"

Bond pulled a handkerchief out of his pocket and passed it over his forehead. His hands were shaking.

"The police!" he whispered. "At the Onyx!"

De Silva's face grew a shade paler, but he did not flinch. "The police!" he repeated derisively. "Well, for myself, I have no objection. I hope you treated them hospitably, my little Bond, in the absence of the owner. Or had you your own reasons for disliking their company?"

Bond's sallow face flushed a deep red.

"They've nothing against me," he muttered savagely. "But you'll laugh once too often, de Silva. They meant business, I tell you."

"What do you mean, 'meant business'?" exclaimed de Silva. "If our flat-footed friends found anything to interest them at the Onyx they are welcome to it. Unless you made an exhibition of yourself! The mere sight of you as you are now would be enough to damn any place!"

"All the same," Bond insisted, "they weren't after any shady massage establishment to-night. They barely looked at the books, but they asked some very queer questions, and they went over the place inch by inch."

"And found nothing, my friend. I do not think they will trouble us again."

There was a spiteful gleam in Bond's eyes.

"They found nothing in the shop," he said slowly. "And, if you ask me, I don't think they expected to. Of course, what you keep in those rooms of yours upstairs I don't know. I didn't go with them."

De Silva stiffened.

"They went into the flat?" he exclaimed, and Bond noted the change in his voice with dour satisfaction. "How did they get in? You fool, you did not show them the door in the office?"

"They didn't need any help from me, I assure you. They merely brought a locksmith with them and picked the lock of the side door. They were up there a good half-hour or more."

"So!" retorted de Silva savagely. "The police pick locks, do they, in this free country! I have an idea that somebody is going to get into trouble."

"Nobody's going to get into trouble, I tell you," returned Bond, his voice shrill with mingled fear and excitement. "Don't be a fool, de Silva. It's serious this time. They had a warrant. I saw it."

De Silva's confidence seemed shaken at last.

"A warrant! In England that is serious, I believe. What happened in the flat? Did they say anything?"

"I don't know. I was downstairs, but they left in an uncommonly good temper. What are you going to do, de Silva? If you're clearing out you'll take me! I'm not going to be left behind to bear the brunt this time."

De Silva glared at him. The man was worse than useless in an emergency. His nerve had completely gone. He looked abject, and yet, under his manifest fear for his own skin, he showed a curious, vindictive satisfaction at the prospect of his employer's downfall.

"What is the matter with you?" snapped de Silva. "Nobody is going to get hurt in this business, unless it is the bungling fool of a policeman who thought he was going to get promotion out of it. If they stripped the paper off the walls they would find nothing at the Onyx. Do you think I am a fool? What are you afraid of?"

"You and your dirty schemes," said Bond bluntly. "Do you suppose I don't know that there's more in this Onyx business than meets the eye? And the fact that you've kept me in the dark as to what it is doesn't mean that I won't get roped in, just the same, if there's a show-down. I want to know where I stand in all this."

"You stand where you have always stood, my good Bond," murmured de Silva softly—"behind the door, waiting to be kicked. But this time there will be no kicking. Run if you want to—I shall not try to stop you; but if you do, there may be things I could tell your friends the police that they would be glad to hear."

"By God, I've a good mind to clear out and let you do your worst!" exploded Bond, and then, according to his custom, capitulated. "What are you going to do?" he repeated feebly.

"Stay where I am, of course. And if you've got any sense you will do the same. Get out now. If the police come here they had better not find us together. It was like you to come rushing round here at the first hint of danger. It is as well for me, my brave friend, that you are not my accomplice!"

"You are going to carry on as usual, then?"

"Of course I am going to carry on as usual. What do you think? Go back to your job, which is to run a respectable and flourishing Beauty Parlour. It is about all you are fit for."

"Well, I've warned you," said Bond, as, gathering together the tattered shreds of his dignity, he took himself off.

It was as well he went when he did. Less than fifteen minutes after the door had closed behind him Detective Inspector Shand was shown in.

He found de Silva back at his letter-writing, a cigar between his fingers and a tall glass by his side.

"Come in, inspector," he said cordially, not attempting to disguise his surprise at this untimely visit.

He rose and pushed the cigar box across the table.

"You will have a drink?"

Shand refused both offers.

"Not at this time of night, thank you," he said pleasantly. "We've taken the liberty of going over your little place, the Onyx. Had to make sure that all was ship-shape, you know. We've had a good deal of trouble with one or two places of that sort."

De Silva laughed.

"You found nothing incriminating, I hope?" he said.

"Nothing except Captain Bond," retorted Shand genially. "We've come up against him before, you know."

De Silva looked startled.

"I did not know you had anything really serious against him. The truth is that he came to me after that affair at the Terpsychorean, and he was in such a bad way that I offered him the job. He seemed to have had such a bad fright that I thought it unlikely he would offend again."

"I don't fancy he was much to blame for the Terpsychorean affair," said Shand thoughtfully. "It was his principal we were after, and we shall get him in the end, I've no doubt. No, we've nothing against Captain Bond at present. There are one or two questions I should like to ask you, Mr. de Silva. Just a matter of routine, you understand."

De Silva settled himself more comfortably in his chair.

"Yes?" he murmured.

"You came to England from the Argentine, I believe? Was it your first visit to this country?"

De Silva nodded.

"Curiously enough, I had never set my foot outside America until I came here. A visit to England was one of the pleasures I had always promised myself, but the opportunity was a long time in coming. I have had to make my own way, you see, and it is not so easy, even in a rich country like the Argentine."

"But you were lucky in the end?"

Shand's tone was one of friendly interest.

"On the whole, yes, though I am not a rich man. I invested what money I could save in some of the smaller cinematograph companies and did astonishingly well. That, by the way, was how I came in touch with that poor fellow Conyers."

"I was going to ask you about that. What was he doing when you first met him?"

"Playing small parts on the films. He was an eccentric dancer by profession, I believe, but I fancy he had never been very successful."

"Did you ever meet him in the company of a man called Piper, by any chance?"

"Piper?" De Silva repeated the name slowly. He seemed to be trying to chase an illusive memory. "Was not he a man who got into trouble with the police? I never met him, but he was pointed out to me by Conyers once in a cafe. They knew each other well, I believe."

"And how did you come to hear of his little trouble?"

Shand put the question carelessly, but he was watching the other man closely.

"Somebody told me that the police were after him before I left Buenos Aires, and later I saw in the papers that he had been arrested in England."

"When did you leave Buenos Aires, Mr. de Silva?"

De Silva smiled.

"This is quite an inquisition, inspector," he said blandly. "But I am only too glad to help you if I can. To be exact, I sailed on January the fifth. I came by a French boat to Marseilles, as I wanted to have a look at Paris on the way."

"And you arrived in England, when?"

"On February the first. Two days before I found and took this flat."

Shand rose to his feet.

"I think that is all," he said. "We've been trying to get in touch with the associates of Conyers in America, and I had hoped you might be able to help us. By the way, I suppose you never came across a fellow called Strelinski?"

De Silva had been nursing the long grey ash at the end of his cigar. Now it fell suddenly, making a little heap on the tablecloth. His face was impassive as he answered: "Strelinski? No, the name is strange to me. But you must understand that I knew very few of Conyers's friends. Most of them, I am afraid, were not very reputable."

Shand gave a sigh.

"Well, it's an uphill business, this digging into a man's past. I'll be getting on my way. Thank you very much, Mr. de Silva."

De Silva preceded him to the front door and opened it for him. Shand, who had been standing on the hearth, close to the writing-desk, waited until his host was across the threshold and in the little hall. Then, as he passed the desk, he dexterously stripped off the top sheet from the block of telegraph forms that lay on it and slipped it into his pocket. A couple of long strides took him across the room, and he was on de Silva's heels by the time the Argentino reached the front door of the flat.

"And the Onyx?" queried de Silva smoothly, as he waited for Shand to pass out.

"Oh, we're not going to worry you there," answered the inspector with a friendly grin. "That was all in the day's work, and, as I say, we found everything ship-shape."

As he went down in the lift Shand reviewed his evening's work. He was not ill-satisfied, on the whole, for Piper had stated emphatically that he had never met Conyers, and he had as good reason to believe him as he had for doubting de Silva. For whereas Piper could have no possible object in denying his acquaintanceship with Conyers, seeing that his alibi on the night of the murder was firmly established, de Silva might have his own reasons for lying. What they might be was, for the moment, a mystery.

Shand fingered the crumpled telegraph form in his pocket. His eye had fallen on it while he was questioning de Silva, and he had commandeered it on impulse, knowing that it is impossible to write on the uppermost form of a packet without making a fairly clear indentation on the paper beneath. These indentations had been plainly visible from where he stood, and it had seemed too good an opportunity to miss, though he had no reason to hope for any luck in that direction.

Once back in his room at the Yard it did not take him five minutes to read the message. And when he had read it he made a jump for the telephone, and by sheer good luck managed to get on to Dalberry immediately.

"Can I see you?" he said. "I've got something here that may interest you."

Dalberry had been on the point of going out, and his car was at the door. He suggested dropping in at Scotland Yard on his way.

"I've got Mr. Mellish here with me. Shall I bring him along?" he added.

"I think he ought to see this. It may be urgent," was Shand's answer.

When they entered his room ten minutes later they found him engaged with two plain-clothes detectives.

"Don't lose sight of him if you can help it, and report to me here at the earliest opportunity," he said, as he dismissed them.

The door had no sooner closed behind them than he turned to Dalberry.

"Have you ever been inside de Silva's flat, Lord Dalberry?" he asked.

Dalberry looked surprised.

"Never. I hardly know the man."

Shand handed him a slip of paper.

"To the best of my knowledge this telegram has been sent from his flat within the last few days. It was certainly written there."

Mellish peered over Dalberry's shoulder and read the message. It was addressed to Mrs. Roma Verrall, The South Lodge, Berrydown, Sussex, and ran:

"Necessary you should leave immediately travel by seven thirty-five a. m. will meet you Victoria. Dalberry."

Dalberry passed the paper to Mellish, his hand going instinctively to his hat, which he had thrown on the table as he entered.

"I never wrote this," he said decisively. "I'll get down to Berrydown at once. I was going to-morrow, anyhow."

He had almost reached the door when Shand stopped him.

"Just a moment," he said. "Half an hour, one way or the other, won't make much difference. Either this wire was sent some days ago, in which case we are too late, or it went today, which gives us till to-morrow morning. I've just put a couple of men on to de Silva, and he won't get out of the flats without my knowledge. He was there less than half an hour ago when I interviewed him in his room. Lady Dalberry, according to the porter, is spending the evening at home. We've got them both bottled for the present, unless de Silva nipped out the moment my back was turned. There's Bond, of course, but he wouldn't be trusted with a job of any importance. You don't happen to know if Mrs. Verrall has left the lodge?"

"She was there two days ago," answered Dalberry. "I told the lodge-keeper to report to me regularly, and I had her letter yesterday. If Mrs. Verrall had left yesterday morning early I should have heard from the lodge-keeper by now."

"That's all to the good, then. If you can get down there in time to stop her from starting to-morrow morning we shall have done the trick. Of course, she may have gone this morning."

Mellish was staring thoughtfully at the paper in his hand. "I don't think so," he said slowly. "I'm beginning to see a certain method in

Lady Dalberry's sudden desire to visit her husband's grave to-morrow. It looks as if in some way she'd discovered that you were proposing to go to Berrydown, and was making plans to keep you occupied for the greater part of the day. What time were you due there?"

"About lunch-time. I was going to take it easy."

"And the South Lodge isn't on the way from the station?"

"No. You turn into the park by the one on the Lewes road. I see what you mean. She was counting on my not looking up Mrs. Verrall till after lunch, which, as a matter of fact, is what I meant to do."

"If you hadn't been fully occupied in entertaining Lady Dalberry and Carol," Mellish reminded him.

"Carol? Is she coming down too?"

It was Mellish's turn to look surprised.

"Didn't you get her wire? I asked her to keep me informed as to her movements, and she telephoned from the Carthews' this evening to say that she and Lady Dalberry were spending the day at Berrydown to-morrow, and that she had wired to you asking you to give them lunch."

"This is the first I have heard of it," said Dalberry grimly. "It seems to me it's time I got on the job. I shall drive straight down there now and spend the rest of the night there. By the time Lady Dalberry arrives I'll have Mrs. Verrall out of harm's way."

"What do you propose to do as regards Mrs. Verrall?" asked Shand.

"I shall take her up to the house early to-morrow morning. She'll be safe enough there for the time being."

"If you take my advice, Lord Dalberry, you'll bring her back to town with you to-morrow night. I'll give you a safe address, where we can keep an eye on her. And get Miss Summers out of that flat as quickly as possible," he added soberly.

CHAPTER XIX

CAROL CAST A side glance at Lady Dalberry and decided that the drive to Berrydown was going to be even gloomier than she had first thought. Her aunt had gone out early that morning—indeed, the girl was still dressing when she heard the hall door close behind her—and she returned soon after ten, her arms full of hot-house flowers to lay on her husband's grave.

Since then she had been silent and preoccupied, and Carol, while blaming herself for her own lack of sympathy, could not shake off the suspicion that her aunt's attitude was one of annoyance rather than grief.

They were now threading their way through the suburbs, and, so far, Lady Dalberry had vouchsafed only the curtest of answers to the girl's tentative remarks. She was leaning back in the car, her eyes fixed on the fragrant heap of flowers that lay on the floor, her face so dark and brooding that Carol had not the courage to interrupt her thoughts. It was not until they were well out of London that she pulled herself out of her abstraction and made a determined effort to atone for her ungraciousness.

"It is too bad of me to be so distrait," she said, with an attempt at a smile. "You have given up your drive with Gillie to come with me, and it is ungrateful of me to behave so badly. The truth is that I find I mind this more than I had thought. Please forgive me, Carol."

"Of course!" exclaimed the girl. "I know how you must feel. Please don't bother about me, Aunt Irma."

"But I do bother, as you call it. And it is better for me to make an effort. Tell me about Berrydown. I saw so little the day I was there."

She questioned Carol closely as to the house and its surroundings, and the girl, who loved the place, was glad to gratify her curiosity.

"How do we arrive, coming from London?" she asked. "There are several lodges, are there not?"

"Only two. One, the South Lodge, is on the Lewes road; the other, the one we turn in by, is at the end of the main drive. It's a much prettier approach. The park's really lovely when it's at its best. Of course, it's early in the year now."

"And the village? Is that on the Lewes road?"

"No. We pass through it on our way. We don't hit the Lewes road at all. I believe the South gates were only put there after the railway came, and are hardly ever used except for the station."

Lady Dalberry relapsed once more into thoughtful silence, and Carol did not interrupt her. Except for an occasional question she did not speak again until they drew up at the gates of the little churchyard.

"Would you like me to come with you, or shall I wait in the car?" asked Carol shyly.

Lady Dalberry bent forward and gathered the flowers into her arms.

"I will go by myself, if you don't mind, my dear," she said, with a little quiver in her voice.

"Of course not," answered Carol warmly. "If you don't want me, I'll leave the car and walk up to the house. I'd love it, and it isn't more than three-quarters of a mile. Then you can follow when you feel inclined."

Lady Dalberry turned to her impulsively.

"If it is such a little way, I too would love the walk. It will do me good after the long drive, and give me time to pull myself into a better frame of mind after my visit here. Go on in the car, my dear, unless you would really rather go on foot. In which case tell the chauffeur to drive on, and I will follow later."

In the end Carol drove on alone, and found Dalberry waiting on the doorstep when she got there.

"Where's our august relation?" he asked. He did not try to conceal his joy at seeing Carol alone.

"Don't be a pig, Gillie," she exclaimed. "She really is upset and miserable, and you must admit it is pretty beastly for her. She's coming on on foot from the churchyard."

Dalberry shot a quick glance at her.

"Walking, is she? Why didn't she keep the car?"

"She seemed to think she'd rather walk. Honestly, Gillie, she is feeling it, and I think she wanted the time to pull herself together. Anyway, when I suggested that I should walk on, she told me to take the car and she would follow."

"I had an idea, somehow, that she might walk up from the church," said Dalberry thoughtfully. "Come into the library, will you? I've had it put more or less in order. It's time this house was lived in again, Carol."

"I know," she said. "I hate to think of it standing empty after all the jolly times we've had here."

They went into the library, a long, low-ceilinged room, brown and mellow with age, leather bindings, and old oak.

"Gillie! How lovely! Just look at the flowers. You didn't arrange those yourself?"

Dalberry was looking down into her face. At her words his eyes shifted suddenly.

"No. I expect we've got old Gibbs to thank for that. She's been beside herself since she heard you were coming. You'll find her gibbering in the housekeeper's room."

Carol turned quickly.

"How horrid of me!" she exclaimed. "I ought to have looked her up at once."

Dalberry slipped cleverly round her and barred the way to the door.

"Wait a minute, Carol," he said.

"What is it?" she asked, with mischief in her eyes.

She had hardly let the words slip before she knew that they would prove her undoing. A second later she was in his arms, and he was kissing her as he had longed to kiss her ever since that day in Mellish's rooms.

When at last he released her there was a new look of hope in his eyes.

"I'm not sorry," he said, her hands held so closely in his that she could not have escaped if she had wished. But she did not try to draw them away.

"Why didn't you do it sooner?" she asked softly. "I might have given you your answer then."

"Is it 'yes'?" he whispered.

Her hands crept steadily up until they rested on his shoulders.

"I might just as well have said it in the beginning," she murmured. "I never really had a chance against you, you know."

It was some time before Carol paid her visit to the old nurse, Gibbs. When she did go she took Gillie with her, and they broke the glad news to the old woman together. Her reception of it was entirely satisfactory.

"Good heavens, I'd forgotten our aunt!" exclaimed Dalberry, suddenly realizing how the time had flown. "She'll be wandering forlorn among the dust-sheets."

They hurried back to the library, but, to their surprise, there was no sign of Lady Dalberry.

"Do you suppose she's lost her way?" asked Carol. "She can't have gone astray between us and the church."

They strolled over to the window and looked out.

"Here she is!" he exclaimed. "No wonder she's late."

Lady Dalberry was walking quickly up the drive. She had just turned into it from the branch that ran down to the South Lodge.

"Then she did lose her way," said Carol. "How clever of you to see her. I was looking down the main drive."

"I had a kind of inkling she might come that way," said Dalberry quietly. "I say, Carol."

"Yes?"

"Let's keep this to ourselves to-day, at any rate, shall we? We don't want a lot of congratulations and things over lunch, and old Gibbs won't spread the glad news till we've had our food. With luck, Lady Dalberry won't hear it till you get to London. What do you think?"

"I'd much rather not tell her," said Carol frankly. "She's so queer and upset to-day, and I've got an awful feeling she might weep over us. It's a hateful thing to say when I'm so happy, I know. And, Gillie, you must try to remember to call her 'Aunt Irma.' She'll be so hurt if you don't."

She spoke with genuine remorse, but as she watched the tall figure in its heavy black draperies approaching the house, she could not control a little shudder of repulsion. Dalberry tightened his grasp and drew her closer to him.

"It's all right, old thing," he said gently. "That little episode in your life closes to-morrow, and after that I shall have a right to look after you."

He pulled her back behind the heavy curtain, and for a moment they clung to each other, then Carol freed herself.

"This is where we dissemble," she announced solemnly, as she led the way into the hall.

As Carol had foreseen, Lady Dalberry was tired and depressed; but she seemed in a gentler mood, and laid herself out to be pleasant to Dalberry. Her appreciative interest in Berrydown went a long way towards disarming him, and Carol was amused to see these two more at ease with each other than they had ever shown themselves, the truth of the matter being that Dalberry found himself in a mood that made it impossible for him actively to dislike anybody.

After lunch they sat for a time over cigarettes and coffee, after which Lady Dalberry expressed her desire to see over the house.

Carol welcomed the suggestion. She had foreseen a rather deadly two hours of desultory conversation before it was time to drive back to town, and she was afraid that the latest antagonism between Dalberry and his aunt by marriage would come to the surface before she could decently find an excuse for departure.

She swung herself eagerly out of the big chair in which she had curled herself.

"Come on, Gillie," she cried, "and do the honours; though I believe I know more about the house than you do."

Gillie rose lazily.

"It's not the best time to show the old place off," he said. "It's all in curl-papers, and it looks pretty dreary and unlived-in."

"The pictures, though. One can see those, I hope," urged Lady Dalberry: "I have heard so much about the Berrydown collection."

"It's a very unequal one, I believe," answered Dalberry. "My grandfather took most of them over from the original owner, and they were a mixed lot, though they are historically interesting. Carol knows more about them than I do."

He led the way to the long gallery, and busied himself with opening and throwing back the shutters. The room, with its shrouded furniture, had a ghostly look, and their footsteps re-echoed eerily on the carpetless floor. The pictures were, for the most part, indifferent contemporary portraits of bygone owners of the place, but here and there was evidence that the sitter had, by sheer luck, placed himself in the hands of one of the masters of his day. There were two Van Dycks, and a Romney that had been the bait of all the big dealers for many a long year. The first Lord Dalberry, who had been one of the few rich collectors justified in relying on his own taste and knowledge, had added to the collection, and it was in his purchases that its value really lay. Carol, who loved the pictures, was only too delighted to act as guide, and she found Lady Dalberry an intelligent, if not very knowledgeable, listener.

When they had exhausted the gallery she led them to the long suite of rooms which, in old days, had been reserved for royalty, and showed them the famous tapestried bedroom where, needless to say, Queen Elizabeth was reputed to have slept during one of her many progresses through the country. According to Dalberry, his grandfather had never been able to find any proof that she had ever stayed in the house, though the original owners of the place, from whom he had bought it, had believed in the story implicitly.

"There's nothing else on this floor," said Carol, as they emerged into the corridor, "except a few uninteresting bedrooms and the old nursery. You haven't changed that, have you, Gillie?"

"Rather not," he assured her. "It's the room I know best in the house. It's where we had all our greatest fun when I used to come here in the old days. Let's get back to the library and stir them up about tea; shall we?"

"I should like to see this old nursery," said Lady Dalberry.

"I can imagine you and Carol playing there as children. Which of these doors is it? This one?"

"No, the one at the end. I'll show you," said Carol.

"I should give it a miss, if I were you," urged Dalberry. "After we grew out of our nursery days it became the schoolroom, and it was' always one of the shabbiest and untidiest rooms in the house. It must be looking ghastly now."

He was too late. Carol had run lightly down the corridor and thrown open the door at the end. Lady Dalberry followed her.

But Carol didn't go in. Instead, she halted on the threshold.

"I'm sorry, Gillie," she said, in a voice of mingled distress and perplexity. "I didn't know you were using it."

Then her bewilderment changed to surprised recognition.

"Why ..." she began, then her voice trailed away into silence.

Lady Dalberry, looking over her shoulder, took in the scene. Instead of being shrouded in dust-sheets, as were all the other rooms on that landing, the nursery was quite obviously in use. It was, as Dalberry had said, a shabby room, but, with the bright fire burning in the grate and the flowers on the much-used round table in the middle, it looked a comfortable one.

And in a big armchair by the fire, a book on her lap and a cigarette between her lips, sat a woman. Lady Dalberry did not miss the look of consternation that Carol's unexpected entrance brought to her face or the quick, desperate signal which had passed between her and the girl, and had frozen Carol's exclamation on her lips.

Lady Dalberry was the first of the little party to recover herself.

"I am sorry, Gillie," she said. "I am afraid that we intrude."

Dalberry stepped forward.

"Not a bit," he said quickly. "I'm sure Miss Bruce will excuse us. May I introduce my aunt, Lady Dalberry, and Miss Summers? They wanted to have a look at the old nursery," he explained.

Then, to Lady Dalberry:

"Miss Bruce is painting the gardens here. She was staying at the lodge, but a burst pipe flooded her out of hearth and home yesterday, and she was obliged to take refuge here. I'm afraid it is rather a makeshift shelter."

"It would make an excellent studio," said Miss Bruce. "I wish now I hadn't left my canvases down at the lodge," she added swiftly, as though aware of the words that were hovering on Lady Dalberry's lips.

"I am so sorry," exclaimed Lady Dalberry regretfully. "I should have so liked to see Miss Bruce's work. You must show it to me sometime, Gillie."

"I will," he assured her, with what seemed to Miss Bruce almost unnecessary fervour.

"Will Miss Bruce not join us at tea?" went on his aunt, her eyes on that lady's face.

"I've just had my tea, I'm afraid," she said quickly. "And now I must go down to the lodge and rescue some of my things."

"Then we will leave you in peace," said Lady Dalberry graciously. "Come, Carol."

They were a silent party as they made their way down the corridor. At the head of the stairs Lady Dalberry halted, a malicious sparkle in her eyes.

"I am afraid we were indiscreet, Gillie," she murmured. "You should have warned us."

Dalberry flushed a rich brick red.

"Not at all, Aunt Irma. She's very busy, and I wasn't sure that she wanted to be disturbed, that's all. I tried to make her join us at lunch, but she wouldn't. The lodge was in such a state that I had to offer to take her in."

For the next hour he tried in vain to get Carol for a moment to himself, but Lady Dalberry, wittingly or unwittingly, frustrated him at every turn. It was not until, just as the motor came round, Carol announced her intention of saying good-bye to Nurse Gibbs that he managed to slip away after her, leaving Lady Dalberry struggling with her various wraps in the hall. In desperation he slipped the bolt in the baize door that separated the hall from the servants' quarters. He found Carol waiting in the passage beyond.

"I say, Carol, I've got to explain," he began urgently.

To his relief there was only amusement in Carol's eyes. "Gillie darling! why on earth did you say she was an artist? My dear old donkey, haven't you got eyes in your head? It wouldn't have taken in a child."

"You recognized her, then?"

"Of course I recognized her. Mrs. Verrall isn't the sort of person one forgets. Why on earth didn't you warn me?"

"I never dreamed we should go into that room. And, come to that, what would you have called her if you'd been in my place?"

Carol's shoulders shook with amusement.

"I must say she played up beautifully, but if you could have seen yourself solemnly introducing her as an artist to Aunt Irma! It was the most transparent thing I've ever heard."

"Well, how else was I to introduce a woman who looked like nothing on earth but a cinema vamp? Joking apart, do you think our aunt recognized her?"

"I don't know, but I didn't like her manner. She's extraordinarily difficult to fathom sometimes. She only saw her for a moment that day she found me speaking to her on the landing outside the flat, and it's quite likely she wouldn't know her again. Whether she did or not, I shall have a horrid drive home, Gillie. She'll make the most abominable insinuations against you all the way, and I shan't know how to defend you."

"Don't you want to know how Mrs. Verrall got here?" asked Dalberry gently. He had realized suddenly that Carol was taking this astonishingly well.

She laughed.

"Were you waiting for me to 'feature' jealous rage?" she asked. "I'm not quite a fool, Gillie dear. Jasper told me he had seen Mrs. Verrall, and that he thought there really might be something in her accusations against Mr. de Silva. I can see his hand behind this. Are you supposed to be hiding her from Mr. de Silva? Because, if so, you're not doing it very well. If Aunt Irma did recognize her she'll tell him about her within the next few hours."

"De Silva's tracked her already. That's why I had to move her from the South Lodge. I'll tell you all about it when we've more time. But I'm afraid I've made a hash of things."

Carol's face was very serious.

"I should get her up to London to-night, if you don't want him to find her. He's too clever not to guess that you'd move her to the house, and even if Aunt Irma didn't recognize her, he'll smell a rat when she tells him about the woman she found here."

Dalberry saw Lady Dalberry and Carol into their car and watched it disappear down the drive. Then he had a short interview with Mrs. Verrall. He found her only mildly perturbed by what had happened, but he realized that she had no reason to connect either of her visitors with de Silva. She was more than anxious, however, to accompany him to London. Since the telegram she had received that morning her one idea had been to get away from Berrydown.

He gave the other car an hour's start before leaving for London. His car was a closed one, and he did not switch on the light inside. It would be practically impossible for any one to see the face of his passenger provided she sat well back in her seat.

He did not leave the park by the usual gate, but drove round by the South Lodge. There he stopped to say a word to the rather surprised old woman who opened the gate to him.

"This is your busy day, Mrs. Baker," he said pleasantly. "It isn't often you have to open this gate twice in one day."

"That it isn't, my lord," she answered. "It's seldom enough any one uses it now. Very worried, her ladyship was this morning. She lost her way, seemingly, comin' from the church."

"I expect she admired the garden."

"Lovely, she said it was. She asked me if I ever let my room at all, seein' that the lodge is bigger than most. Bearin' in mind what your lordship said to me this mornin', I told her I had had a lodger, an artist lady, but that she'd left this mornin' early."

"Did she ask where the lady had gone?"

"Yes, she did; and very disappointed she was when I said I couldn't rightly tell her. It seems that she thought it might be a friend of hers as had talked of comin' down to these parts."

"Well, I shall be seeing her again to-morrow, and I can explain," said Dalberry easily. "Thank you, Mrs. Baker."

He glanced behind him. Mrs. Verrall, who had not missed a word of the little dialogue, was leaning forward, her face white and startled in the light from the lamp.

CHAPTER XX

SOMEWHAT TO Carol's relief, Lady Dalberry seemed to have reverted to the mood in which she had started from London, and preserved a rather morose silence all through the first part of the journey back to town. Then, just as Carol was beginning to congratulate herself on having avoided the dangerous topic of Mrs. Verrall, Lady Dalberry became as talkative as she had been taciturn before.

She opened the ball by asking Carol point-blank whether she had ever heard any rumours of Dalberry's entanglement with the "extraordinary woman" they had seen that afternoon. Carol's suggestion that Miss Bruce was merely what she seemed, an artist who had been staying at the lodge, she greeted with polite incredulity.

"When you have reached my age, my dear," she assured her, "you will recognize such a situation when you see it. Our poor Gillie's explanation was amusingly unconvincing. I am afraid he is leading a wilder life than we either of us realized."

Carol suppressed a smile with difficulty. Annoyed though she felt, she could not help being amused at Lady Dalberry's tone of solicitude.

"If Miss Bruce is what you think, he would hardly have put her into the least presentable room in the house," she suggested.

"It is the room we were least likely to look into."

The truth of this was so incontrovertible that Carol was reduced to silence.

"I have only just learned what happened at the Terpsychorean," went on Lady Dalberry portentously. "Juan de Silva has been admirably discreet, but he let fall something in a careless moment, and I made him tell me exactly what caused the breach between you and Gillie. I can imagine how distressing it was for you, my dear."

"Gillie was ill, as it afterwards turned out," said Carol quickly. "If I'd realized that, I should never have deserted him as I did."

If Lady Dalberry's object was to antagonize Carol she succeeded admirably. Laying her hand on the girl's, she patted it gently.

"My poor little Carol," she murmured, her voice vibrant with emotion, "it is better to face facts now than later, when it is perhaps too late."

Carol released her hand at the earliest opportunity, and for the rest of the drive the conversation languished.

That night Lady Dalberry departed, as usual, to her club, and Carol spent the evening alone. She felt unaccountably tired, and went early to bed. But she could not sleep. She was happier, she told herself, than she had ever been in her life.

To-morrow she would leave the flat for good, and, once she was at the Carthews', she and Gillie could meet as often and as freely as they liked. Owing to Lady Dalberry's vigilance they had been able to make no definite plans for the next day, but she knew that she would find him there when she kept her appointment with Mellish in the afternoon, and they would no doubt spend the evening together.

For a long time she was content to lie awake, absorbed in the thought of her own happiness. It was not until the little clock by her bed struck three that she realized that sleep had become out of the question. She turned on the light and stretched out her hand for a book. The table was empty, and she remembered that she had taken the book she was reading to her sitting-room, meaning to finish it before leaving the flat, and had then spent the evening dreaming in front of the fire.

She got up, slipped on a dressing-gown, and made her way down the passage to her sitting-room to fetch it. She moved softly, fearing to wake Lady Dalberry, whose bedroom she had to pass on her way. The utter stillness of the flat oppressed her, and she instinctively hastened her steps, anxious to get back to the security of her bedroom.

She had reached the door of her aunt's room when she heard a sound from within that made her stop short and put all thoughts of her errand out of her head.

As she turned the angle of the passage her attention had been caught by the unmistakable sound of her aunt moving about her room. This was now followed by a curious rumbling noise, quite unlike anything she had ever heard in the flat before. In the daytime she might have taken it for the creaking of the lift, but she knew that the lift did not work at night, and besides, owing to the stillness of the flat, it was easy to locate the sound. It came unmistakably from Lady Dalberry's room.

It was followed by a sharp, metallic click, like the closing of a spring lock.

For a moment Carol stood listening, but the noise was not repeated. Instead, there was utter silence behind the closed door.

She knocked softly. There was no response. And yet, a moment ago, she had heard her aunt moving. She knocked again, more loudly, with the same result.

Then, with a sudden sick feeling of terror, she remembered a burglary that had taken place some time before in the flat below. The thieves had climbed a gutter pipe and had managed to reach a balcony, from which they had got into one of the bedrooms. Supposing her aunt had been attacked and was unable to answer!

She did not dare to knock again, but stood straining her ears for the faintest sound from behind the closed door. But the silence remained unbroken. Since that last metallic click there had been no movement from within the room.

She hesitated for a moment, then, very gently, turned the handle of the door. Even if the thieves were still in the room she might manage to open the door sufficiently to look in without attracting their attention. But the door would not move, and the fact that it was locked only added fuel to her anxiety.

One thing was obvious to her. She could not go back to her room until she had assured herself that all was well with Lady Dalberry. She might, of course, ring for the night porter, but the possibility that she was merely the victim of her own nerves daunted her. She could see the expression of ironical compassion with which Lady Dalberry would greet an unnecessary incursion on her slumbers.

Then she remembered that the balcony outside her aunt's window ran past her own sitting-room. She hurried back to her bedroom and slipped a dark fur coat over her dressing-gown, then she went down the passage once more and, without switching on the light, felt her way across the sitting-room to the window.

She managed to get the window open with a minimum of noise, though even the slight sound she made in raising the catch seemed to her to re-echo through the flat. Then, moving very carefully, she stepped on to the balcony and peered along it. The rooms lying, as they did, at the back of the house, she had not even the reflected light of the street lamps to help her, but, moving carefully along the dark balcony, she was soon able to assure herself that it was empty. She reached the window of Lady Dalberry's room confident that she had not made a sound which could have betrayed her. The French window was half-open, and from where she stood she could see almost the whole of the room. All that was cut off from her view was the door into the passage and the wall in which it stood. She could see the door into the dressing-room, which stood open. The room beyond was in darkness, whereas the bedroom was brilliantly lighted, both from a centre lamp and two hanging lights over the dressing-table. Carol, after a moment's scrutiny, shifted her position so that she could command a view of the whole room, and discovered, to her amazement, that she had been right in her first impression.

The room was empty.

She glanced at the bed. It had not been slept in, and though the fur cloak her aunt usually wore in the evening was lying over a chair, where she had evidently thrown it on coming in, there was no sign that she had removed any of the rest of her clothes. Carol stood transfixed, her mind trying to grapple with two unassailable facts. Lady Dalberry was not in her room, and the door was locked from the inside.

Then, as she stood hesitating whether to enter the room or not, she heard a sound that made her shrink back instinctively into the protective shadows of the dark balcony.

The sharp click she had heard before repeated itself, followed immediately by the rumbling sound that had so puzzled her. She could trace it now to the heavy, carved wardrobe that stood close to her aunt's bed.

She stared at it, her throat dry and her heart beating wildly.

The doors of the wardrobe stood open, and she could see the sheen of the reflected light on the silk of the dresses that hung in it. Suddenly the light shifted, and she almost cried out as she realized that the dresses had moved.

Then they were thrust aside, and Lady Dalberry, fully dressed and carrying some papers in her hand, stepped out of the wardrobe into the room. Before closing the doors she pushed aside the dresses once more and, reaching behind them, released some hidden mechanism in the back of the cupboard, for there was a repetition of the odd scraping sound, followed at once by the click of a latch.

Carol watched, spellbound, her mind working mechanically the while. This, then, was where her aunt had been the night before when she had been unable to find her in her room. She realized now that behind her aunt's bed must be the party wall that divided her flat from de Silva's. The passage which ran past her own bedroom took a sharp turn when it reached the tiny hall, continuing first past

Lady Dalberry's bedroom and dressing-room, then on past Carol's sitting-room and an extra bedroom. Lady Dalberry's room was, therefore, the first in the row of rooms to the left of the front door. The corridor outside the flats had no window at this end, the two flats meeting across the end of the passage.

It took Carol's brain but a second to register these facts while her eyes took in every detail of Lady Dalberry's movements. She saw her throw the papers on the table by her bed. Something seemed to be worrying her, for she stood staring at them, frowning, her fingers beating an impatient tattoo on the wood of the little table. Then she strolled over to the fireplace and lighted a cigarette. Once she glanced quickly at the window, and Carol, panic-stricken, concluded that she had been seized with the desire to finish her smoke on the balcony. In her fright she almost abandoned her watch altogether, and it was only the intensity of her curiosity that kept her from creeping back to the safety of her own sitting-room.

When Lady Dalberry suddenly threw her cigarette into the fire and turned towards the window she wished with all her heart that she had done so. But her fears proved groundless. Her aunt stopped short at the dressing-table, which stood at right angles to the window, and sat down.

Her back was turned to Carol, but the girl realized that the window behind which she stood was probably reflected in the mirror, and she drew back against the outside wall until her view of the room was limited to the dressing-table and the woman who sat in front of it.

Then, as Carol watched, Lady Dalberry did a thing which made the girl clutch at the wall behind her for support and kept her, for the next ten minutes, glued to the spot, sick with the realization of her own danger, yet too fascinated to move.

When, at last, she crept back along the balcony to her sitting-room she was too terrified to control her movements. The catch of her window slipped out of her hand and it swung to behind her with a noise that brought her heart to her mouth. She did not wait to discover if the sound had disturbed Lady Dalberry, but, like a hunted thing, sped along the passage to her own room. In her blind panic she made a mistake which she was bitterly to regret later. She switched off the light in the passage.

Once safely in her room she began feverishly to dress. She was conscious of one thing only: she could not stay another hour in her aunt's flat. She threw on the first garments that her hand fell on, and, wrapping herself in her fur coat, stealthily opened the door of her room and listened.

There was no sign of any movement anywhere, and the passage stretched ahead of her, pitch dark now and silent as the grave. She dared not risk the noise of the click of the switch controlling the passage light, and was obliged to grope her way as best she could. Her whole mind was concentrated on reaching the front door and getting out of the flat unobserved, and she blessed the fates that had placed Lady Dalberry's room round the angle of the passage, so that she would not have to pass it on her way out.

Very carefully she felt her way into the hall. She had almost reached the door when her sleeve caught in a silver tray that stood on the table and brought it clattering to the ground.

Transfixed with terror she stood clutching the edge of the table, listening for the inevitable sound of her aunt's door opening. But the silence remained unbroken, and at last, by sheer force of will, she shook off the spell that bound her and felt her way in the direction of the hall door.

She found it and, with a blessed feeling of relief, turned the handle. The door opened and a beam of light from the lamp in the corridor outside fell across the threshold.

Then a hand closed over her mouth from behind, jerking her head backwards and stifling the scream that rose to her lips. She made a frantic, ineffectual effort to free herself, but the hand slipped down on to her throat and began to tighten inexorably.

There was no further sound in the dark hall, but, after a short space, the hall door was closed and latched quietly from within.

CHAPTER XXI

JASPER MELLISH was feeling at odds with the world.

A succession of things had happened to exasperate him. The first of these was the arrival of Dalberry the night before. He had dropped Mrs. Verrall at New Scotland Yard on his way back from Berrydown, and had left her in the capable hands of Shand, who had undertaken to find her a safe lodging, after which he had called on Mellish to break to him the rencontre between her and Lady Dalberry. Mellish, who hated to see his plans go agley, had retired to bed thoroughly out of sorts.

He woke next morning to find that Carol's solicitors had made an appointment for him at 9:30 am, which he could not evade, and by the time he had heaved himself out of his comfortable bed nearly two hours earlier than was his custom, he was feeling very peevish indeed.

The business interview was a short one, and he got back to his rooms soon after ten, rather worse tempered, if anything, than when he had started out. The root of his grievance, though he would have hesitated to admit it, was the realization that his guardianship of Carol was about to end. Much as he had grumbled at the responsibility and all the trouble it had caused him, it had kept him in constant touch with her, and the pleasure he had derived from her company was quite out of proportion to the frequent annoyance she had managed to cause him. The thought that, after to-day, he would find himself in the comparatively obscure position of a trustee not only rankled, but made him feel a little forlorn. The truth was that he had grown to look upon her almost as a child of his own, and was beginning to realize, for the first time, the full strength of his affection for her.

"Did you give Miss Summers my message?" he asked, as his man helped him off with his coat.

"Miss Summers hasn't rung up this morning, sir," answered Jervis imperturbably.

Mellish swung round.

"Not rung up? Have you tried to get her?"

"I rang up the flat, sir, knowing you wished to fix the appointment for this afternoon, and her ladyship answered. She said Miss Summers was not at home. I asked if she could tell me where I could find her, and she said she believed she was lunching at Mrs. Carthew's, where she had spent the night. I tried twice to ring up Mrs. Carthew, but the line was engaged."

Mellish's frown deepened. Carol had undertaken to leave the flat early that morning, and go straight to her friends the Carthews, telling Lady Dalberry that she was going to spend the night with them, but there had been no suggestion of her either dining or sleeping with them the night before. He was certain that, when she had left Berrydown, she had had no intention of going anywhere but to the flat. And if she had gone there, why had she not rung him up directly after breakfast, according to her promise?

With an impatient snort he heaved himself once more into his coat. To-day he was leaving nothing to chance.

"I'll go round to the flat myself," he said, as he took his hat from a rather pained Jervis, who was already aware that this was one of those days when one can do nothing right.

Mellish found Lady Dalberry at home.

"I'm trying to get on the track of Carol," he said, wasting no time on preliminaries. "As you know, this is rather an important day for her, and there are certain arrangements I must make for this afternoon. Have you any idea where I can catch her?"

Lady Dalberry shook her head.

"How inconsiderate of her," she said sympathetically. "But you know what these young people are, Mr. Mellish. She dined out last night, and rang up about ten o'clock to say that she was spending the night and would be back this afternoon. She said nothing about any appointment with you."

Mellish looked ruffled.

"Bother the child!" he exclaimed. "I'd better ring her up at the Carthews'. May I use your telephone?"

For a fleeting second Lady Dalberry looked disconcerted. Then she threw out her hands in a little gesture of despair.

"I am so sorry," she cried. "There seems nothing I can do to help you. The telephone has been out of order ever since breakfast. I have rung them up from the hall downstairs, but no one has come yet. I tried it just now. It was no good."

Mellish turned heavily towards the door.

"It doesn't matter," he said. "I can get her from my rooms."

Lady Dalberry rose with alacrity. It struck him that, in spite of her invitation to wait for Carol, she was not sorry to see him go.

On his way out his eyes fell on a photograph of the late Lord Dalberry that stood on a table near the door.

"A good portrait, that, of Adrian," he remarked. "I don't think I've seen it before."

Lady Dalberry winced. Evidently she found it difficult, even now, to speak of her dead husband.

"It was taken in America," she said gently. "It is the one I have always liked best."

"He'd changed very little," went on Mellish thoughtfully. "Did he keep up his music, I wonder? It used to be a great hobby with him."

Lady Dalberry smiled.

"It is nice that you should remember that. He was always playing, of course, and, when he had the chance, he would go to hear good music; but we lived far away from the towns, you know, and it was not easy to keep it up."

"Of course. Just so," agreed Mellish vaguely, as he took his leave. On his way through the hall he paused opposite the telephone.

"Troublesome things," he commented, his keen eyes on the instrument. "I often wish they'd never been invented."

His face was impassive as he stepped out of the lift into the hall of the Escatorial and wished the lift-boy a benevolent "good-morning," but he was seriously perturbed. For one thing, he had seen the cut wires behind the telephone; for another, Lady Dalberry had fallen into the trap he had laid for her with a completeness that, at any other time, would have caused him acute satisfaction. Now he could only wish, with all his heart, that his suspicions had been aroused sooner and that he had thought of applying his test earlier. It was no doubt its very simplicity that had proved Lady Dalberry's undoing, but it was conclusive, for nobody could have known Lord Dalberry for long without discovering that not only was he unable to play any kind of instrument, but that he was so tone deaf as to be incapable of telling one time from another, and detested music in consequence.

Curiously enough, with all his acumen, Mellish had never, until now, suspected Lady Dalberry's *bona fides*. Her papers had been in order; indeed he knew that her credentials had been carefully gone into by the solicitors to the estate, who had found everything above suspicion. Until to-day she had never made the smallest slip. Now the magnitude of his discovery appalled him. He made up his mind to locate Carol at once, and then get into immediate touch with Shand.

He was so immersed in thought that he did not notice a car standing at the door of the Escatorial or see the woman getting out of it until she called him by name.

He looked up quickly and recognized Mrs. Carthew.

"Have you been to see Carol?" she asked. "I've come to return her bag and find out what time we're to expect her to-day."

"She's out," he answered. "I had an idea that she had already gone to you."

"We expected her early this morning, but she never turned up. I want her for a matinee this afternoon. She left this when she dined with us the night before last. I wonder she hasn't missed it."

She held out a gold-mesh bag which he recognized as Carol's.

There was nothing in his manner to betray the fact that he had received one of the greatest shocks of his life.

"I'm afraid I must lay claim to her for this afternoon," he said regretfully. "You know it's her twenty-first birthday, and there are all sorts of ceremonies attached to the day. Very tedious ones, from her point of view, I'm afraid. I'll take the bag, if you like, and return it to her, and I'll tell her to ring you up and let you know when to expect her."

They stood for a few minutes chatting until Mellish, with admirably concealed relief, handed her into her car.

Then he hailed the nearest taxi and told the man to drive to New Scotland Yard.

"I'm in a hurry. Avoid as many traffic blocks as you can," he told him resignedly.

He overtook Shand on the Embankment and picked him up. It did not take Mellish long to put him in possession of the facts, and he was quick to see the gravity of the situation.

"You think that Lady Dalberry is aware that Miss Summers did not spend the night with her friends?" he asked.

"I am certain that the woman who calls herself Lady Dalberry is in this up to the hilt," snapped Mellish, whose anxiety was fast becoming unbearable.

In answer to Shand's swift glance of interrogation he described how Lady Dalberry had fallen into the trap he had set for her.

"I acted on impulse," he said, "and I'm thankful now that I did. It struck me suddenly that her grief for her husband had, all along, been a little overdone. But I can't understand it. It seems incredible that she should have managed to hoodwink the solicitors to that extent. I naturally took her for granted. But I'm certain now that she never knew Adrian Culver."

"I'm on my way to keep an appointment with Mrs. Verrall in my room," said Shand thoughtfully. "She was to be there at twelve, and it's close on that now. We've got all Conyers's belongings at the Yard, and I want her to look at one or two things. They may suggest something to her. I'll send a man down to the Escatorial now to keep an eye on both the flats while I have a word with Mrs. Verrall. I fancy the time will be well spent."

"For God's sake make it as short an interview as possible," urged Mellish.

They found Mrs. Verrall waiting in Shand's room. After a word of explanation Shand went to a cupboard and took out the suitcase she had been looking at when she was surprised in Conyers's lodgings. He placed it on the table and threw it open.

"We found this packet of photographs at the bottom of the case," he said, handing a fat bundle to her. "Will you see if you can identify any of them?"

She ran through them quickly. Most of them were familiar to her, but the names she gave conveyed nothing to either of the two men. She had almost finished her inspection, and was turning over the contents of an envelope full of snapshots, when she gave a sudden cry of mingled surprise and excitement.

"It's the same man!" she exclaimed. "The one whose photo was stolen from me that night!"

She handed a snapshot to Shand. It was of a group of three men, standing in a doorway, with the sun shining full on their faces. No Press photograph could have been clearer.

She pointed to the figure in the centre of the group.

"That's the man! I'm certain of it! The one on his left is Eric himself, and I know the other, a man called Culick." Shand turned the photograph round. On the back was written, in pencil, a date and the names of the three men. The first two were, as she had said, Conyers and Culick. Shand gave a little gasp of triumph as he read the third. It was Strelinski!

"That's what I've been waiting for," he said slowly. There was an immense satisfaction in his voice. "I felt that name would crop up sooner or later. Now we can get to work."

He handed the photograph to Mellish.

"A very nice trio," he went on, "if we're to include the lady who calls herself Lady Dalberry. We've got her, and, unless things have gone very much agley, we can lay our hands on de Silva. But Strelinski's my man! Unless I'm very much mistaken, he's got two murders at least to his count. Do you remember the descriptions given by the steward on the *Enriqueta* and Conyers's taxi-driver? 'Slim, medium height, with fair, almost white, hair.' Look at that snapshot!"

Mellish was looking at it. The man's hair showed white in the photograph, but his face was that of a young man and his eyes had photographed dark, a sure sign that they were brown, not blue.

"I've seen this fellow before, somewhere," said Mellish meditatively. "Let me have a pencil, will you?"

Shand took one from the writing-table and handed it to him. Mellish laid the snapshot flat on his knee and worked on it for a minute.

"How's that?" he said at last, passing it to Shand.

Before he could speak, Mrs. Verrall, who was peering over his shoulder, gave a cry.

"It's de Silva!" she exclaimed.

Mellish had blacked in the hair and eyebrows, leaving the features untouched, and the likeness was unmistakable.

"He did it uncommonly well," he admitted. "But then the man was an actor by profession. And his eyes were naturally brown, which made all the difference. He only needed a sallow make-up and a dark wig to make himself unrecognizable. Conyers must have seen his hair that night, or else I doubt if he'd have spotted him. The man's an artist in his way."

Shand picked up his hat.

"We're up against something bigger than I thought," he said gravely. "The sooner we get a move on the better. I shan't be happy till I see Miss Summers safely out of their hands. The whole of this business was planned months ago in South America, and it looks as if she'd been their objective from the beginning. Why they have waited until now to bring matters to a head, I don't understand."

Mellish laid a heavy hand on his shoulder and propelled him in the direction of the door.

"I do," he answered, with a note of anguish in his voice.

"Miss Summers came of age this morning. She is her own mistress now. She can sign away every penny she's got, and she will, if these people are what I take them to be."

Shand nodded.

"The money's the least important part of the business now," he said soberly.

He glanced at Mellish. The fat man's face was drawn with anxiety.

"I know," he snapped. "We've got to make Lady Dalberry talk. And at once, if we're to get Miss Summers out of Strelinski's hands alive."

CHAPTER XXII

CAROL'S RETURN to consciousness was merciful in its slowness. Her first sensation was one of pain, a dull ache that racked her whole body and a sense of oppression that made even breathing difficult. Then, as she moved her head in an instinctive effort to find relief, the discomfort centered itself in her throat and neck. Still too dazed to reason, she tried to raise her hands.

With a shock that jerked her back into full consciousness of her surroundings, she realized that her arms were bound tightly to her sides.

For a time she lay motionless, her brain growing clearer each moment. She remembered now her frenzied attempt to escape from her aunt's flat and the horror of the silent struggle in the dark hall. Slowly the whole sequence of events came back to her, and she came near to fainting again as the significance of her position dawned on her. She realized, only too well, into whose hands she had fallen, and a sick terror invaded her, leaving her shaking and powerless in its grip.

A sound in a room near by roused her, and, urged by a blind instinct to escape, she managed to raise herself to a sitting position, only to fall back, sick and dizzy, miserably conscious of her own helplessness.

At last her brain steadied and she was able to open her eyes. As she moved her head she realized that part of her discomfort was due to a muffler which passed over her mouth and was tied tightly at the back of her neck. She tried to shift it, but, after a vain effort that made her head swim, gave up the attempt and concentrated her attention on her surroundings.

She found herself in a room she had never seen before. It was well and solidly furnished, and, as her eyes fell on the heavy wardrobe which stood opposite the bed on which she lay, she realized that it was an exact replica of the one in her aunt's bedroom. The window at the other end of the room was draped with thick curtains of some dark material, and, though she listened intently, she could hear no sound of traffic outside. From the general aspect of the room she felt fairly certain that she was still in the Escatorial, and she had very little doubt as to the identity of the owner of the flat in which she found herself. Taking the lack of sound into account she judged that it was one of the rooms looking on to the garden at the back, no doubt the one corresponding to her aunt's room; hence the presence of the second wardrobe, the significance of which she could guess after what she had seen in her aunt's bedroom.

Her heart gave a wild leap and then seemed to stop beating. Footsteps were coming down the passage outside. From her position on the bed she could not see the door, but she heard the handle turn and she knew, without a vestige of a doubt, who was entering the room. She lay rigid, listening to the soft, light footfall on the carpet as the owner approached the bed. A hand came into her line of vision, holding a glass.

"Drink this."

The voice was the one she dreaded most to hear, and a long shudder ran through her body. It seemed in that moment as if all hope left her. Even in the comparative security of her aunt's flat she had feared de Silva; now, alone with him and utterly at his mercy, her terror became almost uncontrollable.

In desperation she twisted her head away from the glass.

"Do not be foolish," said de Silva sharply. "It is only brandy. You will feel better when you have drunk it. Quickly, please!"

She shook her head. His hand was already loosening the bandage over her mouth, but, even if her lips had been free, she could not have spoken.

"You will have to take my word for it that it is not drugged," he went on, "but, believe me, I have every reason to desire to keep you in full possession of your senses. Now!"

He raised her head and, as the muffler dropped, held the glass to her mouth. Half hypnotized by sheer terror, she swallowed a mouthful, and almost immediately felt her head clear and her nerves stiffen. De Silva did not force her to drink more, but set the glass down on the table behind him and picked up the muffler from the bed.

He stood looking down at her, swinging it gently to and fro in his hand.

"I do not wish to use this," he said quietly. "But if you scream I shall kill you. You understand? Things have gone so far now that there would be nothing else for me to do. You will be quiet?"

She nodded, knowing that he spoke nothing but the truth.

"If you will undertake not to be foolish I will put this scarf away, but, remember, any attempt to get help and you will suffer; and you have suffered already, only, this time, you will not come to your senses again."

He fetched a chair and sat down by the bed.

"For the moment," he said, "I am going to do the talking. In the first place, you have perhaps guessed that you have only yourself to blame for what has happened. Believe me, I have never had any desire to hurt you, and, if I could get what I need by legitimate means, I should infinitely prefer to do so. But to-night you forced my hand. It was pure chance that I heard you leave the balcony and was able to act in time, and it is no one's fault but your own that I have been drastic in my measures."

He sat looking at her for a moment in silence, a little smile playing on his lips, then:

"If you had stayed on at the flat you would have married me in time, you know," he said gently.

Seeing the passionate denial in her eyes, he went on:

"Oh yes, you would. By the time I had finished with you you would have had to. In the flat there you were at my mercy, and there would have come a day when your engagement to your fool of a cousin would have come to an end, broken off by you because, knowing what you knew, you would not dare go on with it. Those are the measures I should have preferred to have taken, but, as I say, you have forced me to modify my plans. If you behave reasonably now you have nothing to fear. You will leave this flat a little poorer and, perhaps, a little wiser than when you came into it, and you will be free to marry that solemn prig Dalberry whenever you feel inclined."

In spite of himself he could not control the venom in his voice, and Carol realized that, though cupidity had been his main inspiration from the beginning, his hatred and jealousy of Dalberry had now become almost uncontrollable.

"What do you want me to do?" she whispered.

He rose and pushed his chair out of the way.

"I am glad you are beginning to see reason," he said smoothly. "You know what I want?"

Her throat was so dry that the words came with difficulty.

"My money?"

"A little of your money," he corrected. "You need not be afraid. You will not go to Dalberry with empty hands. There are certain papers of your father's which I happen to know are in the hands of your solicitors. I need not bore you with business details. It is enough to say that they will satisfy my needs. You have only to put your signature to a letter I will give you, telling the solicitors to hand the documents over to Lady Dalberry, and I will not trouble you further. I shall leave England by the eleven o'clock boat this morning, and, before I step on board at Dover, I will undertake to post a letter to Dalberry, telling him of your whereabouts. Until he gets it, I am afraid you will have to put up with a little discomfort, but I can promise you that you will be none the worse for your adventure. If I fetch the letter now, will you please sign it?"

Carol hesitated.

"How can I be sure that you will tell them where to find me?" she said at last, in desperation. "If the servants see you leaving they may not come up here for days. How can you expect me to trust you?"

He smiled.

"For the simple reason that you have no alternative and you are not a fool. I am desperate, and you know it. Do you realize how easy it would be for me to put you away? Just enough chloroform to send you to sleep. A little expedition back to your own bedroom, where Lady Dalberry will find you to-morrow morning with the doors and windows closed and the tap of the gas fire turned on. She will be heart-broken, of course, and, in her evidence at the inquest, she will describe how for some time you have been nervous and depressed. Believe me, it will be easy and, from my point of view, necessary. You will do better to trust to my word and do what I ask."

Now that she knew the worst, Carol's courage was beginning to return, and with it her reasoning powers. Though lacking in experience of the world, she had inherited much of her father's acuteness and sound common sense, and, terrified as she still was of de Silva, she was sufficiently mistress of herself now to realize that his arguments did not ring quite true. He might very well be bluffing. On the other hand, she believed him to be more than capable of carrying out his threats.

"You will gain nothing by killing me," she said, trying to keep her voice steady.

"Except your silence," he reminded her, with a grim note in his voice that sent a shiver coursing down her spine. "You know too much now. Once you are out of the way there is nothing to prevent my staying on here, but so long as you are alive England will be closed to me. It is not much to ask, that you should pay me to go."

He looked at his watch.

"It is nearly five now," he said. "I will leave you half an hour to think it over in. It is all I can spare. I have my own arrangements to make, and I need sleep. When I come back it will be for the letter, and I think you will sign it."

The door closed softly behind him, and Carol was left to her thoughts. At first she found it impossible to force them to any kind of coherence. The fear with which he inspired her and the knowledge that she was absolutely in his power made the temptation to give in to his demands almost irresistible, and yet, deep down in her mind, lay the conviction that his real plans were very different from those he had chosen to reveal to her.

It seemed barely ten minutes before she heard his footsteps returning and realized that she was still in a state of miserable indecision. Every instinct now urged her not to put her name to the letter, but, in this moment of panic, she doubted whether she would have the courage to withstand him.

He came swiftly towards her.

"Well?" he said.

She looked up and saw his face, and knew that part, at any rate, of what he had told her was true.

"I will sign," she answered, in a voice that was hardly audible.

Without a word he fetched a table and placed it by the bed. On it he laid a sheet of foolscap, the upper portion of which he had covered with a piece of blank paper.

She raised herself with difficulty to a sitting position and stared at it.

Below the space he had left for her signature, two other people had already signed their names. One she recognized as that of Captain Bond; the other was unknown to her.

"The witnesses," he informed her, in answer to her puzzled look. "As they were unfortunately unable to be present, I had to settle with them beforehand. I may tell you that they have been well drilled in their parts."

Again she did not believe him. She was convinced that Bond, with all his faults, would never have lent himself to this.

"I can't sign unless you set me free," she said.

He laughed softly.

"All in good time. The stage is not set yet."

He moved to a writing-table near the window and opened a drawer.

"A broad nib is what you generally use, I believe," he continued. "Tell me if I am wrong."

She did not answer. In passing the table the edge of his coat had caught in the corner of the covering paper and shifted it, and the whole of the piece of foolscap underneath it lay open to her eyes. She had only a moment in which to read while, with his back to her, he bent over the drawer of the table, but one glance would have been enough.

This was no letter that he was forcing her to sign, but a will. Her own will, written in the typical script of a solicitor's clerk. Her eyes caught the words: "I hereby will and bequeath," and, farther down the page: "To my uncle's wife, Irma, Dowager Countess of Dalberry." In a flash she realized the diabolical significance of the whole plot. The will once signed, she would die, in the manner so vividly described by de Silva, and Lady Dalberry would step into her inheritance. That she should leave her money to the aunt with whom she had been living would seem natural enough to the outside world. In putting her name to the document that lay before her, she would be signing her own death-warrant.

She glanced swiftly at de Silva. He was already in the act of raising himself. In a second he would turn.

With an effort that wrenched her whole body, she managed to get her shoulder against the rickety little table and send it spinning to the floor. The papers on it fluttered through the air and fell almost at de Silva's feet.

He whirled round to find Carol lying motionless on the bed.

"I was trying to raise myself," she panted. "Cramp! It's horrible ..."

His eyes darted to the papers, but they had fallen face downwards, and there was nothing to suggest that Carol had had any opportunity to read them.

He picked them up and replaced them on the table, carefully adjusting the covering paper. Then, setting the pen and ink down beside them, he bent over to untie the silk scarf that bound the girl's hands.

With the courage of despair, Carol managed to twist herself out of his grasp. She knew now that her one chance lay in her refusal to sign the paper.

"I can't do it now," she sobbed incoherently, her eyes closed so that she should not see his face. "You must give me time. I didn't know what I was saying when I said I'd sign."

There was a silence that she thought he would never break. She was shaking uncontrollably now in every limb, and she did not dare look at him, but she knew he had not moved from his place beside the bed.

His voice came at last, soft and venomous.

"So you prefer the other alternative," he said.

She heard the protesting creak of the mattress and felt it sag as he placed his knee on it.

Then his hands were at her throat. His fingers crept to the back of her neck, and the pressure of his thumbs under her chin began to tighten.

She was past struggling now, and lay waiting for what she knew to be the end. The sense of suffocation increased, and she could hear the blood drumming in her ears.

Then, miraculously, the pressure relaxed and his voice reached her.

"I will give you one more chance," he said. "Will you sign?"

She shook her head.

He raised himself, and she felt that he was standing looking down at her. For an instant the cloud lifted from her brain, and she realized that he had been bluffing, trying to frighten her into signing. Unless he were driven to it he would not kill her till he had forced her to put her name to the paper, and, when he did kill her, it would not be after so crude and incriminating a fashion.

He was bending over her once more, unfastening the silk that tied her hands. He released the left hand and bound the other tightly to her side.

"You will need this one to write with," he told her. "We must not hurt it."

She opened her eyes and looked him full in the face.

"I will never sign," she said, with the courage of despair.

He took a firm grip of her left wrist.

"I think you will," he assured her, with an icy smoothness that was more terrifying than anger.

His grasp tightened and he began, slowly and inexorably, to twist her arm.

Not a sound escaped her lips, though, as the pain increased, tears of sheer agony welled from under her closed lids and trickled down her cheeks. He waited till she was sick and dizzy with the pain, and then abruptly released his grip.

"Will you sign now?" he asked.

Again she shook her head.

He hesitated.

"I do not want to hurt you," he said. "Why not be sensible?"

Then, as she did not answer, his hand closed on her wrist once more.

"This time I shall not be so gentle," he assured her, and waited for her answer.

But it did not come. She lay rigid, her lips tightly closed, steeling herself to bear the agony she knew was coming.

It came. But this time he was to defeat his own ends. There is a point beyond the endurance of human nature, and Carol had reached it.

A shriek that died into a moan of anguish broke from her lips; then her whole body, that had been tense with agony, relaxed, and de Silva knew that she had fainted.

CHAPTER XXIII

WHEN CAROL RECOVERED consciousness she was alone.

The scarf had been replaced over her mouth, her hands were once more firmly bound to her sides, and she could tell, by the throbbing ache and discomfort in her left arm, that it was rapidly swelling. She tried to ease it a little, but the pain that resulted was so atrocious that she gave up the attempt and set herself to bear it as best she might. She could still move the joint, however, and knew that the bone was not broken.

While she was engaged in these tentative efforts to discover the extent of the injury, she heard the slow, reverberating chime of a church clock. She counted the strokes. Seven o'clock. The night was over. Would she live through another day? She wondered. At the moment she felt so ill, so utterly beaten, that she would almost have welcomed death as an alternative to this endless struggle in which she seemed doomed to be worsted. Of one thing she felt convinced—if de Silva touched her arm again, she would give in. She could only pray that he would leave her alone until she had managed to regain at least a semblance of courage.

There was not a sound in the flat. If de Silva were there he must be sleeping.

She tried to free her feet, but the long strips of silk that bound them to the bed were so cunningly tied that they tightened, rather than gave, with her efforts. In desperation she tugged harder.

Suddenly something ripped under the bedstead. She pulled harder and felt the silk slowly give. In another second her feet were free.

She worked her way into a sitting position and managed to get her feet to the ground, but when she tried to stand, she found herself so stiff and cramped that she was glad to sink back on to the bed, rubbing one foot against the other to restore the circulation. Her hands were still bound to her sides, and the change to a more upright position made her sprained arm ache almost unbearably.

And all the time she was beside herself with fear that de Silva would return.

She managed at last to get on to her feet and progress awkwardly across the room. It was an absurd and crablike progress, and, owing to her fettered arms, she could reach nothing higher than a couple of feet from the ground.

Thus it was that, when at last she found what she was looking for, it turned out to be quite hopelessly out of her reach.

Lying on the top of the high chest of drawers, in company with de Silva's hair-brushes and other toilet articles, was a small pair of nail-scissors.

They were placed so far away from the edge that it seemed out of the question that she should ever reach them, until she noticed that, across the top of the chest of drawers, was a runner of embroidered linen.

She listened intently, but there was not a sound in the flat. Gathering all her courage she leaned forward and managed to get the edge of the runner between her teeth. Very carefully she pulled. The runner, carrying with it all the things that were lying upon it, slid over the edge of the chest of drawers on to the ground. The hair-brushes fell with a thud that brought her heart to her mouth, but fortunately the carpet was thick and, judging by the silence that ensued, the noise had not reached de Silva's ears.

With some difficulty she managed to kneel and get the fingers of her right hand round the scissors. By twisting her wrist, she found she could insert one of the blades under the edge of the scarf where it passed round her body. She worked the blade clumsily backwards and forwards against the silk, and it seemed an age before she felt the fabric begin to give. Once it had started to rip her task became easier, but infinitely more painful, owing to the pressure on her swollen arm. White with pain, she strained the silk to the utmost with her right arm, keeping her left as rigid as possible, and with each effort she could feel the tear lengthening. Soon she had her arms free, after which it was an easy matter to loosen that portion of the silk that had been wound tight round her wrists.

The greatest relief came when she slipped the bandage from over her mouth, and could breathe freely once more.

She was standing holding it in her hand, trying to gather courage to attempt the opening of the door of the room, when she heard the church clock outside strike the half hour. The sound had hardly died away before the telephone bell in the hall burst into an insistent clamour.

So unexpected was the sound and so taut were her nerves that she only stopped herself from screaming by a miracle. As she stood there, shaking with apprehension, she heard a door open and footsteps crossing the hall, followed by de Silva's voice answering the telephone. It was the house instrument, with she gathered, the night porter at the other end.

"If it is important, I will see him," she heard de Silva say. "Ask him to come up."

There was a pause, during which she waited in an agony of terror, expecting every moment that he would open the door and look into the bedroom. But luck was with her. She heard him go to the hall door, open it, and admit his visitor.

A confused murmur of voices came to her, and she had a conviction that one of them was that of Bond. She moved closer to the door of the bedroom and tried to hear more clearly, but the speakers were standing near the front door, and the sound only reached her faintly.

Realizing that she was cut off from the hall as a means of escape and that, if she were to get away at all, she must take advantage of de Silva's preoccupation with his visitor, she crept across the room to the wardrobe.

She felt certain that this was built on the same plan as the one she had seen used as a door in her aunt's bedroom, but when she opened it and pushed aside the clothes it contained, she was confronted with a plain surface of solid and immovable mahogany. She searched in vain for the catch she had heard click when Lady Dalberry used the corresponding cupboard in her bedroom, but she could find no sort of projection on the inside of the wardrobe.

In despair she slipped back to the door of the bedroom, hoping that de Silva might be inspired to take his guest to some room farther down the passage. To her dismay he seemed to be showing him out.

She heard the front door open and a man's voice—Bond's, she felt certain now—raised in high anger.

She hesitated. Bond had shown himself a good friend to her once when he warned her not to frequent the Onyx establishment, and he might prove an ally now. In her desperation she was inclined to take the risk. Then she remembered that he was one of the "witnesses" to the will lying on the table, and drew back. As she did so, she realized that, in any case, she was too late.

The front door slammed heavily, and she knew that Bond had departed and her chance was gone.

She guessed that, once he had got rid of his guest, de Silva's first move would be towards the bedroom. Already she could hear his steps crossing the hall. With the instinct of a trapped animal she made for the one place that offered any sort of concealment, the wardrobe.

Only one door of it was open, and behind the other hung a couple of heavy winter overcoats. Slipping behind these she covered herself as best she could and waited, cowering, for de Silva to make his appearance.

She heard the door open, then his sharp exclamation of furious dismay as his eyes fell on the empty bed.

His first move was towards the window. The rings clattered as he jerked the heavy curtains apart. Then he opened the window and stepped out on to the balcony. In a second he was back in the room, and there was a moment's silence, during which she could guess that he had halted, probably arrested by the sight of the strips of silk from which she had freed herself and which she had left lying on the floor.

Then came the dreaded sound of his feet approaching the wardrobe. In another second he would throw open the other door and her discovery would be inevitable. She waited, making herself as small as possible behind the inadequate screen of the overcoats.

He had almost reached the cupboard when he paused, evidently struck by a sudden thought, wheeled and made a dash for the door of the bedroom, slamming and locking it behind him. Carol heard him run through the hall and out through the front door, and guessed what was in his mind. If, as he suspected, she had managed to open the back of the cupboard and escape into the other flat, there was still a chance that he might head her off there. She could imagine him hastening from room to room of Lady Dalberry's flat in search of her.

In the meanwhile, by locking the door of the bedroom, he had cut off her one avenue of escape.

She could only hope that he would jump to the conclusion that she had succeeded in getting away while he was engaged in conversation with Bond and abandon the search. If only he did not decide to make use of the passage through the wardrobe, there was still a chance that she might remain undiscovered.

Paralyzed with fear that he would come through the wardrobe from the direction of her aunt's flat, and knowing that, if he did so, he could hardly avoid seeing her, she waited through what seemed an eternity for his return.

Her luck held. When he did come back it was by way of the bedroom door.

She could hear the sound of drawers being hurriedly opened and shut, and gathered from his movements that he must be packing. He had accepted the fact of her escape, then, and was intent on making his get-away before she should have time to give the alarm. She had heard the church clock strike eight while he was in the next door flat, and she knew that, if he was to catch the first boat train, he would not have any too much time. Now, at last, she began to entertain at lease a glimmer of hope that she might remain undiscovered.

There was a sound that she took to be the closing of a bag or suitcase, followed by the reopening of the bedroom door. It seemed as though the impossible was actually about to happen and he was on the point of leaving the flat.

Her heart leaped and then seemed to stop its beat. For he had turned with an exclamation of impatience, and was approaching the wardrobe.

Dropping the case he was carrying he flung open the second door of the cupboard.

There was a tense silence, broken at last by de Silva's low, mirthless laugh.

"So that was it," he mocked softly. "Almost you got away with it. In another moment I should have been gone, and the bird would have flown. As it is, I am afraid I shall have to postpone my departure, and extend my hospitality for just a little longer."

Carol shrank into the corner of the wardrobe, faint with terror. Then she broke into a frenzied appeal.

"Let me go," she implored him. "I promise I won't say a word to any one, if only you'll let me go. You can go away, and I'll stay here until you've had time to leave the country. No one shall ever know what has happened to-night. I'll give you money, if it's money you want ..."

He laughed again, his face an inch from hers.

"Oh, I shall have the money. I will see to that myself. Come."

He stretched out his hand and caught her by the wrist.

Before she could help herself he had jerked her violently out into the room and on to the bed. Holding her wrists with one hand, he took his handkerchief from his pocket and tied them together. Then he turned to pick up the strip of silk she had left on the floor.

He had barely turned his back before she was off the bed and at the door, trying in vain to turn the handle with her fettered hands.

It took all his strength to overpower her. Once she managed to break away from him, but the advantage she gained was a brief one, and only served to exhaust her.

A few minutes later she was on the bed, bound and gagged once more, and he was standing over her.

"There has been enough of this fooling," he said venomously. "You are not an idiot. Use the brains that have been given you. In the end you will sign. Believe me, if you do it now, before I go, you will save yourself a great deal of unnecessary suffering."

He could see the expression in her eyes change from terror to relief at the mention of his departure.

"I am going," he went on, and her heart sank at the mockery in his voice, "because I have that imbecile, Bond, to deal with. You will be pleased to hear that he has his suspicions, our friend Bond. He very nearly spilt the milk this morning when he came here. If you had cried out! I am going now to smooth him down, but ..."

He paused, his laughing eyes watching her.

"Soon you will have your dear aunt to deal with. I fancy you will find her less patient than I have been."

She would have spoken then if she could, but the scarf over her mouth made all communication impossible. He was watching her eyes, however, and read the message in them as surely as though he had heard it from her lips.

"You will be glad to see Lady Dalberry," he went on softly. "A woman's hand. So much has been written on that beautiful subject. If I were you, I should sign now."

Then, as she made no movement:

"As you will. You gain nothing, you know, by delay. I have left precise instructions as to your treatment, and you may be sure that Lady Dalberry will carry them out."

He paused, apparently enjoying some grim jest of his own, then:

"Neither food nor drink will pass your lips until you sign this letter, I assure you, and your friends will not find you. You are still obstinate? Then I must leave you to your aunt." He was laughing openly now. With a little shrug of his shoulders he swung round and left the room, and she heard the click of the lock as he turned the key behind him.

He was no sooner gone than she tried once more to free her feet; but this time he had done his work too well and the bandage held, in spite of all her efforts. Then, for the first time, her self-control gave way entirely, and she burst into a flood of tears which, once started, she found she could not stem. She cried until, from sheer exhaustion, she could cry no more. Then she lay, in a kind of dull stupor, waiting for the next assault on her courage.

It was over an hour before she was disturbed, and then it was by the entrance of de Silva.

He closed and locked the bedroom door carefully behind him, putting the key in his pocket, and went at once to the wardrobe. As he opened the doors he cast a mocking glance at her over his shoulder.

"How much would you have given to have found this little button?" he scoffed, as he slipped his hand behind the massive wardrobe.

She heard the click of the latch, followed by the sound of the back of the cupboard sliding to one side. Then he stepped through and disappeared, leaving the cavity open.

From where she lay she could see nothing of the room on the other side of the opening in the wardrobe, but she could hear some one moving to and fro, and once, about half an hour after de Silva had left her, the telephone pealed loudly in Lady Dalberry's flat and a voice, which she thought she recognized as her aunt's, answered it. Then there was the sound of the front door of Lady Dalberry's flat opening and she could just hear footsteps and voices in the passage beyond. She heard the front door close again, and then some one crossed the bedroom and approached the wardrobe.

In another second Lady Dalberry stood in the opening.

Her eyes, bright with malice, sought Carol's and held them. Her Ups, scarlet against the white make-up she affected, were parted in a faint, amused smile.

Carol tried to meet her gaze bravely, but, as she looked, the horror that had inspired her blind effort to escape from her aunt's flat returned to her. She tried to turn her eyes away and could not.

Then the figure of the other woman wavered and grew misty, the bandage round the girl's mouth seemed to get tighter and more suffocating, and, for the second time, she fainted.

When she came to herself Lady Dalberry was sitting by the bed. She had replaced the table, bearing the writing materials, at Carol's elbow. On it was a glass filled with an amber-coloured liquid.

"You will drink this," she said shortly. "And after that, my little Carol, you will sign. There have been too many delays. We will finish this business."

She unfastened the handkerchief and freed the girl's mouth, then she held the glass to her lips.

Carol drank thirstily. It mattered little to her now whether the stuff were drugged or not. Indeed there was nothing she would have welcomed more gladly than oblivion, but she knew that Lady Dalberry, in her present mood, was not likely to vouchsafe her even that mercy. The liquid revived her, however, and for a moment brought back some of her old courage.

"I will not sign," she whispered stubbornly through parched lips.

Lady Dalberry smiled and bent forward to untie the bandage round the girl's wrists.

Then, as if in answer to Carol's prayers, the front-door bell of de Silva's flat pealed loudly.

With a muttered exclamation Lady Dalberry rose to her feet and stood hesitating.

The bell rang again, and this time it did not stop. Whoever was on the other side of the door was standing with his finger on the bell. Then, through the insistent clamour of the bell, came the sound of knocking.

Lady Dalberry went swiftly to the door of the bedroom and stood there, listening.

The pounding on the door grew more violent, and above it Carol could hear the sound of a man's voice. He was shouting something indistinguishable.

Lady Dalberry must have caught something of what he said, however, for she crossed the room swiftly and began to refasten the scarf round the girl's mouth. Then she untied the bandage that secured Carol's ankles and, with surprising strength for one of her build, jerked the girl to her feet.

Carol staggered and would have fallen but for the other woman's arm round her waist.

Trussed and helpless, she could make no show of resistance as Lady Dalberry half dragged, half carried, her through the opening in the cupboard into the adjoining flat.

Before Carol could adjust her mind to what was happening she found herself back in her own bedroom. Lady Dalberry only waited long enough to help the girl on to the bed and rebind her ankles. Then, without a word, she hurried from the room, closing the door behind her.

Carol guessed that she was probably engaged in closing the passage between the two flats. From where she lay she could still hear the noise of the assault on de Silva's door. Then it ceased abruptly, and she wondered whether the Argentine's unwelcome callers had departed in despair. Lady Dalberry did not come back, and for a long twenty minutes or so Carol lay helpless, speculating, with a sinking heart, on what her next move would be.

Then the knocking began again, but this time at the door of Lady Dalberry's flat.

Carol heard the front door open, then the sound of Lady Dalberry's voice, cool and faintly ironical.

It was followed by the sound of her own name, uttered by Jasper Mellish, in tones so unlike his usual lazy drawl that it reached her ears even through the closed doors of the bedroom.

Carol tried frenziedly to answer, but the scarf round her mouth proved too effective a gag.

With an effort that sent a stab of agony through her sprained arm, she managed to get her feet to the ground. She raised herself, lost her balance, and literally flung herself in the direction of the door.

She fell heavily, wrenching her arm agonizingly, but she had managed to cover at least half the distance between the bed and the door. By dragging herself painfully along the floor she managed to achieve the rest, only to find that, with her arms bound as they were, it was impossible for her to reach the handle of the door.

With infinite labour she got once more to her feet. For a second she stood, rocking to and fro helplessly; then, as she fell, she flung herself, with all her force, against the closed door.

Then she sank, utterly spent, in a pitiful heap on the floor.

And as she lay there she heard the sound of receding footsteps and the murmur of voices growing fainter, and realized that, once more, she had lost.

Mellish was leaving the flat.

CHAPTER XXIV

As the police car containing Mellish, Shand, and a couple of C.I.D. men drew up before the Escatorial, Dalberry appeared in the doorway of the flats. His face lit up at the sight of Mellish.

"I say, Jasper," he began, "I'm a bit worried ..."

In spite of his anxiety Mellish's lips curved into a grim smile.

"You have our sympathy," he remarked sardonically. "Have you been up to the flat?"

"I've just come from there. Carol's not in. Where is she?"

"That's what I propose to find out. Who told you she was out?"

"Lady Dalberry. According to her, Carol rang up to say that she was at Claridges. Been to a dance there, or something, and stayed the night. That wasn't what she'd arranged to do, was it?"

His eyes fell on Shand and his two companions.

"I say ..." he began.

At that moment Shand, who had been engaged in a low-voiced consultation with the detective he had detailed to watch the flats, joined them.

"My man tells me that no one has gone in or out of either of the flats since he got here, but the porter declares that de Silva went out about nine o'clock this morning and returned at ten," he informed them. "It appears that Bond was here early, between seven and eight. He stayed about twenty minutes, according to the night porter. What brought you here, Lord Dalberry?"

"I rang up Miss Summers at the Carthews', as we'd arranged, and found they knew nothing about her. When Mrs. Carthew told me that she had seen Mr. Mellish coming out of these flats without Miss Summers I began to get the wind up and came round myself. I was just going on to Claridges to verify my aunt's statement when you arrived."

Leaving a man to guard the stairs, Shand herded them into the lift.

"I think we'll take de Silva first," he said thoughtfully. "If Miss Summers is not in her aunt's flat, it's pretty obvious where we shall find her, unless they've managed to get her away, which I doubt."

Arrived at de Silva's door, Shand put his finger on the bell-push and kept it there. There was no response.

Then he knocked, shouting to de Silva to open the door, but there was not a sound from the flat.

"I've got the pass-key here, sir," said the detective he had sent down earlier in the morning.

Shand took it, and in another second they were in the flat.

"Tell Lee to stay on the landing and keep his eyes open," he flung over his shoulder as they entered.

He made for the sitting-room. It was empty, but on the table was a tray bearing drinks and the remains of a plate of sandwiches.

Shand went straight from there to de Silva's bedroom. The door was closed and, when he tried the handle, it did not yield.

Wasting no time he put his shoulder against it and exerted his full strength. There was a sharp snap and the sound of splintering wood as the lock gave and the door flew open.

The room was in disorder. On the floor, near the big wardrobe, lay a closed suitcase. The doors of the cupboard were open, clothes were lying half out of the drawers of the chest of drawers by the window, and it was evident that de Silva had been disturbed in the act of packing.

Shand fell on his knees by the suitcase and snapped it open.

"Full," he said. "He must have cleared in a hurry or he'd have taken this with him."

Bolton, one of the detectives, appeared at the door.

"He's not in the flat, sir," he said. "We've made a thorough search. All the windows are closed and latched on the inside."

Shand rose to his feet.

"Then he's gone opposite," he said. "Must have slipped across just before we came up in the lift. If he used the stairs they'll have got him downstairs by now."

An exclamation from Mellish made him turn.

The fat man was staring at a paper he had picked up from a table which stood beside the bed.

"There's been some devilry here, Shand," he said heavily. "This is Miss Summers's will, though I'll swear she never drew it up herself. I hope to God she's all right."

Shand peered over his shoulder.

"Has she signed it?" he demanded; then, answering his own question: "It's still unsigned! Then you may take it she's still alive. We'll leave a man here, in case our friend comes back, and go over and have a few words with Lady Dalberry."

They crossed the landing to the flat opposite. To Shand's surprise the door was opened at once and by Lady Dalberry herself.

She was dressed for the street and was evidently on the point of going out.

"Oh, Mr. Mellish," she began, "I am so glad you came back."

Then her eyes fell on Dalberry.

"You have met, then," she went on. "I have just been telling Gillie that Carol telephoned just after you'd gone to say that she was at Claridges after all. It appears—"

Mellish broke in ruthlessly on her explanations.

"Lady Dalberry," he said, "we've reason to believe that Carol is in this flat. Will you let us in, please?"

Lady Dalberry laughed.

"Isn't this a little foolish?" she exclaimed. "I have told you that Carol is at Claridges; you have only to ring them up at the hotel to find out if I am speaking the truth."

"On your telephone?" suggested Mellish pointedly.

"Certainly," she answered. "The man came and put it right just after I saw you this morning. It is at your disposal."

She stepped aside to permit him to pass into the hall.

"There seem to be a great many of you," she continued, with more than a hint of good-humoured contempt in her voice. "Are you all looking for that poor Carol?"

"It will save time and trouble if you will tell us at once where Carol is," said Mellish. "If not, we must search the flat."

She shrugged her shoulders.

"I have told you all I know about Carol," she answered. "You will forgive me if I say that I think you are taking a great deal on yourself if you insist on breaking your way into my private apartments. I shall do nothing to prevent you, but that does not mean that I shall swallow the insult meekly. You may be sorry that you have taken this line, Mr. Mellish."

She stepped past him and out on to the landing, Mellish instinctively following her.

Shand came forward to meet her.

"I have a warrant," he said. "I advise you to make no trouble."

She turned to Mellish.

"This is an added insult, Mr. Mellish," she exclaimed, "which I shall not readily forget."

With a dramatic gesture she pointed to the door.

"The flat is open," she continued. "You are at liberty to go where you like. I am sorry I cannot accompany you, but I have an appointment and I am late already. I think you will apologize for this later."

She turned towards the lift.

Mellish stepped forward to stop her, but, quickly as he moved, Shand's hand descended first, with a grip like a vise, upon her wrist. He pushed back her sleeve and bent for a second over her arm.

"Hold her!" he cried, as she tried to wrench herself free.

Lee, who was standing behind her, pinioned her elbows and held them, in spite of her struggles.

Shand's arm shot out once more. There was a furious ejaculation from Lady Dalberry, a frantic effort on her part to escape, and then Shand stepped back.

In his hand was a hat and, attached to it, a flaxen wig.

Mellish was staring at the man still writhing ineffectually in Lee's grasp.

"My God, de Silva!" he exclaimed, in consternation.

De Silva's answer was to step backwards with such suddenness that Lee was thrown off his balance. He stumbled, and as he did so his hold relaxed, and the Argentino wrenched himself free. Shand made a dash for him, only to receive a blow that sent him reeling.

It was Dalberry who tripped the fleeing man as he passed him and fell heavily on top of him, pinning him to the ground until Shand could reach him and snap the handcuffs on his wrists.

Dalberry scrambled up and stood staring at the man who lay, panting and cursing, at his feet.

"He's not de Silva," he exclaimed.

For the prisoner who, in spite of his absurd clothing, bore such an extraordinary resemblance to de Silva, was fair instead of dark, and his hair was so light as to be almost white.

Shand bent down and hauled him to his feet.

"Kurt Strelinski," he said, "I arrest you on the charge of being concerned in the death of Eric Conyers. I have to warn you that anything you say will be used against you."

CHAPTER XXV

LEAVING SHAND to dispose of his prisoner, Dalberry brushed past Mellish and hurried into the flat. He ran down the passage to Carol's sitting-room. Finding no trace of her there, he tried the bedroom.

The door was shut, and when he tried to open it, he discovered that there was an obstruction of some kind on the other side. When he at last got it open and discovered Carol lying huddled on the floor, it seemed to him that his worst fears were realized.

He dropped to his knees by her side and tried to raise her. At his touch she shrank away from him, shuddering.

"Carol!" he cried, beside himself with mingled rage and anxiety. "What is it? Has that swine hurt you?"

At the sound of his voice she raised her head and looked at him. For a moment it seemed as though she were too dazed to recognize him, then the horror slowly faded from her eyes and gave place to an unutterable relief. With a sigh she let her head fall back on to his shoulder.

White with anger he unfastened the bandage round her mouth and, with his penknife, cut the strips that bound her.

Her arms once free she clutched him, clinging to him like a frightened child.

"Hold me tight, Gillie," she sobbed. "Don't let him get me! Don't let him come in here!"

He picked her up in his arms and carried her to the bed; but when he tried to put her down, she held on to him in a frenzy of terror.

"Take me out of this place before he comes back," she begged piteously. "I can't bear any more! Take me away, Gillie!"

He was still trying to soothe her, to make her understand that de Silva would never trouble her again, when Mellish burst into the room, closely followed by Shand.

Mellish took in the situation at a glance.

"We'll borrow your car, Shand, if you don't mind, for Miss Summers," he said. "There's no object in keeping her here, I suppose?"

Shand shook his head. He had picked up the strips of silk from the floor and was turning them slowly over in his hands, his eyes on the girl's swollen wrists.

"The sooner she's out of here the better," he answered, in a low voice. "I'm glad I did not know that that devil had used these when I had my hands on him just now. How long was she tied up, do you know?"

Dalberry shook his head.

"I don't know. She was bound and gagged when I found her. I can't make her believe, even now, that she is really safe from that brute."

Shand hesitated for a moment, then he took a stride to the door.

"Lee, just bring Strelinski in here," he shouted.

Then he crossed to the bed and bent over Carol.

"Do you remember me, Miss Summers?" he said, in his quiet, reassuring voice. "My name's Shand. I spoke to you in the hall one evening. I've been after our friend de Silva for a long time, and now I've got him. He'll never trouble you again."

He put his hand gently on her shoulder and, with the other, made a sign to Lee, who was waiting in the doorway.

He felt the girl start and shrink as Lee stepped into the room with his prisoner. Standing between them and the handcuffed man, he went on:

"You see, you've nothing to be afraid of any more. In another half-hour we'll have him under lock and key, and he and Lady Dalberry will have ceased to exist as far as you are concerned. Looks a bit different without his wig, doesn't he?"

Carol nodded. She was still incapable of speech, but her colour was beginning to return and the fear was passing out of her eyes.

Shand smiled down at her.

"You've had a bad time," he said gently. "But it's over and done with now, and all you've got to do is to forget it. I'll look after the rest."

At a sign from him Lee removed his prisoner.

Shand drew Mellish after him into the passage.

"She'll do now, I think, Mr. Mellish," he said. "I should get her away from here, though. When she's rested and fit, I should like to ask her a few questions."

Shand's opportunity came sooner than he had expected. Once under the friendly roof of the Carthews, Carol pulled herself together with a celerity that was little short of amazing. The doctor spoke darkly of "shock" and "after-effects," but, when a mild sedative and a good night's rest had done their work, even he was driven to admit that all danger of a serious breakdown was over. He raised no objection to a meeting between her and Shand, being of the opinion that, once she had been given an opportunity to discuss the events that had so terrified her, she would have a better chance of dismissing them from her mind.

Thus it was that, less than a week after the arrest of Strelinski, she found herself the principal guest at a select dinner-party in Mellish's rooms at the Albany.

Dalberry and Shand were the only other people invited, and, at Mellish's suggestion, all discussion of the business which had brought them together was shelved until after the dessert.

"Till then, we'll look upon it as a slightly deferred coming-of-age party," he said. "I've been waiting for you to remind me that my jurisdiction is over. You can kick over the traces as much as you like now."

"I'm rather off kicking, for the moment," confessed Carol. "I must admit that there does seem something to be said for that 'safety first' policy that you've been rubbing into me ever since I can remember."

Mellish looked doubtful.

"It's a case of 'the devil was sick,' I'm afraid," he said. "At present you're only convalescent. Once you're properly on your feet again there'll be no holding you."

Carol hesitated for a moment. When she did speak it was with an attempt at nonchalance that seemed slightly overdone.

"As a matter of fact," she announced, stumbling a little over the words, "I have had to give up the career of glorious independence that I have been looking forward to for twenty-one long years. Circumstances have arisen ..."

She broke off, blushing vividly.

"This is very interesting," said Mellish gravely, "and your language is beautiful. Circumstances have arisen ... ?" Carol relapsed into the vernacular.

"Oh bother!" she exclaimed. "The fact is that I came to the conclusion that I'd better have some one to look after me, and as Gillie seemed to want to take on the job, we ... Well, we arranged that he should. And that's that."

"The idea being to get married as soon as possible," put in Dalberry. "Any objection, Jasper?"

"Good heavens, no!" Mellish was beaming. "But you little know what you're in for, Gillie. As for you, my child," he went on, turning to Carol, "you'll find you've met your match. He won't give you your head as I did."

"Speaking on behalf of the Yard, Miss Summers," announced Shand, with a kindly twinkle in his eye, "I may say that the arrangement meets with our entire approval. You've been a bit on our minds lately, you know."

"If it wasn't for the Yard I shouldn't be here, Mr. Shand," said Carol gratefully. "As it is, you're the only person I feel really safe with, even now."

"The occasion seems to call for a toast," said Mellish. "Fetch yourself a glass, Jervis, and wish Miss Summers and Lord Dalberry luck."

Jervis's habitually solemn face creased into a thousand wrinkles.

"One of the happiest occasions I can remember, sir," he murmured confidentially—"if I may say so."

It was not until they were comfortably settled round the fire in the study that Mellish introduced the subject that was of such absorbing interest to all of them.

"I think, if you don't mind, you had better take the platform, Shand," he said. "You've got the whole story unravelled now, and it's complicated enough, goodness knows."

Shand cleared his throat.

"We've got it pretty clear now, I think," he began, "partly from Strelinski's own confession, and partly from what we've been able to get from America. He's owned up to the impersonation of Lady Dalberry, and told us, more or less, how it came about, but, of course, denies having had any connection with either of the two murders. There's no doubt, however, that he worked the whole business, from beginning to end, single-handed, and an uncommonly pretty piece of roguery it was."

He rose to his feet and stood facing his audience.

"The facts, as we have been able to reconstruct them, are, roughly, as follows. When Lord and Lady Dalberry set out for the coast from their ranch in the Argentine, they were not, as has been generally supposed, accompanied by a maid. That maid was a fiction of Strelinski's to account for the presence of the woman's body on the scene of the motor accident. The inquest was held in a small and remote town, far from Lord Dalberry's ranch, otherwise the deception would have been impossible. The disfigured body found lying under the car was, of course, that of Lady Dalberry. Lord Dalberry was driving the car himself, without a chauffeur, and he and Lady Dalberry put up at a small town, little more than a village, for the night. At the inn there, Lord Dalberry got into conversation with Strelinski, who had been travelling with a third-rate theatrical company. The tour had been a frost, and Strelinski found himself stranded, absolutely on his beam ends, without even the money to pay his way to the nearest big town. Practically the only thing he possessed was a bag which contained his make-up and a couple of wigs. Lord Dalberry took pity on his penniless condition and offered him a lift as far as he cared to go. There seems every reason to believe that the accident was a genuine one, because, at that period of the affair, Strelinski had nothing to gain by the death of the man who had befriended him; but when he realized that he was the sole survivor, and that Lady Dalberry's body was mutilated beyond recognition, he was quick to take advantage of the fact. He admits that the people at the inn had heard of Lord Dalberry's unexpected accession to the title, and been interested enough to discuss the matter with him. What he learned from them, combined with certain things he had read in the papers at the time of the accident to the airmail, convinced him that he stood a fair chance of success if he tried to impersonate Lady Dalberry. He had the contents of her luggage to choose from, and, with the help of his own wig and make-up box, he was able to dress the part before help arrived. It was pure bad luck, from our point of view, that Lord Dalberry should have been carrying in the car a dispatch box containing all his most important papers and, what was of even more value to Strelinski, full and carefully kept diaries—small pocket affairs, but with a whole page to each day. It had apparently been his habit to keep these diaries ever since his school-days, and we found eleven of them at de Silva's flat at the Escatorial. He declares that he started the impersonation on an impulse, merely with the intention of getting hold of Lord Dalberry's ready money and anything else of value that might be in his luggage, trusting to luck to get away with the loot before he was found out. It was only after his first night at the hotel to which he was taken, a night spent in going through the papers he found in the dispatch box, that he conceived the idea of carrying the thing through on a much larger scale. The two things that decided him were the fact that Lady Dalberry was unknown to any one on this side of the Atlantic, and the discovery of the whereabouts of Miss Summers. Curiously enough he had worked for a film company in which Miss Summers's father had a controlling interest, and he had been with it at the time of Mr. Summers's death. There he had heard a great deal of gossip concerning Miss Summers and her enormous inheritance, and was now to discover her close connection with the Dalberrys. It was with the determination to get hold of Miss Summers that Strelinski came to England, and it was with this intention that he decided to double the part of Lady Dalberry with that of de Silva. He admits that he hoped to marry Miss Summers, in his character of de Silva, and his failure to make a good impression on her ended in the wrecking of all his plans.

Once married to her and back in the Argentine he would have had things all his own way."

"It would be interesting to know how he proposed to dispose of Lady Dalberry, once he had achieved his object," put in Mellish.

"I imagine that she, also, would have returned to the Argentine, and then conveniently disappeared."

"It's amazing that he should have been able to get round the lawyers, though," commented Dalberry. "It's a wonder they didn't smell a rat."

"Family solicitors are not quite so astute as people seem to think," remarked Mellish dryly. "You must remember that her papers were in order and that, curiously enough, none of us had ever seen even a photograph of your uncle's wife. On the other hand, she answered to the descriptions we had had of her, and we had absolutely no reason to suspect her."

"Also," Shand reminded him, "Strelinski was peculiarly fortunate in one thing. Lady Dalberry's parents were dead and all her other relations were in Sweden and had never seen her, so that they were hardly likely to interfere in his plans."

"What was his connection with the man Smith, on board the *Enriqueta*? I suppose there's no doubt that he had a hand in that affair?"

"None whatever, to my mind, though it's an open question whether we'll ever manage to bring the murder home to him. He'll be convicted all right for the Conyers murder. We've got an excellent case for the jury there, but it's probable that he won't even be charged with the one on board the *Enriqueta*. The probability is that Smith, with whom he had undoubtedly had dealings in Buenos Aires, recognized him on board the boat, and he had no alternative but to silence him. Smith, who was both a drinker and a talker, would have made a hopeless confederate. And, by that time, Strelinski had gone too far to draw back. Smith must have blundered into him that night, and in doing so sealed his own death-warrant; but unless Strelinski makes a full confession, we shall never know exactly what happened. The fact remains that both Smith and Conyers were killed in the same manner, by strangling, and Mrs. Verrall and Miss Summers, who were both attacked by Strelinski, narrowly escaped the same fate."

"If he had dared he would no doubt have killed Mrs. Verrall that night at Conyers's lodgings," said Mellish.

Shand nodded.

"As it turned out, she was his undoing; but she was in touch with us, as he knew by then, and he had taken too many risks already to attempt another murder. As it was, over the Conyers affair, he had sailed nearer the wind than was pleasant. Too many people had seen him, and we have not only got the wire he sent to Conyers making the appointment with him, but the clerk at the post office at which he handed it in has identified him. He has also been identified by the taxi-driver who took Conyers to the Escatorial. His method was an extraordinarily ingenious one, and, but for sheer bad luck, he would never have been found out. During the whole time he was in England he was only seen three times without a disguise: by Conyers at the night club, when his dark wig became misplaced; by the clerk at the post office, and by the taxi-driver. Even Bond had no idea what he looked like. If it had not been for that photograph that we found among Conyers's things, it is doubtful if we should ever have identified him."

"How much was Captain Bond mixed up in the whole thing?" asked Carol. "You know he tried to warn me about the Onyx. I feel I owe him something for that good turn, at least."

Shand turned to her.

"He tried to warn you, did he?" he exclaimed sharply. "He came to us of his own accord after Strelinski's arrest. He'd evidently begun to get cold feet soon after the affair at the Terpsychorean. We're not holding him. Whatever his suspicions may have been, he seems to have known very little. He did manage to get into the flat over the Onyx shop and found some woman's clothing there. He concluded that de Silva was meeting a woman there, and had shut off the flat as a convenient place for such assignations. Later he came to the conclusion that the woman was Lady Dalberry. If he warned Miss Summers, it was probably on account of the use to which he thought de Silva was putting the flat. As regards the will Strelinski tried to make you sign, there seems no doubt that Bond's signature was got under false pretences. He had no suspicion as to what the paper was when he signed it."

"I can't help feeling glad he's going to get off," said Carol. "He's such a miserable little creature, but there's something rather pathetic about him, all the same."

"There was nothing pathetic about the way he doped me," remarked Dalberry. "Just abominably efficient, I should call it."

"That was the one really stupid thing Strelinski did," said Shand thoughtfully. "He drew suspicion on himself by that drugging affair, and he must have known that he could gain nothing by it in the long run. Even now, I can't get at his motive for doing it."

If he had been looking in Carol's direction he might have seen the colour deepen in her cheeks. She knew instinctively that Strelinski's motive had been neither more nor less than an insane jealousy of Dalberry, and that he had risked the over-setting of all his carefully-laid plans to give vent to it. She kept her own counsel, however, and the three men never knew how nearly Strelinski had come to grief through the unexpected workings of his own heart.

"What was the nationality of the fellow?" asked Mellish. "Without that dark make-up it was easy to see he was no South American."

"According to his real passport, which we discovered among other papers at his flat, he was a German Pole whose parents emigrated to America when he was a boy of about sixteen. He has told us that much himself. He's got all the vanity of the born criminal, and is ready enough to talk about himself. It wouldn't surprise me if he ended by admitting to everything. He's the sort that not only confesses, but boasts of what he's done. He's not an unusual type, though he's cleverer than most of them. You did us a good turn, Mr. Mellish, when you blacked in the hair on that photograph. I admit I hadn't seen the likeness."

"I wish I'd gone a step further and spotted the likeness to Lady Dalberry," said Mellish ruefully. "You beat me badly there."

Shand turned to Carol.

"That's a thing I've been wanting to ask you, Miss Summers," he said. "When did you realize that de Silva and Lady Dalberry were one and the same person?"

Carol caught her breath. Even now she did not care to dwell on her vigil on the balcony outside Lady Dalberry's bedroom.

"I was watching through the window," she said, "and I saw Lady Dalberry come through the opening in the wardrobe. Did you find that, by the way?"

"Not until Lord Dalberry had given us your message," answered Shand. "It was a clever dodge, and ridiculously easy to carry out. Where Strelinski had the wardrobes built we haven't been able to find out, but he must have brought them to the Escatorial and then, with his own hands, hacked his way through the partition between the two flats. You see, owing to the fact that the Escatorial was originally a hotel, there were no party walls between the flats, and he had nothing but lath and plaster to deal with. The sliding doors are on the wardrobes themselves, and there is merely a rough hole through the wall behind them. He had another quite neat adaptation of a cupboard at the Onyx establishment. That, by the way, was a perfectly genuine business venture, but its real object was to provide him with a place outside the Escatorial where he could change from one impersonation to the other if the occasion arose."

"He used it on the night of Conyers's murder, I imagine?" said Mellish.

"Yes. He worked that very cleverly. He sent Bond to Paris with a view to getting him safely out of the way and leaving the coast clear at the Onyx. Then he dropped his disguise altogether and sent his wire to Conyers, meeting him later, still undisguised, at the restaurant. He entered the taxi with him, giving the driver the address of the Escatorial, strangled him, stopped the cab and got out, taking care that the driver should see him clearly. He then made straight for the Onyx, where he got into his Lady Dalberry disguise, and arrived at the Escatorial just in time to view the corpse. He then slipped through the wardrobe into his own flat and was able to open the door to me in his night clothes when I called to ask him if he could identify Conyers. That was why he was never seen to come in that night, and got us all puzzled as to his alibi. The whole thing was amazingly ingenious, but the cleverest part of the performance, to my mind, was the way he manipulated his voice. Both de Silva and Lady Dalberry spoke with marked foreign accents, but whereas hers was guttural, almost German, his was clear and precise, just what you would expect in a South American. And the difference in voice was astonishingly clever. But I want your story, Miss Summers."

"It's simple enough," explained Carol. "I saw Lady Dalberry come in and sit down at the dressing-table. You can imagine my surprise when she took off her wig and began to remove the grease-paint from her face. The moment her wig was off I knew she wasn't a woman, and a moment later, in spite of the light hair, I recognized de Silva. My one idea was then to get out of the flat, and, if I hadn't made a noise shutting the window of my sitting-room, I should have succeeded. As it was, he heard me, and caught me just as I was getting out of the front door."

Dalberry stared at her in astonishment.

"Do you mean to say that you never saw Lady Dalberry and de Silva together all the time you lived in the flat, and the fact did not strike you as extraordinary?" he exclaimed.

"It seems incredible, doesn't it? But, looking back, I realize that I never did see them together. You must remember that, on more than one occasion, I believed him and Lady Dalberry to be together in her sitting-room; and once, at least, I was convinced that she was in the next room all the time I was talking to him, and was very angry when I went to find her and discover that she was not there. De Silva then went over to his flat, and five minutes later she appeared. I did think it odd that he always made a point of coming to the flat when she was out, but I had my own explanation of that. I'm afraid my vanity was to blame there," she finished, her colour deepening.

"What beats me is how de Silva tracked Mrs. Verrall to Berry-down," said Dalberry.

Shand grinned.

"He had us beat there. I'm afraid we underestimated his intelligence. The truth is, he simply used his brains. He had already caught Mrs. Verrall going into the Albany, and tracked her from there to Conyers's old lodgings. He knew that she had been badly frightened and that she was in touch with Mr. Mellish, and, through him, with Lord Dalberry. If Mr. Mellish wanted to get her out of London, Berrydown was a fairly obvious place for him to choose. I imagine he went down there as soon as he found she was no longer at her old address and located her. The rest was easy."

"How did you jump at the double impersonation, Shand?" asked Mellish.

"I didn't till the last minute," Shand admitted. "It was due to one of those little slips that the cleverest criminals are apt to make. When I interviewed de Silva on the night of Conyers's murder he was wearing a rather gaudy gold and platinum watch-bracelet. He was in his night clothes, and I was naturally on the lookout for any indication that he had not really been roused from sleep as he pretended. Well, a good many people do sleep in their wrist-watches, but somehow, this one struck me as incongruous. When Lady Dalberry was flourishing her fist under my nose, I recognized the watch or one so like it that I decided to take a chance. It *was* a chance, I admit. Anyhow, I grabbed her hat, and, sure enough, there was the flaxen-haired man I had been looking for ever since that night on the *Enriqueta*."

THE END